If Connie loses her standing in society, she risks losing everything...

except Alex.

When country widow Constance Rattigan finds herself in a notorious London brothel instead of at the altar, only one person can save her from the auction block. Alex Vernon walked away from Connie once before, when he discovered her engagement. Now that her fiancé has betrayed her, Lord Ripley doesn't intend to leave her again. But Connie has other ideas... She won't marry him until her name is cleared.

Alex decides to make Connie's wishes come true, but it's not that easy, even with the help of his powerful relatives known as the Emperors of London.

Books by Lynne Connolly

Rogue In Red Velvet

Published by Kensington Publishing Corporation

Rogue In Red Velvet

Lynne Connolly

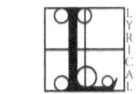

LYRICAL PRESS
Kensington Publishing Corp.
www.kensingtonbooks.com

Lyrical Press books are published by
Kensington Publishing Corp. 119 West 40th Street New York, NY 10018

All Kensington titles, imprints, and distributed lines are available at special quantity discounts for bulk purchases for sales promotion, premiums, fund-raising, and educational or institutional use.

Special book excerpts or customized printings can also be created to fit specific needs. For details, write or phone the office of the Kensington Special Sales Manager:
Kensington Publishing Corp.
119 West 40th Street
New York, NY 10018
Attn. Special Sales Department. Phone: 1-800-221-2647.

First Electronic Edition: April 2014
eISBN-13: 978-1-61650-564-6
eISBN-10: 1-61650-564-8

First Print Edition: August 2014
ISBN-13: 978-1-61650-587-5
ISBN-10: 1-61650-587-7

Printed in the United States of America

Chapter 1

March, 1754

The library door crashed open, shattering Connie's peace and admitting the last man she wanted to be alone with. Pretending unperturbed tranquility, Connie put her pen in the standish. She clasped her hands on top of the book she'd been working on to still the trembling his presence caused.

Wide-eyed, chest heaving, the normally elegant, cool Lord Ripley, slammed the door and put his back to it.

She met his blank, dark stare and cursed her fluttering pulse. Whatever had put him in this state, it couldn't be trivial.

He blinked, straightened and assumed the town bronze most of his sort used like a cloak, covering whatever he felt beneath. He gave the perfectly tied strip of linen at his neck a twitch, arranged his sleeve ruffles, then straightened his wig. As poise and elegance returned, he transformed from a hunted fugitive to a gentleman and pushed away from the door. He strolled to the old, scarred table at which she sat. "Here you are."

What a ridiculous statement. "I believe I am." She read a line in the journal before her, more to look away than because she needed to, and took a steadying breath before she met his eyes once more. "May I help you, Lord Ripley?"

"I merely wondered why you lock yourself away here every day, Mrs. Rattigan. And I came to see if I may assist you in any way."

"I'm perfectly fine, sir. I doubt you could help me, or have any interest in doing so." She'd avoided him for three days and wanted none of his games. She didn't care why he'd shot in here, only she wished he'd shoot out again, just as fast.

"Is it something too difficult for my paltry brain? Are you a bluestocking, ma'am, that you labor here day after day without joining the revelry?" In full control, his society manners polished as ever, he walked to her side of the table and loomed over her.

Her heart beat faster and her breath quickened. She worked to hide his effect on her and castigated herself for a fool. He wasn't interested in her in that way, much less when she had her hair scraped back in a knot, wore no cosmetics at all and had donned her old clothes in preparation for the dusty work. She was just an excuse, an escape from something. Or someone. She was no empty-headed miss. She was a respectable widow, but it didn't stop her becoming tongue-tied. "I—I—"

"You find yourself bored by our antics. You'd rather study Plautus, or is it Marcus Aurelius?" Chuckling, he leaned over her shoulder, flipped the book closed. With one long finger, he traced the name on the cover. "Saucy stories perhaps?"

The door opened and admitted Miss Louisa Stobart, one of the young ladies invited here to meet Lord Ripley. Connie's godfather had confided to her that he might choose a bride from among them.

Now she understood why he'd shot into this room like a pursued fox. Miss Stobart had been the most assiduous of Lord Ripley's pursuers, indefatigable in her chase. He'd been escaping her.

For a change, Connie was in charge. How delicious.

Lord Ripley straightened and gave Connie such a look of pleading that she almost laughed. "Help me," he mouthed, before assuming his easy smile and facing his tormentor.

She would have preferred that he said that in different circumstances, but what she dreamed at night remained between her and her pillow. This would do. A little gentle revenge was called for. She slid the book over to his lordship and pointed at random. "Here is a word I cannot read, sir. Do you see?"

"No, ma'am." Bending over her shoulder, he peered then looked at her.

Far too close, his breath heated her cheek and her heart quickened. This close, he'd see her reaction for sure. Inwardly, she groaned. She hadn't bargained on him doing that. She should have shoved the book away from her.

His eyes widened slightly. He turned his attention to the book. "I think it says wormwood. An old spell book?"

She laughed. "An inventory, sir. As you well know."

His shoulders relaxed under his country-coat. In an ordinary man that slight movement might remain unnoticed, but Connie had spent the last few days watching him surreptitiously. He was the most handsome man she'd ever seen and while she could tell herself that she was merely observing, it did no good. For the first time in her life, she longed to be younger, wealthier and socially higher ranking. Then she could compete. Instead, she'd dressed in a practical country gown that would survive hedgerows and house dust, and hidden away here. "Yes, of course. Wormwood."

Thank goodness he straightened.

Miss Stobart stood on the other side of the table, her delicately draped pink silk gown mocking Connie's sturdy dark green garment. Miss Stobart's was a fashionable ideal of a gown to be worn in the country, sprinkled with exquisitely embroidered spring flowers. Miss Stobart's gaze skimmed over Connie and to his lordship. Her ruby lips pursed in a winsome pout. "Sir, I had hoped we could take a turn in the gardens. I quite thought you had promised me at breakfast."

"I had no idea." He glanced down at Connie. It was her cue to say something.

"I'm so sorry to interrupt your"—*Courtship? Pursuit?* —"walk. Of course you must go."

Miss Stobart drummed her foot against the wood floor, maddening in the quiet library. "Indeed sir, I quite thought you'd forgotten me, so I came to find you." Her voice was sweet; her foot was not.

"I beg your pardon, but I had promised today to Connie for some time now." He gave her an easy smile.

Connie stared at him in astonishment. He'd used her first name. She wasn't aware he even knew it. When he put his hand on her shoulder, she nearly leaped up. His skin wasn't in contact with hers, due to her modest gown and fichu, but it might as well have been. She felt it like a shock of recognition. Of what she didn't want to consider.

"Connie and I are old friends." The familiarity of her first name implied he was much friendlier with her than anyone had imagined. "When she mentioned her task, I immediately volunteered to help. Her—er—errand is something I am particularly interested in."

Not to mention, he didn't have the faintest idea what she was doing. She'd never discussed her project in company and nobody had expressed an interest except for her godfather, whose commission this was.

He was casting her as his rescuer when he hadn't asked her first.

"It is a special project I've been meaning to undertake for some time." Should she lie, draw out the moment? She wasn't used to being the center of attention.

Miss Stobart fixed her cold, blue eyes on Connie, probably for the first time since she'd arrived.

Connie gave the young woman her sweetest smile. "My visit here provided the perfect opportunity."

"A bluestocking?" That was the second time in ten minutes she'd been accused of that. Did everyone in society who opened a book get accused of that?

Miss Stobart's lips curved in a superior smile. She clearly considered herself the victor in this encounter. After all, who would not? Connie was below the notice of a young lady of marriageable age and considerable fortune.

"Not exactly." She glanced at the book.

Leaning over her once more, Lord Ripley flipped the volume over, revealing the faded label on the front. "It's an inventory of the house from the sixteenth century. Family history is important."

Damn, she couldn't torment him anymore. He'd guessed right. "Lord Downholland has particularly wished to gather all the documents pertaining to the house in one place. I merely offered to assist him."

"And I offered to assist Connie," he said smoothly, back in control. "I'm sorry, Miss Stobart, but her claims had precedence."

Wonderful. He was fast making an enemy on her behalf. Miss Stobart would resent her intensely if she came between the chase and ensnarement of her quarry. "I'm only doing this until my fiancé arrives."

Miss Stobart relaxed, nodded regally. "I see. But Lord Ripley has other commitments."

"I'll be down directly, ma'am." He walked to the door and held it open. "If you would not mind waiting for a few moments, I would greatly appreciate the time."

Miss Stobart swept through and he closed the door behind her.

Breathing deeply, he slumped against it. He met Connie's gaze and smiled. "Thank you."

So that was what she was good for. A distraction. "I'm not prepared to act as your chaperone, sir."

Laughing, he waved a hand in one of the most elegant movements she'd ever seen. "I would be eternally grateful to you if you did so." He sauntered toward her. "I never thought I'd be in need of one, to be truthful."

Connie resisted the temptation to move away. She was not afraid of this man, or intimidated by him, even though he had just gone from being the object of her fantasies to a real live human being. His panic, his silent appeal for help had transformed him in her eyes. Although, sadly, his appeal remained.

Seizing her hand, he dropped a kiss on the back, and immediately restored it to her. "I can't thank you enough, ma'am." He grinned wickedly. "Connie."

"I wasn't even aware you knew my first name."

"I do."

How did he know her name when she wasn't even aware that he'd noticed her? Had he made a point of learning it?

"Connie, I truly appreciate your help. Is there anything I can do for you in return?"

"You can answer this. Why is it so important to avoid Miss Stobart?" She dared to turn around and look at his face, bracing herself for the visual contact, as she always did when she looked at him. "You raced in here as if the hounds of hell were after you. Surely you have enough address to avoid her?"

He perched on the table by her side. Too close.

Anger was taking the place of curiosity. She no longer cared about the social gulf between them, or her dowdy appearance, or anything else other than the consideration that he had treated her badly. "Sir, I'm a widow, from the country, but I'm not prepared to be treated as if I don't exist."

His eyes darkened as he gazed steadily at her. "I owe you an apology. I am truly sorry if I implied anything of the kind. I meant it. I owe you a favor. Anything."

The devil take him. What she could do with was an extra pair of hands, and someone who knew how to read the spidery old writing she was fighting every day. She folded her arms. "Very well, since you ask. I want an assistant in this task. I agreed to help my godfather gather the books he'll need to compile a family history. It's proving more difficult than I imagined. Some of the books are heavy and stored in virtually inaccessible places."

His broad shoulders eased. "I would be honored to help."

"Even if it meant getting a speck of dirt on your clothes?"

"Even then." His lips curved in a disconcertingly attractive smile.

Meeting his eyes became more difficult and she fought the urge to fidget. She'd have to change her chair, it was becoming most uncomfortable. "I'm working at this task most of the day. Until my fiancé arrives."

"Dankworth, yes." He snapped the name as if Jasper had done something to annoy him. "I should wish you happy, I suppose."

"Content will do. Thank you."

He quirked a brow. That irritating smile returned. "Contentment only? You don't wish for wedded bliss?"

"Not in the least. A rational partnership is my dearest wish." It was the truth. Love had done nothing for her. She wished for a comfortable marriage that would improve the lot of both parties, nothing else. She'd decided that years ago, and now her ambition was within her grasp, she'd do nothing to change it. "The marriage will suit my godparents, who have been kind to me and have no child of their own to inherit their estate."

"They know about Dankworth, then?"

Did he? Eyeing her pen, she wished she could take it up again and lose herself in the old inventories. She didn't want her decision questioned in this way. What good would it do? "They know he can be foolish on occasion. Marriage will settle him and ensure heirs for the estate." She tired of this game. This man was only baiting her. "I understand you're here seeking a bride, sir. You won't find one in this room."

"Will I not?" He leaned forward, pressing home his advantage. His citrus and spice scent was altogether too seductive. His low voice hinted at unforgiveable sins. "You're not formally betrothed yet, ma'am."

"I will be very soon." She wasn't very good at flirting, never had been. She scraped back her chair, got to her feet, and made a business of shaking out the skirts of her drab green gown. "You cannot show the guests such discourtesy. They are here for you, at least a good many are."

He grinned wryly. "It would be more discourteous to run away screaming. If I don't have this escape, I might very well do that." He stood, took a few paces toward the door, and turned back, the skirts of his country coat swinging around thighs that filled out his breeches creditably. "I see I must confide my predicament and throw myself on your mercy. Miss Stobart is determined to trap me into a connection I have no desire to acquire."

Miss Stobart had either ignored Connie or treated her with barely concealed contempt since her arrival. Connie had heard rumors as well as witnessed Miss Stobart's relentless pursuit of his lordship.

He sighed and scrutinized the silver buckle on his shiny black shoe. "I suspect my father put her and her mother in the way of finding me here. The old man wants me married and as soon as possible. The truth is, I was caught in a compromising position with Miss Stobart at a ball and I decided to leave London for a while until the affair blew over." He lifted his hand as if to run it through his hair, but he was wearing a fashionable wig.

From the color of his brows, she'd say his hair was dark underneath and she had an irrational but powerful desire to see it for herself. To touch it, in a way entirely forbidden to her. Annoying that this unwanted desire wouldn't leave her. His confession didn't endear him to her. *Compromising position* could mean anything from a private conversation to full-blown seduction.

"The incident happened at a ball," he continued. "Miss Stobart said she'd torn her gown and asked me to help her pin it. So there I was kneeling at her feet in an anteroom when her aunt dramatically flung open the door. She'd been clever enough to bring witnesses."

That wasn't so bad. "Didn't you explain your task?"

"They chose not to believe me. Miss Stobart swore it was a declaration of marriage. It was not, but my absence from town was advisable. She chased me here." He closed his eyes, and when he opened them they were filled with surprising bleakness. "I must sound like the veriest coxcomb, imagining every woman in the house after my hand."

"No indeed, sir. You are from one of the foremost families in the land, accepted everywhere, and in possession of a large fortune. Why should you not think that?." Since he was being so honest, why should she not do the same?

He arched a brow. "If I said I wanted to be desired for myself, I'd sound foolish. But it's true. Connie, I have few friends, people I can be honest with. It would be a privilege if you allow that between us."

Friends? Damn, but she still wanted more. Not that she could have it, and Connie had become used to not having what she wanted. Friends would do. "Very well."

"And I'll devote a portion of every day to helping you."

"Thank you, sir." Exquisite agony to have this man so close, but she'd bear it. Worse that she was liking him more.

"Alex."

She blinked. "I beg your pardon?"

"I want the privilege of calling you Connie. In return, you must call me Alex, especially in private. You do me a great favor, helping me to avoid the ladies, particularly Miss Stobart. She's done everything she can to compromise me."

"What about me? Won't I be compromised?"

"You're a respectable widow, soon to be formally betrothed. You told me so yourself."

He had her there. "And in any case, I'm of an age where I cannot be expected to be on the hunt. Isn't that right?"

"I wouldn't say that." He raked her with his eyes, once, twice, from head to toes.

Every part of her body tingled. How could she bear this? "I'm eight and twenty, sir. I'm far too old to consider husband hunting seriously, even if my arrangement with Jasper didn't exist." He might as well hear the truth. "If it weren't that my godparents had chosen me, I'd be well on the shelf."

"They might consider you decrepit. I certainly don't. But you have my word, Connie, I'll behave. Just don't leave me to their mercies." When he moved back, she caught the scent of citrus and masculinity. He was too real, with her in this room, a man rather than a symbol of power and influence.

"Why don't you just leave?"

He shook his head. "I promised my father I wouldn't. He's an old curmudgeon, but he's the only father I have. In a week, I will be kicking the dust of this admittedly charming house off my heels. I just need help until then."

So he could help the old widow woman sort out the dusty books. The situation appealed to her underused sense of humor. If she could bear his presence, and since he'd dropped his society mask she found him much more agreeable, then she could watch the play unfold and smile. As a widow she was allowed more leeway than others, and even if rumors came her way, she was safe. Jasper would arrive any day now and then her quietude would be at an end. She would be an engaged woman. "Very well, but not for long. Until you leave."

"Thank you, Connie. You do me a great service and I won't forget it."

She might as well make use of him. "Be warned, Lord Ripley, I intend to work you hard collecting volumes from the dustiest rooms in the house."

"Alex."

He must look at all women that way and the gullible thought he did it just for them. More fools they. Connie wouldn't join them.

* * * *

Alex left the library smiling. If Connie Rattigan thought her plain gowns and quiet demeanor had prevented him looking at her with more than usual interest, she was much mistaken.

Her determination to avoid the house party had intrigued him at first. Then he wondered how she could think of becoming betrothed to anyone belonging to the Dankworth family. Of course he was biased, since his mother's family were constantly at odds with the Dankworths, but Jasper, in his opinion, was a typical example of the breed. He didn't deserve her. Glad to find her betrothed absent from the party, he'd looked at Connie and liked what he saw. The more he looked, the more he liked.

Discovering her lair had become an obsession that had lightened the otherwise dull visit. He'd traversed several corridors more plainly decorated and much narrower than the more gracious ones in the main part of the house. But he'd failed in his quest.

So it was ironic that he'd found her by accident. He had been escaping the wiles of Miss Stobart. Running away. He'd wandered into the older part of the house, to explore a little. Like many country houses, this one had been added to over the years. Lower ceilings and narrower corridors than in the modern part of the house attested to its age. He'd ducked into an old library, lined with shelves of books that looked read instead of just for show.

When he turned a corner and discovered the lady facing him full-square, his smile vanished. If he wanted to get past her, he'd either have to retreat or beg her pardon and squeeze past. The narrow corridors that a moment ago had seemed quaint now took on a more sinister aspect.

Another lady chased around the far end of the long hallway, no doubt determined to prevent any tete-a-tete. Good for her.

"Ladies, would you both care to accompany me in a stroll around the gardens?" Acceptable, and he could make an excuse and leave them with each other. Perhaps they'd come to blows. A man could only hope.

Alex considered himself an easy-going man but these two had driven him to distraction. So much that he'd left London and taken up the invitation for a quiet gathering, only for them to discover where he'd gone and follow post-haste. The Downhollands were too genial to turn them away.

Even more reason to pursue the fascinating Constance Rattigan. He'd never met a woman before who drew him as she did. The fact that she was about to be married, or contracted anyway, made her safer than the two women who confidently came forward and took an arm each. Also infinitely better company. She conversed like a sensible woman, and while he tried to be a gentleman, he took note of her luscious figure and her lovely features almost without thinking.

Strange feeling. Must be the Yorkshire air, he decided, as he made the necessary detour to the south entrance, heading for the gardens.

Chapter 2

Alex had helped Connie with her tasks for three days now but that had been clean work, cataloguing and capturing family histories from the more salubrious parts of the house. Nobody had touched this storeroom for years, but she'd found it quite by chance when she opened the wrong door. To her this room was a treasure-trove. To anyone else, a dirt trap holding useless old books.

Connie climbed down the ladder and banged two books together to get rid of the worst of the dust. She found the resulting cloud quite impressive but she drew breath at the wrong minute and coughed, dropping the volumes.

Turning away, she fumbled for her handkerchief and discovered one thrust in front of her nose. Too overwhelmed to wonder who the newcomer was, she mopped up the resulting stream of tears, finished coughing and turned around, ready to thank her Good Samaritan.

Before her, holding the books, stood Alexander, Lord Ripley. Although dressed simply, in a dark green cloth coat and fawn colored waistcoat, she would never confuse his garments with something produced by a country tailor and here she was, in the same old gown as before, only now it was covered in centuries-old dust and grime.

Her breath quickened, her heart beat faster, exactly as they had when she'd first met her late husband. And look how that had turned out.

One dark brow moved a fraction and he smiled, the warmth filling her with a sense of camaraderie. "Such a gentleman," she murmured before she could stop herself. Then she clapped a hand to her mouth. "I'm so sorry. My father always said I shouldn't be allowed into polite society on my own."

He gave a sharp bark of laughter. "He was wrong. You're quite right, ma'am. You nearly had had me in unseemly laughter twice at dinner last night with your drollery. You have a way about you, don't you?" He turned and put the books on the large deal table that dominated this small room and flipped open the cover of one. His gaze sharpened. "My word." He bent and examined the contents.

Surprised by his interest, she opened the other and was similarly intrigued. She'd come here to unearth a few inventories but had become interested in the much smaller books that rested by the side of the larger tomes. Receipt books and notebooks from centuries ago, even older than the Jacobean books she'd discovered yesterday. She planned to clean them and take them to her room for some bedtime reading. What had begun as a way of keeping away from the tedium of the house party had gained a fascination of its own.

That reminded her of her errand to this dusty storeroom. However interesting the smaller books, she still had to collect the inventories, a task that had just become much easier. "Pardon me, sir but would you mind helping me with the other books up there?"

He gazed at her as if she really mattered to him, instead of forming a convenient distraction. His eyes radiated sincerity.

Did he look at all women that way? Was that part of his fabled charm?

"Alex," he reminded her. He glanced up and his eyes widened. "You were planning to get them down by yourself?"

"Well, yes. I know Lady Downholland's staff is rather busy just now. I had planned to take them down carefully and balance them on the steps of this ladder. I brought it from the large library, so I could be sure it was safe."

"You brought it here on your own?" He seemed incredulous, his voice rising.

"It doesn't weigh a great deal and it's not far, if you take the short way." She planted her hands on her hips. His attitude irritated her. As if a woman didn't carry a can of hot water to his bedroom every morning. "I'm not *entirely* helpless. Women aren't, you know."

He grinned, the dimple at the corner of his mouth deepening. "I understand." He executed a small bow. "And I beg your pardon, ma'am." Alex shifted his attention to the books on the table. "Receipt books instead of inventories. History interests you?"

"Somewhat." She shot him a brief glance, not wishing to prolong the moment and receive another of his penetrating gazes. "I shouldn't say that, should I? My aunt has it that men don't like women with too many opinions."

He laughed. "I've just managed to escape a group of women who think that."

Before he laughed again, she put her foot on the bottom rung of the ladder. "If I could pass you the books I want, would that work? I don't think it would do the other way about."

"No indeed. If I dropped them they might squash you."

Now it was her turn to laugh. "I'm not that fragile."

She levered out the first book with a great deal of care and even more dust. Without looking down, she called out, "I fear I'll make an enemy of your valet. I'm so sorry. I didn't realize these had been here quite so long."

He coughed. "It's of no matter. I'm here and waiting."

With the book balanced on the top of the ladder, she glanced down. He'd stood where he couldn't see up her skirts. That alone warmed her to him, since another man might have taken advantage, although she had foregone her hoop today in favor of a quilted petticoat, so the task wouldn't have been so easy. Neither would climbing ladders. "Thank you sir."

Comprehension lit his eyes. "Think nothing of it. I don't steal."

It came as a shock to realize he'd known what she meant. Peeking would have been just that. She hadn't given him any sign that she wanted him to, or shown any sign of not caring. So yes, it would have been stealing something from her. Her feelings for him shifted a tiny bit and she added respect for liking. Desire she must set aside. Not for her.

She concentrated on getting the book down the ladder. He took it from her when she'd gone down three rungs and he lifted it without seeming effort. It had taken a lot of work to get the book down even those three rungs. Without him, the task would have exhausted her.

There were four tomes in all. Each had collected its load of dust and she could do very little when she tipped the book and another tranche of the heavy, feathery stuff slid off the top.

A bout of coughing erupted from below. He had suffered worse than she. An old cobweb dangled from his wig at the back and grime streaked his face. Now he looked human, normal. "There," he said. "Now we're equal."

Hardly, but she'd let that pass. "The others aren't as bad. That one was the worst."

He lifted his strong, capable hands and she let go of the second tome. Without a tremor, he hefted the sizable, heavy volume and laid it gently on the table.

The next book proved easier to shift. It slid off the stack without dislodging more than a cloud of dust and a dead spider, probably the previous inhabitant of the web now decorating Alex's wig. Again he took it and laid it aside as if it weighed no more than a modern novel.

The fourth book held an unexpected treasure; another thick wedge of dust that had formed on the exposed corner of the tome. It landed on him, but apart from coughing until his eyes watered, he made no protest. "Please don't concern yourself, ma'am," he said, smiling. "I find this experience much more to my taste than making polite conversation with the other guests."

Shamefacedly, because she should really not keep the guest of honor here for herself, she headed for the door. She'd left a table on wheels there with a duster that was completely inadequate for the task. She passed the duster over the surfaces of the tomes, but they weren't much better after she'd used it.

"I think," he said gravely, "that we might use the tablecloth."

"Oh you wonderful man!" she cried in delight.

From somewhere he'd produced a slightly grimy, plain linen cloth. "How do you know it's a tablecloth?" she asked.

"It was in a small drawer at the end of the table."

She couldn't imagine why anyone would bother covering this cheap deal table but she was glad of it. She shook out the cloth and applied it to the books, managing to complete the task without raising more than one cloud of dust. When the books were reasonably clean, she wanted to peek inside them but her hands were filthy. She couldn't risk it.

"If we take the books to the library, we can send a maid to finish the job and reconvene after we've washed and changed." His cheeks were begrimed, his fashionable wig covered in a fine mist of grey and cobwebs hung from one sleeve.

"Oh Alex, you shouldn't have helped me. Your beautiful clothes, I'm so sorry. I dressed in my oldest—"

He caught her hands and again a thrill of recognition went through her, a sensation she refused to give way to.

"You are a delightful sight, Connie."

Her name had never sounded so good on anyone else's lips. *Stupid*, she berated herself.

"Shall I tell you why? Because what I see is good, honest enthusiasm. No dissembling, no concern about how you look, how you might feel. It's marvelous, especially after the artifice of London." A shadow crossed his eyes.

"I'm unfamiliar with artifice. I can keep quiet, be tactful and polite but I never had much occasion to use it."

"Did you not use it when your husband courted you?" His dimple returned, hinting at a smile.

She swallowed, pushing her memories back where they belonged. That was gone and done now. John was dead and she was here. "No. We'd known each other most of our lives. However, it turned out that I didn't know him as well as I'd thought." She snapped off her words and hastily passed on to a subject he couldn't dispute, cutting off any possible questions about her last remark. She'd nearly betrayed something so intimate she'd never told anyone else. "He died from a fall from his horse. It was dark and he shouldn't have been riding so fast. "

"I see. When did that happen?" He didn't say he was sorry, as convention required of him, but gave her a considered look.

Somehow that made it better, because John's death hadn't come as a tragedy to her. "Two years ago."

"So you're out of mourning and looking for love?"

"Out of mourning." She smiled and pulled away, turning back to the books. "And to be truthful, the state of widowhood is far preferable to— to being single." She'd nearly committed the unpardonable offence of admitting how difficult she'd found her marriage at the end. Despite Lord Ripley—Alex's flattering comments about honesty, she couldn't be that honest with him. With anyone, for that matter. "My arrangement with Jasper suits us both and my godparents, who have been extremely generous to me, wish it to happen. We will sign the settlement this visit and marry very soon."

"It sounds eminently practical." Turning away, he lifted the first book. "We should get this done and then we can make ourselves respectable once more." He half turned with a smile. "Unless you think that cobwebs should come into fashion? It would be amusing to try."

She laughed, the recent tension broken. "If I attempted anything of the kind, people would only make fun and say something about my eccentricity."

"I could do it." He sighed. "My cousin Julius and I provoke a few reactions from time to time. Though I doubt I could describe him as completely respectable, either."

She'd read about his cousin, the haughty and influential Earl of Winterton. She paused for a moment, remembering the eminence of this person helping her stack old books. He knew the greatest in the land, called a duke Grandfather, and here he was with her, doing this.

He put the books on the trolley, effectively preventing her from doing any of the heavy lifting by blocking her access with his body. So she gave up her attempts to snag a copy and instead stood ready to maneuver the vehicle out of the room. He opened the door for her and she pushed it out.

Steering proved harder when the trolley was burdened with the four heavy books and several smaller ones and she exerted considerable pressure to keep the wobbly wheels on course. Until, at the end of the first corridor, he stood in front of it. She was concentrating so hard on keeping it steady that she barely avoided crashing into him.

Determination in his eyes, he took the end of the table and shook his head. He wouldn't allow her to go any further. "I'll push. You lead the way."

With an exasperated sigh, she straightened, ignoring her aching back. "Very well."

They'd just reached the passage that led from the minor rooms where they'd come from to the larger, more stately apartments, when Miss Stobart appeared from nowhere and made them stop by the simple expedient of stepping in front of them.

"Dammit!" Connie exclaimed, before she could control her unruly tongue.

The woman turned a freezing eye onto her. "You may go."

Connie put her hands on her hips. "I may?"

The woman ignored her as if she didn't exist and addressed Alex. "Aren't you glad to see me?"

Considering the frown on Alex's face, that was a most unwise question.

"As you can see, Miss Stobart, Mrs. Rattigan and I have endured a dust storm. We cannot engage in idle chit-chat at this stage."

He returned to his task.

The lady shot Connie a startled glance of recognition. Connie gave her a regal nod.

The exquisitely formed Miss Stobart emphasized her figure with tight lacing and a white flower-bedecked gown, matching shoes and pretty lace at elbows and neck. She made even more of her assets by the way she thrust her bosom forward. Or rather, up. The contrast with Connie's practical clothes and disheveled appearance couldn't have been more obvious.

"I have been walking in the gardens and I'm *quite* exhausted." She fanned herself vigorously. "Could you not escort me to my room, my *dear* Lord Ripley?" Miss Stobart was a handsome woman but someone should tell her that some men preferred not to be pursued quite so vigorously.

Tired of being ignored, Connie took hold of the table and nudged his lordship aside. "I can see you have other obligations. Thank you very much for your help, my lord, but I can manage from here."

Alex stood foursquare, as solid as a brick wall. He wouldn't budge. "I wouldn't dream of it, dear ma'am." He nodded to the lady in white. "Good day, Miss Stobart. No doubt I'll see you at dinner."

When he eased the trolley forward, she moved aside. "Of course."

Luckily, the library was empty. As Alex wheeled the trolley to the back of the spacious room, Connie checked all the window embrasures, just in case, because she suspected his lordship was in a temper and could well become indiscreet.

His cheekbones were tinged with red and his eyes spat fire. But she refused to become involved in a situation she knew little about. She should really make her excuses and leave. "I really am grateful for your help."

"Yes." He puffed out a deep breath and closed his eyes, before opening them again and meeting her gaze. He leaned against one of the wing armchairs then drew away and brushed his sleeves. "I apologize for Miss Stobart's behavior. She had no right to make the assumptions she did."

Connie laughed and ruefully regarded her grime-bedecked gown. She wasn't even wearing lace, just linen sleeve protectors. No wonder Miss Stobart thought she was a maid. "It's hardly surprising. I'm not exactly dressed like a guest and I was trying desperately to avoid her attention."

"She shouldn't make that kind of instant judgment." Alex frowned. "She behaved poorly."

"Perhaps she's under some strain. Anyone can behave badly if they feel stressed."

He raised a brow. "Miss Stobart was reared in the heart of society. She should control herself better. In any case, she should not be here." He sighed and pushed his fingers into his hair, dislodging his wig. It fell to the floor with a *flump*.

What would his short, dark hair and well-shaped head feel like under her palm, if she curved her hand around it? She pushed her mind away from the unruly thought. She'd never know.

With an unnervingly sincere gaze, he took the three steps that separated them. "Allow me to explain. I won't ask you to do anything that compromises you."

"Like being in my godfather's library alone with you and with the door closed?"

He gave a startled laugh and looked around as if noticing they were alone for the first time. "By God, yes. Should I open the door to assuage your sense of propriety?"

Connie couldn't help it—she smiled. It could have infuriated him, a man boxed into a corner but instead he joined her and that was, perhaps, even more dangerous. Because he had the most attractive smile she'd ever seen. Sensuous with a touch of wicked humor and totally irresistible.

"I'm older, on the verge of thirty. Safe." She smiled ruefully. "And sometimes lonely." She swallowed, fighting back self-pity.

"But you're not desperate." He took her hand, his touch balm to her loneliness. "I can tell. There's a scent, an air, or something."

Rich, handsome, high-born, he was probably pursued as hard as any partridge in August. The foolish image forced a laugh out of her. "I was reared to think of the men as the chasers, the women as prey but it's the other way about with you."

"It is truly charming to meet someone so honest," he said. "And I don't mean that in any derogatory way. You should come to London. You'd be a sensation."

She wouldn't let him turn her head. That was foolish talk. "Lady Downholland spoke of holding a ball to celebrate my marriage to Jasper." She was looking forward to expanding her experience, living a little.

"I fear then it will be too late." He released her and moved away. "We should go." He picked up his wig in one fluid movement. "Though I'd rather stay here, dust or not."

Chapter 3

For the next several days, Connie avoided the many entertainments her aunt had set up. Jasper had still not arrived but he had sent word and apology that he would be late, kept by a tedious business affair in town. He was, he said, putting his estate in order before his marriage, so he wouldn't have to attend to it after.

In the company of the other guests, Alex treated her with polite respect, but no more. It suited her, she told herself stoutly. At least neither were pretending their friendship was anything other than he had said but she did wonder why he hadn't bolted from his unwanted, ardent suitors before now.

Escaping from the prospect of what promised to become an excruciating musicale one afternoon, she made her way to a small storeroom, where she found another nest of family books. Thankfully, these were collections of letters, bound into volumes, rather than the huge inventories and she carried the half dozen books into the library, to the table she had commandeered for her use during this visit.

She paused in the doorway. "Good afternoon, sir."

Alex glanced up and smiled, then returned to his book. He'd come here for the last few days, poring over the receipt books she'd found the day she met him. "Did you know they made their own spirit here in the old days? It was called raspberry cordial but from the ingredients listed here it contained considerably more than raspberries and water. They were skilled at the use of the still. Ladies could indulge in spirits without appearing unladylike, one imagines."

"And ratafia is different?" She put the books down at the end of the table. "Flavored with almonds but completely lethal. I've seen one of my aunts take glass after glass and not able to stand up at the end of the evening. Aunt Joleta is famous for the problems she has with her legs. It isn't her legs, it's her balance."

He looked up, a smile wreathing his features. "I have relatives like that. One of my aunts never goes anywhere without her sedan chair and a pair of sturdy footmen to carry her around. Sometimes I look forward to old age. They call it eccentricity. In me it would be something far worse."

Age would suit him. She doubted he'd lose his power or that magnetic presence.

She shook her head. "Sometimes it's because they have nothing else. They're missing something."

He straightened. "Sometimes it's because they aren't satisfied with what they have."

"Are you speaking from experience?" She should really put a guard on her tongue, but with him it was so easy to say what she thought.

He nodded curtly. "I've known people like that. They destroy everything to get what they want. Then they don't want it."

"Will you be like that?" She shouldn't have asked such an impertinent question and turned away, picked up one of the books. "I'm sorry. I always say too much. I try so hard not to but it happens. Could you pretend I didn't say that?" Usually she had no problems with people she didn't know well but she found herself relaxing far too much around him and not reminding herself who he was and what he represented. Money, power, influence.

"No." He sounded closer.

His proximity disturbed her, sent her heart racing and tightened her throat. Even now, even when she couldn't see him or feel him, she sensed him. The scent of his light citrusy cologne washed over her in a seductive wave. Ignoring it was no longer possible, although she'd tried to do it for days now.

"No, I won't pretend. People do that too much. You're charming, Connie, and you shouldn't let people cow you."

While not shy, she was so very aware of what people said about her. A childhood of blurting out inappropriate comments had only added to her discomfort in company. She was supposed to not care but she did and sometimes it hurt too much, even when the criticism came from people she didn't particularly care about. "I should have a thicker skin."

"Or someone who understands you and wants to take care of you. Do you think Jasper Dankworth will do that?"

She didn't look on Jasper as a soul mate. "I'm sure I can learn to live with my unfortunate vulnerability. Please don't concern yourself."

She turned, the book she'd picked up, forming an effective barrier between them. "I found some letters this morning. Shall we see if they connect with the entries in the inventories?"

He returned to the inventories. "What dates do you have?"

"This one is 1589."

She flipped through the letters. "These are a quarter of a century later. A shame because they won't marry up. What about the other inventories?"

She was glad of his help with the heavy books they'd collected in the dusty storeroom, now thankfully properly cleaned. He spread them out on the long table and she opened the letters and flipped through them. At least they'd been bound in roughly date order. She fetched the other documents and books she'd discovered and they matched them to the books by date, occasionally reading out juicy extracts, showing the quaint habits of a bygone age, or strange connections with their own.

Slowly a picture formed, of people and the way they lived. Not dry historical characters but living, breathing people. "I love this."

He glanced at her. "I can tell. You glow when you make a new discovery. In a way, it's a shame you don't hire yourself out doing this kind of work. My father would employ you in a heartbeat." He leaned back in his high-backed chair, one he'd pulled over from a nearby window embrasure. "You could make a career of it."

"The Downhollands have an interesting history." Her heart quickened. She'd dearly love to, but because of her birth, her status and her sex, she had little opportunity. "Careers are for men."

"Tell that to the florists of London, the women who run successful businesses in the city and for that matter, the housekeepers and lady's maids."

She turned with a smile. "That's a very enlightened point of view."

He shrugged. "It's a practical one. I've never ignored what I can see and experience." The expression in his eyes heated, and their gazes locked and held. Slowly he got to his feet and stood over her.

She didn't give way this time. He gazed at her and this time she met the warm, desirous expression in his dark eyes, the way he crowded her, as if to protect her. But danger lay in his closeness, an intimacy she didn't know how to manage. Her body responded, softening and dampening for him.

"So what am I experiencing here?" he murmured. Someone on the other side of the table wouldn't have heard him clearly.

She licked her suddenly dry lips. "I don't know."

"I think you do." His arms went around her, holding her close to his strong body and he brought his mouth down to hers.

She expected fast ravishment but what she got was slow seduction. His lips touched hers, then he grazed them, adding a final, loving touch that she couldn't resist.

He held her in his thrall, spellbound and finally she admitted the truth of her feelings for him. She wanted him, so much, and even though she couldn't have him, she'd at least have this. She'd lain awake longing to know what his kiss was like, how he'd feel.

Exquisite, that was how. His tongue flicked out and touched her lips, outlined them. The featherlike brush sensitized her, readied her for him, made her want to feel him deeper, more intimately.

She parted her lips, just a little. He darted his tongue in, tasting, then out, then with a groan, he tilted his head and pressed his mouth more firmly over hers, sealing them together. She grasped his waist, impatiently shoving his coat aside, getting as close as she could to that firm, male skin. Only his waistcoat. He spread his hands over her back and held her close, making her feel absurdly safe, all the time plundering her like a pirate. He swept his tongue into her mouth, exploring her like a man dying of thirst. She gave a single sigh of acceptance and relaxed back into his arms, letting him support her.

She'd never experienced anything like this, this sense of oneness, of two people striving together toward a mutual end. He tasted wonderful as he marked his presence on her heart and soul, there for all time.

He devoured her, taking her mouth in a ravishment more complete than she'd ever known. This wasn't a kiss—it was lovemaking.

When he drew back, he gazed at her from under heavy lids. "Who'd have guessed you'd be so irresistible?"

His words, just breathed against her lips, reflected her own feelings. Except she'd half expected it and never thought she'd have the chance to discover if she were right. "We shouldn't be doing this."

"No, we probably shouldn't." He held her, watching her with an intensity that missed nothing. Connie stayed where she was, aware of the danger but lulled by his very presence.

"So what happens now, Connie?"

She was damned if she'd stop now. The recklessness she'd suppressed for most of her life emerged, blinking into the daylight. For once, it would get its way. Her last chance to taste true desire, she wasn't about to give this up. But there was this, and there was reality. "By the end of this visit,

I expect to be formally betrothed to Jasper Dankworth. At the moment I'm a free agent with an understanding, no more."

"Is that an invitation, Mrs. Rattigan?" He gave her a wicked smile.

She didn't know what to say.

"I won't do anything you don't want and we'll do nothing more than kiss here. Anyone could come in."

Startled, she jerked back.

He hauled her back again. "We have a little cover and enough time." He dropped a kiss on her nose. "Sweet. You taste sweet."

"Honey for breakfast." She gave him a cheeky grin. Connie struggled to regain her common sense but the more he gazed at her the more impossible it became to do so.

"Or your own dulcet self." His eyes darkened and gleamed.

She wasn't experienced enough to interpret but it was warm and it heated her all the way through. "What is it?"

"I have a compulsion to taste you all over, discover where your honey is the most delicious." He swallowed and his muscles tensed around her. "But I will be content with what I can see. For now." He kissed her throat, flicked his tongue out and followed the strong tendon down to the hollow of her throat, where he lingered and soon had her gasping his name.

"I've never considered Alex a particularly wonderful name." He breathed the words over her neck, so intimately. "But when you say it, I can't imagine a better one. Say my name again, sweetheart. Just like that. As if you want me."

Oh God, she did, she did want him. How could a simple kiss have escalated to this? To this yearning? She was drowning in him, in her need for him. But she'd only known him for a very short time. She couldn't let him take this much further, although how could she stop him when she wanted it so much? This was dangerous, really dangerous.

He caressed her waist and she felt it through all the layers she wore as if he branded her skin. She turned, trying to get close to him and he laid one sweet kiss on the upper curve of her bosom before he returned to her mouth.

He took his time, tasting her, coaxing her response. Tutoring her. She gave him everything he asked for, opening her mouth to his onslaught. His hand shook when he clasped her wrist and stroked the inner skin.

How could such a public part of her body be so sensitive?

His thumb slid up her arm, toward her elbow. He slipped his fingers under her sleeve and gave the inner part of her elbow the same treatment, all the time taking her mouth in kiss after kiss.

Hungrily, she gave him as much passion as he gave her, willing to follow him wherever he wanted to take her. As long as he didn't stop.

He glided his hand back down her arm, gripped her wrist and drew back. "No more," he said, gasping for breath. "You try my control."

Disappointment flooded her being. She wanted more, so much more.

He smiled down at her. "You've not had much experience, although thank God you're not a complete innocent. But I'm further along this path than you and I know that if I press myself on you now, you'll accept me but you might regret it later."

With a rough growl, he bent and took another kiss. She gave it, moaning into his mouth, the sound setting up intimate vibrations.

He tore his lips away from hers. "We can't. Truly, Connie, we can't. You're close, so am I. I only have so much self-control and I want you so much."

At last, she understood this went two ways and women had power in this situation, too. Nobody had explained that before and she'd never seen it. She'd lost her mother early, too early to make an impression on her. She'd been brought up by her loving father and a succession of nursemaids and governesses. Even he'd gone now. And he couldn't have told her about this. Her marriage hadn't shown her that either. Nor the friendships she'd made with men in the local assembly rooms and on the hunting field before her marriage. *Nobody*. Just as nobody had told her about this yearning.

His hands shook before he took a deep breath and firmed his hold on her. "Come. Sit."

She never expected him to respond like this. A dalliance was all she'd expected from this practiced seducer, someone to give her one precious experience before she entered the marital state for the second time. The secret place between her legs had dampened. And it angered her that she didn't know what to call it. No coy, feminine euphemisms, she wanted to *know*. How could she have lived this long, been married and know so little about herself? He would tell her, if she asked.

She pushed her thighs closer together.

Holding her hand, he took her to the chair he'd occupied and she sat while he drew up another similar one and sat next to her. Immediately he reached for her hand again. He brought it to his lips and kissed her palm but then lowered it. They sat together, hands clasped.

"You've never experienced that before, have you?"

She shook her head.

"It's simple lust. We'd have done something stupid, or I would. With the door unlocked and in a public room, I'd have thrown your skirts over your head and taken you." He watched her, seemingly in control of himself but under his plain maroon waistcoat his chest moved more strongly than usual. "Why aren't you pulling away, scared?"

She had stopped being scared of the truth years ago. "Because it's true. You'd take me and I'd let you." At this moment, she didn't care. He could have her any way he wanted her.

With those cold words, he'd been trying to push her away but they didn't succeed.

He glanced down at her skirt, then up. "You shouldn't move like that. Or I *will* take you, dammit." He swallowed and took a couple of deep breaths. His fine woolen waistcoat moved and the gold buttons glinted in the sunlight streaming in from the large windows to one side of them.

Fortunately, this room wasn't on the side of the house where people would be strolling and taking the air. Her blood went cold. She hadn't even thought about someone seeing them. He'd swept her away, but she had to admit she'd done some of the sweeping herself.

"Let me tell you a story. I've talked about my cousin Winterton before, haven't I?"

She nodded. Oh, yes, nobody could miss reports about the Earl of Winterton.

"He's glorious. He awes everyone when he puts his mind to it. I can do it but not as magnificently as he does. Julius is the pink of the ton, the arbiter of fashion."

"I read that about you, too."

He laughed, a low rumble. "You have?"

"We can read in the north."

He squeezed her hand. "I know that, believe it or not. Yes, if you read a newspaper, you'll have come across their names. Julius and his brother Augustus. Julius had more to take out on the world. Augustus escaped in classical study and fled abroad, but he can be as flamboyant when the mood takes him." He paused, glanced at the books spread out on the table then he looked back at her. Completely grave now. "In society we have a reputation for recklessness. Daring and nerve, they say, though people call it other things too. I only take chances when I think the rewards will be worth it. I don't take chances with other people's fortunes, with their futures. Do you understand me?"

"I'm beginning to." Sense was returning. She cursed its necessity.

"Ten years ago Julius would have taken you without hesitation, if you'd been willing. I wouldn't have done it then and I'm not about to do it now. That's where Julius and I part company. You know why I won't do it?"

She shook her head, and disappointment flooded every cell, every part of her. He wasn't going to let her give herself to him.

"Because I like you. And because if we wait, we'll discover if we're meant to be, or not. This could be the beginning of a friendship and we could ruin it by plunging into lust. Or it could be something else. Or we might never meet again after this house party." His smile tensed. "Dammit, don't look at me like that."

When he tugged on her hand, she fell off balance and he hauled her into his lap. He threaded his hand into her hair, under the knot she wore during the daytime, dislodging the pins. Strands tumbled down her back, tickling her neck. She met his mouth, open and as ravenous as before.

He moaned, the sound vibrating against her lips, enhancing their closeness, echoing hers to him.

More, she wanted more. She curved her arm around his neck, holding him close, cursing her inexperience that she didn't know the wiles that would keep him close.

After one deep kiss, he pulled away and stood, only holding her waist until she was steady on her feet. "I find you completely irresistible, which is why I have to resist you." He drew away, leaving her cold and bereft. "I'll quit this house soon. I've confronted Miss Stobart, told her I have no intention of connecting myself to her. It was uncomfortable, but I needed to do it. Now I must go and tarnish my reputation even further."

She blinked. "What do you mean?"

"Julius has written to me. He's done his best to face down the scandal I left in London but Miss Stobart has friends and rumors are spreading, especially since we're at the same house party." His lips quirked in a sardonic smile. "I stayed because of you, but you know that, don't you, Connie?" The smile disappeared. "He suggests I go back to town and flirt with everyone. Flirt to the edge of danger. I can do it without becoming attached and it's the best way to get the whole affair with La Stobart condemned. Once town witnesses the mood I'm in, its interest will disappear in a welter of different women and they'll consider her one in a long line. I'll make sure to keep to the ones who know how to play the game. So I'm off to do my duty." He got to his feet, gently put her aside and strode to the other side of the table. "Connie, I told you this because I didn't want to lose your good opinion. Know that I do this for a purpose, not because I wish it. Will you write to me?"

Her wayward spirits soared at the affirmation of his regard for her. "I think not." Otherwise, her heart might ache too much. A clean break would be harder at first but better later on. She could get on with her life with no residue, nothing to give her a constant reminder of what she could have had. A man who wanted her for herself, not for the land she could bring or the children she could give him. "I'm embarking on my second marriage. This one is practical."

"And your first one was not?" He was too perceptive, this man, reading between the lines to her true meaning.

Yes, she had loved John once. She met his direct gaze. "Not entirely. But it didn't work out the way I thought it would, so this time I'm going into the union with practical considerations uppermost. I've lived in a small community and I know that kind of existence will not suit me for the rest of my life. Marriage to Jasper will enrich my experience."

He listened to her, really listened, his gaze intent. He gave a short nod. "You're right. It will. He's a man about town, or he fancies himself as such. And London life will suit you. You're not made for the provinces."

She thought of her perfectly comfortable life in the north and her utter, utter boredom there. Maybe this interlude was an illusion but she wanted to remember it, put a frame around it and revisit it when she felt better, stronger.

He walked to the door. "I will never forget you. If you ever need a friend, write to me. I will come. Be assured of that. Have a good life, Constance Rattigan. You deserve it. Never expect anything but the best and it will come to you."

She very much doubted that.

She didn't watch him leave. Her eyes were clouded with tears, but she forced them down, swallowed and lifted her chin, as she'd always done, facing the world head-on. She would allow herself the indulgence of tears later, if she needed them. Then put the experience behind her, wrap it in gossamer as a precious memory, and let it go.

Jasper arrived the day after Alex's departure.

Chapter 4

The contract now bore Connie's signature.

"And here," said Brigham, her godfather's man of business.

She signed. And again. Then it was done.

Jasper bent his head and followed suit. Then the two witnesses, Brigham's assistant and Downholland's land steward. Their task concluded, the witnesses bowed and left the room.

She would marry Jasper Dankworth. Her life and position settled, just as she'd wanted it. But that was BA. Before Alex.

She should be happy but she could think of nothing but the man who had streaked through her life, not the man standing before her now.

Jasper took her hand and smiled, seemingly delighted. She should be thrilled to marry such a promising prospect.

"You could wed before you leave this house," Lord Downholland said with a genial smile. "Extend your visit and we can arrange a license for you." Her godfather, a constant presence in her life, removed his gold-rimmed spectacles and set them on his broad, oak desk, scarred with centuries of use, but the one piece of furniture he refused to relinquish to his wife's passion for refurbishing the house.

Jasper's expression dimmed at his lordship's proposal, his brilliant blue eyes clouding over. "I'm sorry but I have to leave for London tomorrow. I have a business matter that won't wait." He turned to his lordship. "I could return but I have another idea. Why don't you come to London too and we may marry there?"

Lord Downholland heaved a hefty sigh. "I hoped to have this matter settled quickly." His brow furrowing, then he smiled. "But if you need the time, yes, I believe that would do admirably. If Connie comes to our London house, she could spend a week or two with us first. She can see the town and meet our friends."

Who wouldn't be excited at the thought of spending time in London? Even if the man she'd said goodbye to had left the house headed in that direction? But in town there were mantua-makers, toymakers, theatres and balls. That would prove enough stimulation to prevent her dreaming of something she could not have. Or someone doing something. With her.

She gave her godfather a brilliant smile. "I would enjoy that very much."

Lord Downholland rubbed his hands together. "That is settled, then. We shall visit London in a few weeks, after the assizes." Her godfather was a local magistrate and had ambitions to become the Lord Lieutenant of the county in time, so he couldn't excuse himself from that duty.

Her life was about to change. "I should like to go home for a short time. I've wound up most of my affairs but one or two matters are still outstanding."

She needed to bolt home, like a rabbit returning to its burrow. To sleep in her bed on her own, make her own decisions for herself.

Alex had gone and it was as if he'd never been there, except that people still talked about him. It was as if a comet had shot through the house and then disappeared without a trace, just the memory of its brilliance. But she wanted that week or two to work him out of her system, dream about him and then determinedly forget him. After that, she'd get on with her life and not look back. Truly, she would.

Jasper bowed, his smoothly handsome face revealing nothing beyond an appropriate smile. Tall, beautifully attired in crimson broadcloth, his lean frame fluid in its movements, he was the kind of man most women would die for. Not her. She preferred someone more powerful, darker—someone she must forget.

"Would you come for a walk in the garden with me, my dear? It's a bright day and we've been cooped up here for so long that I for one would appreciate some fresh air."

She gave him a smile similar in nature to his own. "Thank you. That would be most agreeable." Like strangers at a dinner party discussing a promenade. Not future life partners.

Lord Downholland resumed his seat behind the huge desk and donned a pair of wire-framed spectacles. "If you wouldn't mind giving me a few minutes more, Connie, I would appreciate it."

"Of course, sir." She bade her betrothed farewell, waited until he'd bowed again and left the room, and retook her seat. She folded her hands in her lap.

"I'm delighted you accepted this offer." Lord Downholland spoke as if he was addressing a public meeting.

Connie had accustomed herself to that. Uncharacteristic irritation almost drove her to tell him to get on with it.

Lord Downholland continued to speak in measured tones. "I have asked you to remain behind, because I wish to make a few matters clear."

Connie couldn't imagine what he meant. "Is it the morality clause? It is of no matter." The caveat that if she were proven to be of dubious moral character, the contract was in default and Jasper could claim her estate in lieu of damages in an expensive breach of promise case.

Her godfather retained his avuncular smile. "No, it's not that. We have no reason to concern ourselves with your excellent character. Jasper wished for it, and you didn't object, that is all." He paused, and lost the smile completely. "Connie, we are aware that you are no youngster but you are still capable of bearing heirs."

Shock ripped through her, nearly sending her to the floor. So cruel, to mention this. But so necessary. Her throat went dry and tight. "Children? Sir, you know I haven't had the best of fortune—"

"We understand that. But you *have* given birth. Many women lose babies but you came through the ordeal and you are as healthy as ever."

Every day she thought about her baby, the tiny scrap who hadn't given even one cry. These days the grief had stilled to a dull ache. It was how people told her it should be, but she couldn't help but feel a pang, an echo of the awful pain she felt after her only baby died. Her own personal sorrow, not one she wished to burden others with.

Her godfather nodded and awkwardly patted her shoulder. "You are to feel under no compulsion or regret. We proposed this marriage in full knowledge of your history. This house and estate does not depend on direct heirs. There is no entail. That is how I could choose to leave this estate to my sister's son, in default of a direct heir. If you do not produce an heir, you may take the next in line into the house and train him in preparation for his new role." His kindly face, creased with concern, revealed his understanding of her concerns. "No, that is not why we chose you, dear Connie. You are a sensible woman and Jasper needs a guiding hand. A young woman wouldn't have suited him, or coped with his moods. He needs a steadying influence. You have guided a wayward husband before. That is the reason, dear Connie."

"John wasn't completely faithful." It choked her to say it. So many mistakes that she'd sworn never to let love into her life again.

Lord Downholland *smiled*. "We know, my dear. You quelled any possible scandal and handled the affair most carefully. Connie, Lady Downholland and I are proud of what you made of your inheritance and we have hopes that you and Jasper will together do even more to improve this one. Jasper is merely skittish, that's all. His relatives on his father's side are powerful, but untrustworthy, and we wish to give him a better chance in life. There is goodness in him, I'm sure of it." His ruddy country features were as dear to her as her father's. As was the inevitable egg stain on his waistcoat. He'd never quite managed the skill of breaking open a boiled egg without spilling the contents and he loved them. His valet must despair.

That was the real reason they'd chosen her. Not because his lordship and her father had corresponded for most of their lives, not because Lady Downholland was her aunt as well as her godmother, not because she was intelligent or beautiful or they wanted to show her kindness. But because she was managing and they wanted her to "guide" Jasper.

Her godfather put the second page of her marriage settlement back on the desk. It lay slightly askew on the small pile.

Precisely as she felt, she realized with a sudden shock. This didn't feel quite right any more. Ever since her encounter with Alex.

Too late. She'd gone too far, signed the documents. She had to go through with this. It would enrich her life immeasurably in all but one area. "Thank you, sir. I am immeasurably blessed that you and Lady Downholland have chosen to treat me with such kindness."

The other, unspoken, requirement would be that she did as the Downhollands bid her. Since they were in their mid-fifties and in robust health, she had no illusions of inheriting early but Jasper's estate and her own would give them plenty to live on in comfort. "I will, with your permission, join my intended husband in the gardens."

Revealing nothing, she got to her feet in a smooth motion. During John's affair and after, she'd had plenty of practice hiding her real emotions and her skill came to her aid now. She smiled then curtseyed to her godfather before leaving the room.

Pausing only to find a straw hat, a shawl and a pair of gloves, Connie headed outside. It was a bright day, although the chill of early spring still permeated the atmosphere. A light shower had sprinkled the leaves and buds with sprays of water, splitting the light into shards of brilliance.

Too early for most flowers, although a few snowdrops were nestled by the side of a box hedge. She bent and touched them.

The velvet petals caressed her fingers when she touched them, their creamy white reflecting on her skin. She stood and walked through the rose garden, the paths presenting a pleasant walk for anyone, although the roses were only in tight bud as yet, none of their color showing.

It would be a good year for the rose bushes. How was her garden faring in this season of growth and new life? In a few days, she would find out.

Alex had been wiser than she'd thought. If he'd shown her any more passion, what she'd wanted from him so badly, she'd never have returned to this path, never looked at her future husband without remembering another man. She sent Alex silent thanks and set her mind to her future husband. Young, handsome, fond of her and possessed of a good fortune. Not many women were so lucky.

Jasper stood at the edge of the garden, waiting for her, his red coat a startling contrast to the greenery. His mouth was barely curved in the slightly supercilious smile he habitually wore. She couldn't blame him for that expression. Few people studied their own expressions in the mirror and he was probably unaware of it.

She walked toward him and tried to concentrate on his fine figure and fashionable air. Any woman would be glad to be seen with him.

She smiled back. "So you're leaving me?"

"Yes, I am. I'm so sorry. It's a small matter but I do want to conclude it. I want our union perhaps more than you do." His lips skimmed her cheek then he murmured, "Have I ever told you of the other advantages of marriage?"

"I've been married before." She repressed a shudder at the thought of sharing a bed with Jasper. For no reason other than that she had experienced the caresses of someone she wanted more than anyone else. She could do this, and she would. The breeze caught at the brim of her wide hat and she put a hand up to straighten it.

"Ah, yes but I heard John Rattigan was a brute of a man. A woman like you needs gentle handling, careful loving." His smile turned warmer. "Am I right?"

Considerate of him. "I can't imagine where you heard that. John was a big man but good to me, in his way." She had brazened everyone down during her marriage. She wouldn't change that now. Pride demanded she retain the secrets that were no one's business but her own. Crossly, she untied and retied the bow on her hat, pretending it needed adjusting. "It's true that my first marriage wasn't everything I expected but we managed pretty well."

"What was it, then?" He put his hands on her waist.

She allowed it, tried to relax into the embrace. They stood in the shelter of a high hedge, not in sight of the house. "We had a love match. Unfortunately, it turned out more infatuation than love but we came to an understanding. We managed." The words came out by rote. She'd told herself so often she almost believed it.

"We'll do more than manage," he said. "I promise you that."

When he pulled her closer, she didn't resist. His arms about her didn't feel right, although he held her close. Too close. His heat branded her stomach through the thin silk of her gown and she swallowed the urge to shove him away.

His mouth opened over hers in flagrant invitation and hers opened underneath. As she'd been taught and not by Alex. She could do this. She _could_.

Although Jasper was gentle with her, she didn't enjoy his kiss. Too wet, too invasive, his tongue forging a path into her mouth. He took instead of persuading her to give.

When he cinched her closer, she pushed away with a small laugh, feigning embarrassment. "We can't, Jasper. Not here."

He didn't let her go. "Where, then?" His eyes were still cold but his mouth slightly open.

She fought an urge to wipe her mouth. She'd persuade him to kiss her a little less like a wet fish and more like—no, just not as wet, was all. "When we're married, Jasper. And not in the garden."

"Oh come on, Constance, you've just admitted you're not a shy virgin." He squeezed her and grinned. "You could probably teach me a thing or two. So should we anticipate the ceremony? Just a little bit?" He planted another kiss on her lips. "The morality clause doesn't apply to us, you know."

She covered his lips with her fingers, stopping him kissing her again. "Perhaps when we're in London." She didn't want to appear prudish but he was rushing her. She wanted time to herself, the space to forget one man and anticipate another. The breeze rustled through the leaves of the rose bushes and the hedge behind them. It was getting up. Likely it would rain soon.

He smiled against her fingers. "Very well, but tonight. If I promise to take care, will you receive me?"

One night? Yes, perhaps she should start now. It would give her a path to follow, something to look forward to, because she couldn't deny she'd missed the physical side of marriage sometimes.

Lord Downholland would attend the assizes, go to London and she'd join them there. The banns would go up and they'd wed three weeks later. Very neat.

"Very well." Commit herself now, put space between her and the events in the library.

She was the recipient of his most fervent thanks, which almost made her change her mind. But he didn't kiss her again, for which she was truly thankful.

* * * *

Before dinner, she received a note scribbled by her betrothed.

My dearest Constance,

I have received information that means I must leave for London instantly. Some small confusion about the estate that necessitates my presence in London. I apologize for my hasty departure, particularly since we had such delightful plans. But I hope to expedite this matter that prevents our union and be with you much faster. Have patience. Return to your home and I will contact you as soon as the matter is concluded.

A pang of guilt shot through her because her first, instinctive reaction was relief. The next time they met, she'd be closer to her wedding day, caught up in the plans. And further away from this house and the memories it held.

All she had to do was forget Alex's kisses that had opened her up to possibilities she'd never considered before. Passion, consideration, someone who valued her for what she was, not what she had. Even love.

Chapter 5

By the time the season proper started, just after Easter, Alex's social life was in full swing. He attended balls, flirted with every eligible lady present and worked hard to put the rumors of Miss Stobart and himself behind him. After the balls, he went to the gaming hells, gentlemen's clubs and other interesting establishments and enjoyed those, too. However, the matchmaking mamas were closing in and after one such evening Alex felt like a fox pursued by particularly rabid hounds.

He went to bed alone and when he lay there, he felt alone.

He woke in the morning and tucked his hands behind his head, staring at the folds in the blue canopy above his bed, his mind in a forbidden place.

He'd been out of sorts since he'd kissed Connie Rattigan. The rawness of his emotions would wear off, the sensation of waking up every morning and missing something, specifically the sight of silken hair the color of rich honey on his pillow, her blue eyes gazing into his with sleepy welcome. Stupid to imagine such things, even if that vision had chased his sleep away. It would go. It *must*.

He just couldn't get Connie out of his head, where she had no place. She was marrying a Dankworth, for Christ's sake. It was hardly likely their paths would cross a great deal in the future.

He'd visit White's today. The matchmaking mamas couldn't follow him there.

When his valet came in with the can of hot water for his wash and shave, Alex rolled out of bed and with minimal help dressed in record time. He went for the louche and casual, tucked his neckcloth half inside his shirt in a style he was making popular. It saved time, too. He wasn't so much in a hurry that he didn't choose his new Brussels lace frills for his shirt and his new short sword, cut steel and lethal but very pretty. City wear and a display to make. An Emperor had to make his mark.

He picked up the letter on the tray and broke the seal. An invitation from his cousin Julius for that night. Yes, he'd go. He liked Vauxhall Gardens and with the greater prize of the Earl of Winterton, heir to a dukedom, no less, the mamas might leave him alone.

That evening, Alex attended Vauxhall Pleasure Gardens, at the invitation of his cousin Julius. Julius the Magnificent. A pretty place, if a trifle tawdry, but it amused Alex, normally. Tonight he couldn't crack a smile.

"Isn't that your Downholland's heir, Alex?" Julius perched on the low parapet separating their box from the dance floor but rose hurriedly, his rich blue velvet coat swirling around his legs when the flimsy barrier creaked under him. The candles in the sconces against the wall quivered as Julius stepped inside the box. One day this place would go up like a bonfire, but hopefully, not while they were here.

Julius was as fair as Alex was dark, and society had invented several fanciful names for them on the angel and devil line that amused neither. He'd described Julius to Connie as glorious, and he was surely that, his clothes of the finest, glittering with brilliants, his maquillage in place, and his fair hair covered by a fashionable wig.

Julius took the seat next to Alex and grimaced when he saw the sight opposite them. The dance floor was well illuminated, so when the promenading couples moved away the view was as clear as day.

Dankworth sat in a booth opposite them, in the company of some decidedly raffish individuals.

Alex had seen condemned men celebrate their execution day with the same kind of feverish exuberance. Was it because he was marrying Connie soon? Alex would have been anticipating the day with eagerness, not dread. Alex shuddered. "He's affianced to Lady Downholland's niece. It could mean trouble." The bastard didn't deserve her.

He couldn't hear Jasper Dankworth and his cronies, but they were chortling, their mouths wide with amusement. Several empty wine bottles stood outside the booth, waiting to be collected, and the elegant supper Vauxhall served to its patrons was scattered around, bits of wafer-thin ham dotted over the yellow and green paint.

Julius frowned. "Why is that trouble? What is Lady Downholland's niece to you?"

Oh hell, Julius had noticed the extra venom in Alex's tone. His cousin knew him too well.

He'd better pay attention to what he said.

Alex chose to tell the truth. If he couldn't trust Julius, he couldn't trust anyone. "I met her at the Downholland's. At first I asked her to help me avoid Miss Stobart, but our acquaintance became much more than that. She wasn't officially affianced, but I could offer her nothing. Or I thought I could not. After a few days? Her future was waiting for her. I came away. I like the woman a little too much. Now she's signed her marriage contract, so I can't lay claim, or even stake an interest."

He shrugged, making light of the matter that weighed his heart down worse every day. "It was a passing flirtation." If he said it often enough, perhaps he'd eventually believe it. "I don't want to see her married to someone who'll treat her with less than respect."

Julius fixed him with a look far too perceptive, his blue gaze glittering with speculation. He turned back to the scene in front of him. "Alex, what do you see?"

"A man disporting himself before tying the knot." Alex curled his lip at the sight of the booth opposite.

Dankworth had his hand down the bodice of the nearest woman, who was undoubtedly a tart, although dressed in the highest kick of fashion and not cheaply either. He was laughing uproariously at something one of his friends was saying,

"I see desperation." Julius was right. Dankworth was celebrating too hard, too feverishly, as if he had little time left. Despite his determination to keep his distance, Alex had learned some depressing facts about Dankworth. He had no right to interfere, but he wished he had.

Alex grimaced, acknowledging the truth and reached for his wineglass. He took a sip and replaced it carefully. "He's been playing too deep. He's a regular player at Hell in Whites, and God knows how many more places. He'll have to work hard to right his losses. He's living on expectation. He's a man of modest means, but as Downholland's heir he can call on new lines of credit."

"I'll investigate, shall I? Ask a few questions?" Julius leaned back and crossed his legs, the picture of elegance.

"I already have. I asked Fox, who only leaves White's to go to the House. Dankworth is consorting with the kind of man who'll wager on anything, including if Lady Barrett's next child is finally a boy."

"I had fifty on that one myself," Julius shot his cousin a shamefaced grin. "After five girls, I doubt her ability to produce a son. I saw some bets of upwards of a thousand in the book."

"One of them might be his." Alex jerked his chin in Dankworth's direction. "He's down far too much for a man of modest fortune. One more night and he'll have lost most of what he has left then he'll be punting on the expectation. He will gain Mrs. Rattigan's estate on their marriage and no doubt he'll receive some kind of allowance as Downholland's heir."

"I see." Julius poured himself another glass, his movements leisurely. "If I were you, I'd write a warning to Mrs. Rattigan. Tell her how matters lie. Then she can make her own decision."

Dankworth abandoned his booth and strode toward another. In the other booth, new entrants were settling, namely Miss Louisa Stobart and her family. Tonight was turning into the kind of evening Alex preferred to forget.

Miss Stobart appeared to advantage, her gown a confection of white and pink designed to make her appear sweet. More like candied roses than a real living, breathing woman. But a voracious chaser, as Alex had reason to know. She'd returned to town as game as ever.

Unbidden, a picture of Connie came to his mind, her hair tousled, cobwebs hanging from the sleeve of a severely practical gown. The only adornment she needed was the smile that melted his heart.

She'd spoiled him for other women. Not even the most practiced courtesan would be able to raise Alex's attention right now. His father favored Louisa Stobart but Alex couldn't bear marrying a woman with no conversation outside the latest fashions and the people she knew, moreover, one with such a spiteful streak. Louisa wasn't kind to anyone, least of all her friends. Her fortune gave her the leeway to say more than others, and at present society considered her a wit.

Dankworth offered Miss Stobart his arm. She took it and stepped through the small opening separating her box from the dance floor. Now the picture of propriety, he promenaded around the edge of the area, stopping to chat with the various occupants.

"He's distancing himself from the raffish crowd he was with." Alex watched the scene with distaste. What was Dankworth doing with Miss Stobart? He couldn't court her. He was already betrothed.

"He's coming this way," Julius murmured. "I suggest you make yourself scarce for ten minutes, Alex. Give me the field. Besides, he'll know you're angry with him. You're not good at hiding that particular emotion."

Good advice. Alex slipped out of the door at the back of the booth. After a pleasant stroll around the gardens that helped to calm his wayward mood, Alex returned in better spirits.

Julius met him with grim news. His face was as still and hard as stone. "Dankworth is announcing his engagement to Miss Stobart. He introduced me to the lady he has just asked to marry him."

"Why would he do that, when our family and his are at odds?"

Julius shrugged, his well-cut coat settling back into place without a ripple. "I was charming to them."

Alex's sick anger returned threefold. He'd kill the man. "He's affianced to Mrs. Rattigan. They've signed the contract."

Julius's mouth settled into a flat line. "But nobody in town knows that. I suspect he finds himself under the hatches and he needs something more than Mrs. Rattigan can give him. Is the betrothal well known?"

"Not in London." The Downhollands didn't visit frequently and their estate wasn't large enough to excite interest. Dankworth couldn't marry two women.

"I smell danger, Alex. He's cornered and cornered rats become dangerous. The first thing is to warn Mrs. Rattigan. Tell her that we will investigate the situation and wait on her instructions. Suggest that she contacts Lord Downholland and if she trusts him, ask him to act on her behalf."

"I will most certainly write to her," Alex said grimly. He would write it that night, as soon as he got home. And one to the Downhollands, too. Damn his local stint as magistrate, Lord Downholland should be attending his heir in town.

At least Alex could ensure that Connie was in possession of the facts. She needed to act. And perhaps, if she decided to break the contract, Alex could repair the mistake he made. He should never have left the field for Dankworth, and had he known what a cad Dankworth was, he wouldn't have done.

Chapter 6

"Letter for you, Missus."

Connie had long stopped trying to get her housemaid to stop calling her "Missus." Saxton came from a family that had served the local gentry in these parts since records began, or so they had everyone believe. If Connie commented too strongly, they'd have called her "stuck up" and relegated her to the younger daughters and sons of the Saxton clan, the ones who needed training—a subtle kind of punishment that was just as effective as sitting in the stocks.

Connie took the letter from Saxton's hands—no salvers here, as at the Downholland's—and used her butter knife to break the seal, which was so blurred as to be unrecognizable. But this letter had come a long way. It was grubby, the seal chipped. Had he written to her after all? Her heart lifted stupidly. "When did it arrive?"

"But two minutes ago. I thought you might like it now, since you're breakfasting alone." By which Saxton meant the vicar hadn't just popped in to discuss some triviality with her. The vicar was a greedy man and Connie's cook made good breakfasts.

"Certainly and thank you." She'd risen several hours ago and ridden out on estate business after consuming only a few slices of buttered bread and tea. The wind this morning was a lazy one, going right through her instead of around her and she'd looked forward to her meal, which she was now relishing in solitary splendor.

She was glad she had no audience other than Saxton. Had Alex defied her wishes and written to her after all? Fumbling a little, she folded the paper open.

My dearest Sweetheart,
I cannot wait to make you mine.

Everything is in train for your arrival. The Downhollands wish our union as soon as possible and I concur in that desire most fervently. I regret I cannot ride North to escort you to town but you will find a hearty welcome on your arrival. Please write and tell me of your plans. I will arrange to have you met and taken to the Downholland's London residence.

I find that I miss you more than I thought I could ever miss anyone and I need your love and support. I miss your tantalizing presence, your perfume and your good sense and I want to present you at Court.

Yes, that is my main reason for asking you to come to London with all haste. I have obtained an invitation to attend St. James's and if I were married before my visit, that would include my wife. I cannot decline such a treat on your behalf and I don't hesitate to remind you that it would aid our fortunes, too. A honeymoon and a season of sightseeing would be conducive to your spirits, would it not?

I am fortunate to have made the acquaintance of several influential people in town and I can promise you an enjoyable time during our stay. I have several appointments with men in the City, by which I hope to increase our holdings and secure us a greater income. I have also renewed my acquaintance with my second cousin, the Duke of Northwich, and he has kindly extended an invitation to attend his house for tea after we are wed. When we are done with London we will return to our home with all due dispatch and begin our married life in complete amity.

I understand the stage leaves for London every day from Carlisle, so it might be better if you catch that, or if you require more comfort, a post chaise should prove adequate. We should think of purchasing a good travelling carriage on our return home.

I wait impatiently for your letter,
Yours, etc.
Jasper Dankworth.

Of course, Alex wouldn't write. She'd told him not to. But she couldn't deny the sense of hollow disappointment filling her now.

Saxton should really have left the room but she was no doubt waiting for some juicy titbit that would enliven the Saxton household when she went home at the end of the week.

Connie schooled her features, put the letter gently face down and asked for more tea. The maid bustled out, the lappets of her cap whipping out behind her in her haste to leave the room.

Connie had some mending to do after breakfast, which left her clear to think. As her fingers flew over the sheets and the handkerchiefs, she pondered the letter. Apart from the lack of transport, it seemed a reasonable request but she was puzzled that he hadn't sent a carriage or arranged for a post chaise, much as she disliked that form of transport.

Or at least, that the Downhollands hadn't done so. They had arranged for one for her recent visit to their house.

If he'd obtained an invitation to a presentation at court, that was a coup, although she'd have to buy a mantua, an old-fashioned gown she'd have no use for afterwards. Or she'd wager she could hire one.

She dropped the sheet she'd darned and picked up a handkerchief that needed edging.

Jasper's protestations of love and passion seemed a trifle overdone but gentlemen often paid extravagant compliments in the hope they would receive more in return. Hastily, Connie moved away from that thought, although she would have welcomed the attentions of someone else in her bed and concentrated on turning the corner of the handkerchief neatly. Alex was someone she must never think of again, except as a passing acquaintance.

By the end of a relatively restful afternoon, she had made her decision. She was to dine at the vicarage that night and as Saxton helped her dress, she put matters in train.

"I need a ticket to London on the stage next Wednesday. Two tickets. Inside the coach, please. I've written a note to Mr. Dankworth, telling him of my arrival and I want that sent as soon as possible." She picked up the string of amethyst beads she'd inherited from her mother. Not as grand as most London ensembles, but it would do. It would certainly do for tonight. She straightened so Saxton could tighten her stays.

"I'll require someone to accompany me. I'd prefer you, Saxton, since you're a sensible woman and unlikely to let the sights overcome you but if you decide you cannot, Benton will do. I'll be marrying Mr. Dankworth in London. We'll hold a ball when we return to celebrate the event locally." They could hire the Assembly Rooms in local Pantown. "Saxton, can you please stop tugging at my laces? That's quite tight enough."

Although Connie was standing with her back to Saxton she could see her in the mirror. The maid's round face flushed beet red. "Sorry ma'am." She must be overset, because she didn't call her Missus. Or maybe she was excited. The untypical fumbling was a clue. "I'll tell Harrison about the letter and I'll send him to buy the tickets in the morning. Just wondering, ma'am but why don't you hire a chaise?"

"I don't see why I should pay a fortune to travel in that kind of discomfort. It's fast, to be sure but the roads aren't suitable, or at least the ones we took weren't. So I might as well pay a modest amount and still be uncomfortable."

The only way she'd travel in comfort was on a good road, preferably a turnpike, in a well-sprung, private vehicle, taking its time. Since she couldn't afford that, she'd make do with the stage.

"Yes, missus."

At least they were back to that.

* * * *

Could people die of boredom?

When Connie thought there was nothing new to say about the weather, one of her fellow passengers on this godforsaken vehicle thought of something else.

The occupants of the inside of the coach were so respectable they could have given her vicar a run for his money. They discussed the weather, the French, who they hated to the last man and woman, the strangeness of the Londoner and the irresponsibility of the ruling class. Especially its young men who did nothing that they didn't want to.

Connie could have disabused them of that notion but she chose not to. However much the motherly woman sitting opposite her probed and poked, she enlightened her no further.

After the first day's excitement and the first night's uncomfortable lodging, when she shared a sagging rope-bed with her maid, Connie spent most of the next day's travel catching up on her sleep. The days passed until they had only two more nights on the road before they reached London.

By the time they reached Leicester, she was heartily sick of travelling. When the coach stopped for a meal and a change of horses, she took the air with Saxton in tow. Better than eating food she didn't really want in the stuffy taproom of the inn.

"Come, Saxton."

The maid accompanied Connie, grumbling under her breath, her stout figure wobbling on the uneven cobbles of the coaching inn yard.

They strolled along the street, Connie relishing the fresh air and the lack of tedious gossip.

She paused in front of the window of a print shop, looking for amusement in the caricatures. She scanned the images on display then her attention returned to one in particular. Her heart missed a beat.

In the center of the window, larger than the other offerings was hung a print of Alex and his cousins in their imperial finery. They appeared incongruous in the center of London society because the printmaker had dressed them in the style of their namesakes. So Alex had a breastplate and Roman kilt and his cousin Julius a purple-edged toga.

Alex's family was an important one. Even someone in a provincial town like Leicester would know who they were. They didn't need the joke explaining to them.

Finally the death knell tolled on her hopes. She had no chance of attracting such exalted figures and no right to expect it.

The man she'd met and dallied with wasn't for her. She didn't move in his circles, wouldn't know how to conduct a dinner discussing events of the day, events the guests would have direct involvement in. She couldn't swan around a ballroom pretending to be one of the great and the good. Alex would marry a woman who could do all these things and she'd be a credit to him. Not for Connie the fate of being caricatured for the amusement of the nation. Few people knew who she was, or would, once she married Jasper. Mrs. Dankworth, even Lady Downholland couldn't evoke that kind of attention.

Her mood plummeted. She was going to London to marry Jasper then she'd retire with him to Yorkshire, or her home in Cumbria, and take her place in local society. She'd never see Alex again.

The prospect filled her with a numb sorrow. Until now, she hadn't realized what Alex had done to her. He'd spoiled her for other men.

Saxton tugged her shawl. "They won't wait for us, missus. We have to go now."

She'd turned, slightly dazed, and headed back to the inn and the hated coach.

That she'd met him seemed a dream. That she'd kissed him seemed impossible. Alexander Vernon, Baron Ripley, heir to the Earldom of Leverton. No, not her, not him.

She'd put him behind her with all the strength of will she could muster.

When they reached London, she assumed it wouldn't take long to reach the *Belle Sauvage* on Ludgate Hill, where they were disembarking.

However London proved much larger than she'd supposed and it took an hour for the unwieldy coach, weighed down with travelers inside and on the roof, to reach the center of the city. The travelers separated into two groups, the ones who had been before and took it all in with an air of weary cynicism and the ones, like her, who watched, fascinated, as the city passed the windows in all its variety.

They passed through a couple of hamlets first, villages with a prosperous air and modern, well-constructed houses, any of which would have provided a suitable dwelling for a lady of her style and circumstance. The road led into the main part of the city, past dilapidated buildings of disreputable appearance, half falling down and propped up with beams and then rows of neat houses, small but with an air of comfort and well-being. Every building bore streaks of soot. Something she hadn't expected but should have done. So many houses belching smoke all day must produce this kind of appearance. She'd have had her house scrubbed every month but perhaps the battle was too much for the people who lived here.

Finally, they swung up Ludgate Hill and the magnificent dome of St. Paul's Cathedral towering majestically over the buildings clustered around it. Its classical magnificence and its sheer size dwarfed and scorned everything else around it. Breathtaking.

She promised herself a visit there, as well as the Palace of Westminster and the Banqueting Hall, all that remained of the old palace of Whitehall, which had burned down seventy years before. Her spirits lifted at the thought, more, to her shame, than at the thought of meeting Jasper again.

She recalled the history of London from her books, the books she'd spent the nights before her trip poring over. Anything but remembering how close Alex was to her here, how she could pay a visit and see him again. But she would not.

How would she cope with that? From what Jasper had said in his letter, he'd started to move in those circles. She couldn't avoid Alex. She had to steel herself to the possibility of meeting him, pretending a slight acquaintance. Anything more would appear encroaching. And the chance of seeing him with a woman, one who could claim him for her own. Perhaps he'd offer for Louisa, pretty, young and rich, everything Connie wasn't.

She suffered from an infatuation, she assured herself, as she had many times before. Nothing more. It would pass. It *had* to pass.

* * * *

Connie had become adept at climbing down the tiny steps of the coach on to the cobbled yard of yet another coaching inn. Except this one was the last in her journey and the last she'd need to face for some time. She felt cramped, tired and ready for bed, although it was barely four in the afternoon. Food didn't appeal. She was too weary to eat. Not that Saxton felt the same way, if her rumbling stomach was to be believed. Connie ought to take pity on her maid.

"Let's eat something while we wait to hear from Mr. Dankworth."

Saxton nodded. "I'll see the bags unloaded first, missus."

Connie had almost forgotten them.

Saxton snagged a passing ostler by the simple expedient of grabbing the waistband of his breeches and waving a shilling under his nose. She barely came up to the man's chest. "That trunk and that bag."

The man climbed up to get them down.

Connie went inside and headed for the nearest unoccupied table.

A man dressed in plain but serviceable clothes stopped her. "Mrs. Rattigan, is it?"

"Why? Who wants to know?" She was dressed plainly, her pearl necklace tucked under her fichu. She could have been anyone from a shopkeeper to a lady.

The man handed her a folded note addressed in her future husband's handwriting.

Dearest,

The man who gives you this is one of my servants. You may trust him. He will take you to the Downholland's house after you've eaten and refreshed yourself. I am looking forward with eager anticipation to seeing you again. We will marry as soon as possible. I can hardly wait. - J

A brief note and to the point but Jasper's care for her touched her. She smiled up at the man, her spirits lifting. "Yes, I'm Mrs. Rattigan."

"Are you alone?"

"My maid is in the yard, supervising the luggage. She'll join us shortly."

The man gave a brief nod. "There are some private parlors here. I have bespoken one of those for your comfort. If you'll come this way, I'll return for your maid."

"That sounds good." She followed the man to the parlor, which was small and comfortable. He furnished her with a glass of wine from the decanter on the table.

She eyed the basket of bread with more avidity than she'd imagined she could have a few moments before. Jasper's note had relieved her growing tension and worry that she might have to fend for herself and her maid for at least a night.

The wine tasted good enough and she'd downed the first glass without really noticing, wondering if she could put her feet up on one of the stools and relax for an hour. She wondered where her maid had got to when the latch rattled.

The world rocked under her feet. As if her perception had suddenly developed an echo and followed her rather than coming with her. She heard the man saying the same thing twice, saw blurred double images of him. More tired than she'd thought. With a sigh, she sank back on to the hard wooden settle. Her senses telescoped and unconsciousness washed over her.

Chapter 7

Connie groaned then stopped because it hurt too much, the sound reverberating around her head. Submitting to the inevitable, she rolled over and vomited, a bare second's warning between coming awake and her stomach rebelling.

Someone held a foul-smelling pot under her chin.

She was grateful all the same, as she was beyond doing such things for herself. Her hair fell around her face until someone yanked it back. The roots pulled but she strained forward and expelled whatever noxious substance had churned in her stomach. She couldn't speak, could only gasp, regaining her breath.

The person leaned her back against a hard surface.

A bedroom, adequately but roughly furnished. Something gauzy and shimmering draped the bed and burning pastilles heavily perfumed the air. A thin stream of smoke spiraled up from a pottery cottage on the mantelpiece. She closed her eyes. "Am I still at the Belle Sauvage?" Even speaking made her head throb.

"No, dearie, you've moved on. You're in my house now."

The voice was female and the accent unfamiliar. She squinted up and spied a woman, her face creased with so many wrinkles she seemed timeless, as if she'd defeated death. She wore a gown of youthful yellow with fancy lace ruffles and a cap that fluffed around her iron-grey curls like a morning raincloud.

Connie didn't like the oversweet smell but approved of the other things, like the soft bed and the way the drapery masked the over-bright sunshine outside. "So where are we?"

"Covent Garden."

If that meant something special, she missed it, but considering her state, she was lucky to remember her own name. Her head swam and throbbed and her limbs felt like lamb's wool. She forced herself to concentrate.

The room was small and strangely decorated but that might be the difference in taste between her home and London. The luxurious bed contrasted with the other perfunctory and cheaply made fittings. But she wouldn't dare criticize. They might toss her out and the way she was feeling, she couldn't risk that. But she didn't know anyone who lived in Covent Garden, unless the Downhollands had leased a house here. "Is this a lodging house?"

"Just so, dearie." She didn't like the familiar "Dearie," but let it pass. "You must have eaten some bad food. So you need to eat some good to build up your strength and then we'll see about getting you out of bed."

She covered her eyes with one hand. "Not yet."

"No, not yet. But I'll bring you something light on a tray and then we'll see how you feel. Keep sitting up and I'll bring you a fresh pot. Maybe two."

"Can you contact my fiancé, Mr. Jasper Dankworth, please?"

"He knows."

Connie sat very still, thinking but her mind whirled and she couldn't concentrate. Someone was shouting in the corridor outside and she wished he would stop.

* * * *

If Alex had thought to cast off his sole remaining parent by moving out of the house his father owned in London, he was doomed to disappointment.

Father dropped around regularly, this time to share breakfast with him. "You disappoint me, boy." Lord Leverton presented far too colorful a figure at breakfast, his blue coat and green waistcoat magnificent in their disdain for each other.

Alex enjoyed breakfasting on his own but today he had to make conversation and think on his feet. Alex reached for the coffee pot. "Refusing to offer for Miss Stobart?"

"Precisely. A considerable heiress and ripe for childbearing."

"I don't want for money, sir and I'm not your only son." He pushed his plate aside. Bacon could lose its appeal very quickly in the right circumstances.

His father glared. "I thought La Stobart had you but you slipped out of that one. Then she chased you and I thought she'd snare you but here you are, still unattached."

"Not Miss Stobart, Father."

"Pick somebody. I want the succession settled before I pass on. It's time. You know it. I know it." The picture of robust good health, his father glared at him, his dark eyes beacons of disapproval.

"I will, Father, but I haven't met the right woman yet." One face came to mind and he dismissed it, as he'd got in the habit of doing recently.

Lord Leverton snorted. "You've met many women who would have made you an excellent partner in life. You're just too fussy. Or you prefer bachelorhood. There is no reason you should not go along the way you always have after your marriage. You've always been reasonably discreet with your mistresses. I don't even know if you have one in keeping at the moment."

"No, sir. The last one proved a bore in the mornings." He sipped his coffee. At least he didn't have those tantrums to cope with any more. "Do women think they get more money if they scream a lot?"

His father's gruff laugh echoed around Alex's snug breakfast parlor. "It works with a lot of men. Don't say you've never given a ladybird a diamond brooch just to stop her squawking in the morning."

Alex gave a reluctant grin. "Can't say I haven't, Father. But I want more than that in a wife. And I don't want a spiteful woman with no more sense than hair, either. Miss Stobart has a smallness of mind that would, I fear, pall very quickly." He added something bound to appeal to his father. "She would not make a good countess. I want an equal, someone I can talk to, discuss matters with, someone to share my life with—" The expression on his father's face shook him.

No longer displeasure but an open vulnerability that made Alex uncomfortable. His father concealed it in an instant. Enough to tell Alex how much he still missed his wife, Alex's mother. They'd all loved her, sweet with a core of tempered steel, but she'd been taken from them by smallpox ten years ago. Alex missed her, too. Did he want to marry a woman who would mean as much to him, even if it meant that one day he'd have to live without her?

Yes, the answer came, resoundingly and with no caveats.

"Some of us are lucky enough to find that," his lordship said. "But I married young and I'd filled my nursery by the time I was your age."

"You never married again," Alex said softly.

His father cleared his throat. "No need. I'd done my duty. Time for you to do yours." His voice lowered, even though there was nobody else in the room. "Look here, Ripley, it's not just that. I worry for you, sometimes. You can go on as you are but you need to move on with your life. You could have taken Louisa Stobart and made her into what you wanted. Or left her in the country once you'd done your duty. All she needs to do is give you a few children."

"I don't want that, Father. I want a woman who knows a little of the world and what she wants."

"So is that who you met in Yorkshire?" His father tucked into a devilled kidney with every evidence of relish, making Alex wait for his next remark. He experienced no inclination to fill the silence and poured himself more coffee.

Lord Leverton cleared his mouth and took a few gulps of tea, seemingly oblivious of the fraught silence. "You came back very thoughtful and I thought finally you'd met her. When I realized it wasn't La Stobart, I wondered who it could be. A few young ladies just happened by that week, I'm guessing, once they knew you were in the house. So which one was it? Look, I won't ask much but that you find someone you like. I keep finding these women for you but if that's not your taste, we'll forget them. It's not good for you, not good for the title either. I want you married before the season's out."

"That wasn't the reason I came back thoughtful." Not entirely, anyway. "That was because of Jasper Dankworth."

"I wonder you concern yourself with him." Lord Leverton's aristocratic nose flared, a reminder of his opinion of Jacobite traitors who wanted nothing more than to plunge the country back into serfdom, the subject of his one and only speech in the House.

"He is contracted to marry one woman but he's courting Stobart. Actually announced his engagement."

His father put his cutlery down and leaned back, raising his black brows. "There's more than altruistic interest here, isn't there?"

Damn the man, he wasn't supposed to notice. "That part doesn't matter. The whole business of leading two women on doesn't taste well in my mouth but I'm waiting on events. I wrote to the woman he's deceiving and told her I'd be her friend in this matter but I've had no reply. For all I know the marriage contract could have been voided and Dankworth is free to move on." Alex shrugged and reached for his cup. "It's not my concern, Pa."

Except if that proved to be the case Alex would order his travelling coach readied for immediate departure to Cumbria. The only reason he'd walked away from that contract.

Now he had grown up, Alex rarely used the nursery name for his father. A slip he regretted, because his old man would notice but he couldn't change it now.

"You do as you think fit, my boy. Just don't do anything to disgrace the family name and find a bride quick smart, you hear me?"

Wearily, Alex promised to do his best.

After his father left, Alex decided to return to White's and take a look at the betting book but before he could leave the house, a knock fell on the door. One of his footmen opened it to a messenger. The footman transferred the missive he paid for to a salver and brought it to Alex, despite him standing at the far end of the hall the whole time. The tyranny servants wielded over their masters demanded the transfer. God forbid that his retainers would allow Lord Ripley to take a letter directly from the note bearer.

Alex took the letter with a word of thanks. The tattered cover and the crossings out and redirections made it difficult to identify at first, but eventually he recognized the letter he'd dispatched to Connie. It had never reached her.

That meant she didn't know about Dankworth. Alex tapped the letter against his open hand, wondering if he should send her another. On the whole, he thought not. He'd visit her instead. Once the notion had taken hold when he was with his father, it wouldn't let go. He could travel as quickly as a letter if he took a fast carriage.

He turned to ask his footman to summon his butler to make the arrangements, but someone rapped on the kitchen door with an agitated tattoo.

"I'll discover what the trouble is, my lord," the footman said.

"No. Let me." Instead of going down the backstairs, which would cause untold turmoil in the servants' hall, he went outside. He flung the front door wide and descended the shallow steps to the street.

At the bottom of the area steps, outside the servant's door, a woman, dressed plainly like a servant, stood hammering on the door. "Please, I need help!"

"Come up," he said, fascinated by the distraction.

The woman looked up, eyes wide in her white face. "I—I'm sorry, sir but I'm at my wits' end. My mistress has vanished into thin air."

"Who is your mistress?" Color tinged her broad cheeks.

"Mrs. Rattigan."

That name. No, it couldn't be. But it was. "Come up. Was it me you wished to speak to?"

"Yes, sir—my lord." She hurried up the area steps and followed Alex into the main part of the house.

Leaving a curt instruction with the footman on his way past that he didn't want to be disturbed, he entered the study,. Alex bade the woman sit then took his place behind his desk. "How did you get my address?"

The maid glanced away, flushing guiltily. "We—we shared a room on the journey, sir. Mrs. Rattigan muttered your name once or twice in her sleep. Your first name and I recalled you were at the house party. You gave Mrs. Rattigan your address, sir."

That sounded plausible, and he vaguely remembered this woman from his Downholland visit. "How does Mrs. Rattigan need my help?" Anything he could do he would. Anything. Alex racked his brains to think of something he wouldn't do and came up with nothing.

The woman's teeth were chattering. He wouldn't get anything out of her in this state. When she reached up to untie the strings of her bonnet, her hands shook. "What's your name?"

"Saxton, my lord."

Alex snatched the brandy decanter from the sideboard, poured a generous measure and pressed it on her. "Here, drink. I didn't mean to be so abrupt."

If he didn't take care, Saxton would need considerable help to explain her story quickly and articulately.

"N—no, my lord, it's not that." Teeth rattling against the glass, she sipped the liquor. Then she took another sip and sat clutching it as if afraid it would get away.

Alex pulled up another chair and sat next to her. Although alarm coursed through his body, he didn't drink. "Now tell me what happened from the beginning."

"Yes, my lord. I'm very worried for Mrs. Rattigan. I didn't know if I should write to her godfather but that would take days if he's not in town and I asked but nobody knew of him. And I didn't want to wait."

She was wringing her hands, her knuckles white with the pressure she was exerting on them. Wringing her hands, she looked around as if afraid of her actions in coming here. "What has happened?"

"He wrote to her, sir, told her to come to London, where they would be married. We travelled down by stagecoach." She didn't say who *he* was. She didn't have to.

"Stagecoach?" asked Alex, amazed. "Why not a private carriage?"

"Mrs. Rattigan doesn't keep a travelling carriage, sir. She misliked the chaise that brought her for the visit to Lord Downholland's. It made her ill, she said. So she might as well be ill for less cost."

He nodded. That sounded like Connie, ever practical. Nevertheless, it annoyed him she'd taken that step. He'd have sent a more comfortable carriage for her and he wagered her godfather would have done so, if she'd asked. Typical of her not to make a fuss. "So you travelled down on the stagecoach. When did you arrive?"

"This morning, sir, at the *Belle Sauvage*. And just like Mr. Dankworth promised, there was a man waiting for us. He gave my mistress a note. I stayed behind to supervise the unloading of the luggage and to ensure it was stowed safely on Mr. Dankworth's carriage. I discovered that there was no carriage. Then I went to find my lady and although I made the landlord go through every room, I found no trace of her. Nothing, my lord. He said he'd taken her to a private room and bespoken refreshments, but he didn't know what happened after that. And the luggage had gone, too. He didn't care, didn't seem to understand that my lady wouldn't go somewhere and leave me behind." Her hand shook when she put the empty glass on the table.

Dear God, what had that villain done? "You found nothing?"

"Nothing. You believe me, sir? I don't know where else to turn." Tight lines formed around her mouth, and her face was bleached of color.

"Of course I believe you. You did the right thing, coming to me. Please speak frankly. If we're to find where she is, we must act quickly."

She breathed a long sigh of relief. "Thank you, sir. I was afeared you wouldn't believe me, or you wouldn't be interested. You might be thinking I should have found Mr. Dankworth, being her intended and all. But he sent the note, my lord, so it could be him that took my mistress."

"You're sure she's been taken?"

The maid nodded. "She wouldn't have gone anywhere without telling me, or leaving me a message. The landlord was very certain she hadn't. The luggage had gone, too, loaded into a hackney carriage, according to one of the ostlers. She just wouldn't have left me, sir. I've been with her family all my life. She brought me with her because she could trust me."

He was sure, too. At least, sure enough to act on the assumption, because delay could be fatal. If it proved a hum, then he would appear foolish, but that was a risk worth taking.

He held her frightened stare "I don't trust Jasper Dankworth. You may have confidence that I will do everything in my power to find your mistress."

His stomach churned when he considered the possibilities if she'd found Dankworth. Undoubtedly, he was behind this abduction.

"She could be dead." The maid clapped her hand over her mouth.

"No," he said firmly. "We must assume she's alive."

Though there was a strong possibility Dankworth had done away with Connie, a thought that turned his innards to liquid. If Dankworth had hurt one hair of Connie's head, he would pay for it. Connie had people who cared about her, who wouldn't stop until they found her—including himself. Jasper had the most to lose if she died so the authorities would call on him first. No, if he were Dankworth—God forbid—he'd take another course.

If Dankworth wanted to kill Connie, surely, he'd have waited until they were married. Then he would be sure of her property. Maybe he was desperate. Was there a way he could get hold of Connie's money without marrying her? She'd signed the marriage settlement. Were there other provisions?

"I'll go to the inn and retrace the man's steps. You stay here. I'll give instructions for you to be incorporated into my household as a maid."

"Th-thank you my lord but I have a good job—"

"No, you don't understand. You are a witness, Saxton. If something has happened to your mistress, they may be looking for you." He hadn't thought it possible that she could go any paler but she managed it. Plus, the Dankworths rarely left loose ends behind. Otherwise they'd have been attainted after the 'forty-five. "We'll call you Robinson while you're here to protect you from discovery. You know the duties of a housemaid?"

"That's what I am, my lord. I've been with Mrs. Rattigan for a number of years, so she brought me with her when she came to London."

"Did you linger at the inn?"

"No, my lord. I came straight here once I realized she'd gone."

"We will assume you weren't followed but I'll tell the servants to stay alert for any lurkers."

She bowed her head. "Yes, my lord. Thank you, my lord." She looked up, her eyes widening. "You'll find her?"

"Don't tell anyone your real name or purpose here. Servants talk. As soon as I find Mrs. Rattigan, I'll let you know." He stood and put his hand on her shoulder to prevent her doing the same. "Stay here. I'll send the butler to fetch you and show you your room. The secret remains between us, Robinson. If asked, say the staff registry sent you. Clear?"

"Yes, my lord."

Alex raced from the room and took the stairs two at a time, shouting for his valet and butler. He gave terse instructions to Grayson and ordered Wentworth to find him something plainer. "I want to look unremarkable."

"My lord." The valet raised a brow but complied.

Soon Alex emerged in a plain brown coat and russet waistcoat. A little fine but people of all classes used the *Belle Sauvage*. And a useful array of weapons about his person. Grayson had a chair waiting for him.

Alex climbed in and ordered the chairmen to run. They covered the distance in excellent time, so he gave them considerably extra. They touched their caps and said, "My lord."

He hoped nobody overheard. Passing as an ordinary, though wealthy citizen would get him faster answers here. He strode into the inn and called for the landlord. He used enough arrogance that the landlord appeared in good order, wiping his hands on his apron. He was in a beer-stained waistcoat and shirt only, even with this chill in the air, demonstrating how busy he'd been this morning.

"My relative, Mrs. Rattigan. Is she here? I must apologize to her for my tardiness, but I assume you made her comfortable while she waited for me." He had to raise his voice to get over the raucous atmosphere of the inn. People yelled for custom, for attention, for an ostler.

The landlord frowned. "We ain't got nobody of that name here."

"She'd have arrived on the stage from the north, earlier." He tapped his foot on the scrubbed boards. "Come, man, I don't want her to wait any further."

A few passers-by cast them curious looks, but none seemed particularly interested. Just in case, Alex repeated the name. "Mrs. Constance Rattigan. She is surely here."

Nobody showed any special interest or came forward.

"I'll check in the book, sir."

The landlord was back with the waybook in a few minutes. He glanced down today's manifest. "The carriage arrived, sure enough sir, and her luggage was unloaded." He balanced the large book expertly in one big hand. "It's not here now. She's gone, sir. Did you send someone to collect her, perchance?"

Alex slipped the landlord a few coins and asked him about the man who had come for the lady who owned the luggage. "If I don't find her my mother will be more than angry." He gave a mock wince.

The landlord grinned, displaying a few yellowed and crooked teeth. A very few. "Well then, sir, here's all I know." Oh yes, he'd been waiting for that vail. "A man came for her. He gave her a note and she went with him fast enough. She had a private parlor and I furnished a bottle of wine and some bread. She seemed a bit—tired, if you get my meaning when she left." The man came close to winking. "Imbibed a bit."

Alex's fury nearly choked him. Not drunk but drugged. And the landlord would have hidden that information from him for the sake of a few coins. He had to keep in control of himself or he'd learn nothing more. "Is the parlor still free?"

"Yes, sir."

"Then show me."

The man led the way, dropping his book off at the desk on his way past. The inn seethed with humanity, everyone bringing their smells and noise with them. The rumbling noise of the great coaches reverberated through the building at regular intervals. Vehicles arrived, disgorging their passengers or picking them up. Yells came from outside, as people called for their luggage and servants or greeted relatives. Alex walked past it all.

As he passed through the main room, one group seemed to be leaving and another arriving, so the effect was rather like the tide coming in and going out again. He battled his way through, gathering a few curses and keeping his hand on his purse as he followed the landlord to the private parlor.

It was a small room with hard wooden benches and a dark table, with the stains of hard use. A plain decanter stood on the scarred table, empty but not clean. Some residue remained. Alex removed the stopper and sniffed it, and detected a tang, chemical, oily, he couldn't quite identify it. Ah yes, now he had it. His mother used to use the substance for headaches.

He handed it to the landlord. "What do you make of this?"

The landlord sniffed the stopper. "It's off, sir. Doesn't smell like my house wine." Deep creases furrowed between his thick brows. "What's all this about?"

He would tell the man what he expected to know and what would evoke the landlord's sympathy. "My cousin is a considerable heiress. I'm afraid that someone has abducted her."

"You don't say." The landlord stared at Alex, blank-faced.

Alex shoved the decanter under the man's nose. "Just smell this. That isn't off, it's had something added to it. Mrs. Rattigan was drugged. This reeks of laudanum."

The landlord of one of the most prosperous coaching establishments in London wouldn't bother to get himself involved with an abduction plot. Not now the practice was illegal.

He slipped his hand in his pocket, around the butt of his pistol. "I want to find my cousin before nightfall." He kept a grip on the decanter with his left hand.

The landlord stood in front of the door, hands on his substantial hips. His rolled-up shirtsleeves displayed impressive roped muscles. "How do I know it's not you who's the abductor?"

"How do I know it's not you?" That would ginger him up a bit. "I won't give up until I find everyone who is behind this."

Finding the drugged wine gave him hope, because it meant she'd left here alive. If they wanted to kill her, they'd have poisoned her outright. With only the decanter as slender evidence, he had no case in law. He couldn't go to the authorities yet. He needed more information.

The landlord studied him for a moment, dark eyes thoughtful. "All right. Wait here, sir. I'll ask the servants if they saw anything else."

Alex examined the room in the ten minutes the landlord was gone, scrutinizing the sparse furniture and the floor but he found nothing else. Not even a button.

The landlord returned, closing the door carefully behind him. Alex kept hold of his gun. "I didn't see the lady leave, sir, I just found the parlor empty and all the wine gone, so I assumed she'd drunk the wine and the man had taken her quietly home."

If the man had adulterated the wine, he probably dumped the remaining contents, probably out of the window. "Go on."

"One of the kitchen staff saw a man carrying a woman out a side entrance and into a hackney. He winked at her and said his wife was drunk and my maid thought nothing more of it."

Oh God. Bile rose in Alex's throat. But a hackney meant local. He released his pistol to find his purse. He thrust a few more guineas at the landlord. "Did she recognize the hackney driver?"

"No, sir."

"If you see him, send word. I'll take the decanter with me and keep it safe." He wouldn't let the only evidence he had out of his possession.

Not bothering about disguising his identity any longer, he reached inside his coat for his case and gave the landlord one of his cards. "Don't tell anyone about my visit. If I can use the element of surprise, I have a better chance of trapping him and of finding the lady. That is, make no mistake, my first priority. Contact me if you hear anything, no matter how trivial."

The landlord nodded. "I will indeed, my lord. I don't want that kind of reputation around this house. I've already tried to scare away the women who meet country girls off the stage. You know the ones. They just go further up the street but at least I'm trying to stop them. That's more than the landlord at the *White Hart* does." He shoved a finger under the edge of his wig and scratched his skull.

Alex resisted the impulse to step back. Who knew what lurked under that wig? "Besides, the magistrates are making things difficult for the doxies. Probably about time."

Alex marked the information in his mind. He might find allies there, if he needed them. He would take anything from anyone right now if he found Connie alive and unharmed at the end of it.

Leaving the inn, Alex hailed a passing chair, ruthlessly shouldering another man aside to reach it first and ignoring the yells and curses that followed them.

Jasper Dankworth lived in a lodging house in Red Lion Square. Not the most fashionable address but handy for the main centers of interest for the fashionable world. Alex raced up the steps and a Superior Being opened the door.

"Is Mr. Dankworth available?"

The servant had lifted his chin so high he was forced to stare down his nose at Alex, even though Alex had a few inches on him. "No, sir. I believe you may find him at White's club."

Alex smiled grimly. White's was very selective about who they allowed in, so if he'd been dunning Dankworth, he'd just been sent to the rightabout.

He reached into his purse and jingled it, hoping this man belonged to the house rather than to the man. "When do you expect him back?"

"I really couldn't say, sir."

Alex withdrew a guinea and regarded it soulfully. "Do you know where he spends his evenings?"

The man's rheumy gaze wandered to the bright gold. "At balls and various establishments, sir."

"Tonight?" He would track him down wherever he was. He had no time to spare for niceties. He withdrew two more coins. A damned fortune to this fellow but well worth the investment.

"I believe he is attending an establishment in Covent Garden, sir."

Sadly, the man couldn't say which one but that narrowed Alex's quarry down nicely. Adding another coin to pay for the man's silence, Alex handed over the goods and went home to regroup.

He barely waited for the footman to open the door, ran straight through and barreled up the stairs. "Wentworth!"

His valet, good man, came immediately to his call.

"I need something fancy. I'm off to White's. And be snappy, please. No, I don't care what it is, just choose something suitable."

Alex handed over the decanter. "And see this is taken care of. Lock it away just as it is, dregs and all. It could be evidence."

The valet stared at the cheap container then placed it on a side table within his sight, where it looked incongruous against the finely cut, sparkling crystal. "I will attend to you first sir, then the item."

Wentworth arrayed Alex in dark green dull satin, with a cream waistcoat and Méchlin lace at his wrists. He added a sapphire stud to his neckcloth, his large gold and emerald signet ring to his finger, popped a watch and a snuffbox in his pockets, and changed his plain street sword for the fine jeweled steel one.

Alex intended to use it if he had to. He grabbed a cocked hat trimmed with gold braid. He would do.

* * * *

White's was full. Nothing daunted, Alex strode through the public rooms in search of his quarry. He even ventured into Hell, were several fellows hailed him and asked him to join them. Considering how well he could cheat, a skill he deployed as a party trick, they must be desperate. Although he'd never done it when there was money on the table. He'd do it now, if it meant he could discover Connie's whereabouts. That was a measure of his desperation.

But he showed none of his agitation, none of the worry that was screwing his gut into a tiny knot. Instead, he strolled through the rooms, exchanging the time of day but not stopping, until he reached the inner sanctum.

There he was, in one of the leather-upholstered wing chairs scattered in an informal arrangement through the room. By each chair, stood a small table and the one by Dankworth's sported a decanter of brandy. Alex generally preferred to leave his spirit drinking until later in the day but each to his own. Even if he'd rather shove the decanter, stopper and all, down the bastard's throat. He had no proof, no absolute proof but every instinct in his body told him he was right and Dankworth was responsible for the abduction of Connie Rattigan.

Dankworth brightened and stood to greet him. But he wasn't alone, so Alex couldn't grab his neckcloth and strangle him with it. Instead he performed a languid bow and let his lids droop over his eyes, although he couldn't respond to Dankworth's "Good to see you, Ripley!" with a similar response.

He managed to force a smile. "You're up early, Dankworth."

"I am, indeed. Or rather, I haven't been to bed yet. I cannot imagine what I did before I came to London."

Dankworth waved to a nearby chair and a waiter brought it over to join the little cluster around Dankworth.

Alex greeted the other men, all gamblers and rousters, although of the highest rank, which meant they had money to burn, and took his seat.

Alex knew better than to wade in with his demands. It was hardly likely that the man would admit to the atrocities without compunction. The best he could hope for was some clue regarding her whereabouts. "Been around town since I saw you last, Dankworth? I saw you at Lady Roxborough's last week, didn't I?"

"You did," Dankworth replied. "The lady was kind enough to invite my betrothed and myself."

"Ah yes," Alex took the hook Dankworth dangled in front of him. "I understood you were engaged to someone else? Mrs. Rattigan, the pretty widow?"

Dankworth shrugged. "The match was suggested by my uncle. But we decided we did not suit. I fell in love with Louisa the first time I saw her."

"Do you plan a long engagement?"

Dankworth shrugged and picked up his glass. "We don't see the need. We're signing the contract soon." Oh yes, the bastard knew. He would dispose of Connie's claim on him swiftly and then grab his heiress before she could change her mind.

He'd see about that. While he didn't want Louisa Stobart for himself, she didn't deserve a cad like Dankworth. Nobody did.

As soon as he found Connie and had her safe, he'd write to the Downhollands, who would have a great deal to say about the proposed match. He prayed that Connie had a clause in the contract so she could void it. Of course, if Dankworth signed a second contract before the first was legally voided, that would do the trick. The last thing he wanted was to draw attention to the abduction, but needs must. If he needed to, he would. "Out with the old, on with the new?" he murmured languidly.

Dankworth sneered. "Something like that. It would have been a perfectly adequate match for me to marry Connie. But you must agree that she isn't the most exciting of women."

Alex kept his composure, but only years of practice enabled him to do so. "I found her interesting, attractive and a pleasure to talk to." And beautiful, alluring beyond compare.

"You sound like a lover yourself. Well, she is a widow. Fair game, I'd say."

A chorus of "Oh-ho's" made the rounds.

Despite his reservations about the earliness of the day, Alex accepted a brandy. He needed something. Fury roiled inside him and if he weren't careful, he'd pick a fight and end up on the Heath in the morning with a smoking pistol in his hand and a price on his head. Dankworth wasn't worth it. Alex had more important things to do.

"Ripley likes high flyers," Denbigh informed Dankworth in a *sotto voce* so loud anyone standing on the other side of the room could hear it.

"One at a time and exclusive," Alex admitted, "Even though they want to rule the roost. And although they are admittedly the most charming and the most civilized of whores."

Dankworth snorted. "They're all whores. What does it matter what they're like outside the bedroom? All I ask is that they're clean and they spread their legs when I tell them to. I don't expect good conversation while they're doing it. In fact I prefer their mouths full of something that impedes speech."

If Dankworth had hurt Connie, he'd destroy him. And more. Jasper Dankworth would hang for his crimes. After Alex had killed him, of course.

There was no stopping Dankworth now. "Virgins are generally sweet and succulent and they can be tutored."

"Plan to turn your future wife into a whore in the bedroom, do you?" That came from Fox, who didn't sound amused.

"Not at all," Dankworth responded. "Respectable women have to be approached differently. But eventually I prefer them on their knees. It just takes a little longer." He took a deep draught from his glass and reached for the decanter. "Heard about the event tonight?"

A few people murmured a name Alex didn't recognize, "Cratchitt."

Dankworth brightened. "I've never been to a slave auction. I'm looking forward to it. There are some virgins for sale, I believe and the others are new to the market."

"Few of them are real virgins." Alex working hard not to show his interest. This was it. That was what the blackguard had done. If Connie appeared in public offering herself for sale, that would prove her lack of morals. "Where is this house?"

"Covent Garden."

"The Garden itself?" Houses on the piazza and bordering the square were more expensive than the ones on the nearby streets, or the shacks by the market. Alex went to one house in that area for the gaming and he half hoped, half dreaded to hear it would be held there. "I haven't heard of it. Is it Mother Dawkins's?"

"Next door," Fox said. "And Dawkins is furious about it. She says it brings down the tone of her side of the square." The gathered crowd sniggered. "She's worried the new woman will take her custom. She has that glorious Academy on Wednesday nights and her girls are always exquisite, but sometimes a man wants something a little—wilder."

Alex didn't, though he wasn't about to mention that now. He had a healthy male appetite for a lovely woman but that was as far as it went. Dankworth was positively salivating and his blood ran cold.

Now he knew when and where Connie would show up. But he didn't know how. Or where she was now. He had the rest of the day to make his plans but it wouldn't be easy. Whatever it took, he'd do it. He needed to call on the magistrates in Bow Street and then to Mother Dawkins, who owed him a favor or two.

Chapter 8

Alex stood on the steps of the best whorehouse in London, taking in the arena of his upcoming battle. Covent Garden was in many ways the center of London, especially at eleven in the evening. The whole world ended up in Covent Garden sooner or later. This was later.

Standing on the corner of the Garden and King Street, Mother Dawkins's establishment plied its trade. The flambeaux either side of the door illuminated the visage of one of the bullies she employed to keep order, scarred and weathered but dressed neatly in a parody of livery. Alex nodded to him and the bully returned the favor.

He was leaving the house, not entering it. He'd made a bargain with the madam, using all the advantages he had, preparation for what he hoped would happen next.

He'd dressed carefully and gorgeously, in crimson figured velvet and gold. Nobody would miss his presence tonight. Even Mrs. Dawkins, who had seen men come through her doors in full court finery, too eager to go home and change after visiting St. James, remarked on it.

A large ruby glinted at his throat and another on his finger. In his pocket he had a richly enameled snuffbox and a small, loaded pistol, while the small sword at his side while decorative, was no mere ornament. He was dressed to kill, if necessary.

He strode past the flambeaux, down the steps and went next door, where a similar set-up waited for him. He glared at the footman, not at all intimidated by his beefy presence and the man opened the door. Alex entered.

Mrs. Dawkins's house held flamboyant furnishings and bright décor but it was done with wit, as if someone knew they were doing too much, cramming too much fine furniture into a space. This house held no irony, and Alex didn't feel like smiling at the green striped wallpaper, the cherries tumbling down the white stripes and the extravagant mahogany furniture. A large chandelier hung from the ceiling, winched too high because there wasn't room for a full drop otherwise. The lady of the house came forward, hands outstretched.

Thin, bony hands. Alex bowed over one. Chicken skin covering the skeleton. He straightened and examined his hostess with experienced eyes. Good imitation Brussels lace but since lace was the most expensive part of an ensemble bar the jewelry, he'd forgive her that. A slight edge of crudity was evidenced in her clothes, although they appeared reasonable. Or maybe he would think that of anyone who ran a house like this. No, he shouldn't blame her. She might be an innocent party in all this.

Who was he trying to fool? He certainly didn't fool himself. She *must* know. Had she a crop of drugged virgins from the country? It wouldn't be the first time that had happened in the Garden; many men had depraved tastes the people here in these establishments were only too pleased to cater to.

"My lord, I'm delighted to see you here tonight."

"Dankworth assured me of a good seat," he murmured and she smiled broadly in response, almost cracking her heavy maquillage. "You know who I am?"

"Who but a lord could dress in such a refined fashion and with such excellent taste?" The woman spoke like a Londoner trying to talk like his people. Too refined, or *refained*, as she pronounced it, to be real. She enunciated every word carefully, every syllable precise and clipped. In other circumstances, he might have found it amusing but he was so far from being amused tonight that he thought he might never laugh again.

"Very perceptive, madam. Your name, Dankworth says, is Mrs. Cratchitt?"

"Just so, sir."

"I don't think I've seen you around before." The woman, who must have been in her fifties by the look of her, gave Alex a flirtatious flutter of her eyelashes and a grin that made him shudder. He'd known good-looking fifty-year-olds, but Cratchitt wasn't one of them.

Seeing a creature of Cratchitt's age simper gave Alex shivers and not the good kind. "I'm not alone in this venture, my lord. I have powerful backers. I hope you will visit us often. We offer the discerning gentleman a measure of something he will not find elsewhere."

People in these houses needed considerable outlay to set up in this way. So somebody or several people with money to spare had helped her. Alex filed the information away in case he needed it later.

"You have girls fresh to the trade upstairs, I heard?" He hadn't, but it was a reasonable guess.

"Indeed we do, sir. They are eager to enter their new profession. I have girls fresh from the country." And other parts of London, most likely. She leered. "Virgins, my lord. The auctioneer knows the value of his charges. We have rooms available to enjoy your purchases any way you wish, equipped with a variety of playthings."

The house had previously been a notorious House of Correction, which had moved to larger premises on the other side of the square after public demand led to overcrowding. Mother Dawkins had complained when the screams grew too loud but they'd rubbed along well enough for the most part. Perhaps they'd left some items behind.

He forced a smile. "It sounds charming. And how do we pay for our purchases?"

Her crimson-bedaubed mouth turned down at the corners. "We ask for a note of hand for the auction, my lord, or valuables. After that, you may use credit up to a certain value, to be redeemed at the end of the month."

"At a good rate of interest, I presume?"

"Naturally, my lord."

He waved his hand negligently. "It's acceptable."

The bully came forward to take him upstairs. Alex couldn't hope to take these men on his own. He could try but he had a few other tactics to use first. And pockets full of guineas. He'd tried to get into the house earlier in the day in the hope of getting Connie out before the auction, if she was there at all, but it was barred tight and a maid had yelled out of a window for him to come back tonight. He had no choice but to play it Dankworth's way.

Up to a point.

Alex's heart sank when he entered the room, though he ensured no one would deduct anything from his demeanor. The great, the wealthy and the debauched filled the room, all three qualities often embodied in the same person. About thirty gentleman, at his best guess, none of them his close allies but all of them members of society. And two who had been at that benighted house party at Lady Downholland's. Damn. That meant they'd recognize Connie, should she appear.

Not including Jasper Dankworth. Alex gave him a curt nod and moved on.

The bully showed him to a chair towards the rear of the room. Alex made great play of flicking his handkerchief over the upholstery and then settling the wide skirts of his dress coat before he sat. He leaned back, affecting every appearance of boredom and waited on events.

They began the proceedings with a hackneyed show of half-dressed house girls chained together, whipped by a slave driver. Their appearance would gratify the gentlemen present whose tastes swung that way.

Alex yawned, using his handkerchief to cover his mouth, flourishing the white cloth in a way he knew would garner attention. The madam stood by the door, watching the proceedings. At least the man had given him a seat with a good view.

Years of keeping his emotions private came to his aid now, as Alex affected the appearance of a man of fashion vainly looking for amusement.

Dankworth leaned forward in his chair. A slavering dog couldn't have made a better display of excitement. Spittle gathered at the corners of his mouth and his bloodshot eyes were wide and avid with excitement. He clasped his hands, the knuckles white.

Shouts and catcalls greeted the show until one of the women bared a breast. Mrs. Cratchitt finally moved forward when approving whistles replaced the catcalls. "These ladies will be available for personal visits later, gentlemen. They will be serving drinks during the auction. We don't want you dying of thirst, do we?"

One wag called out, "Is this a long auction? Should we send out to a pie shop?" It got more laughter than it deserved. Alex spared a tight smile. He couldn't have cracked a laugh at the moment, not to save his life. Only to save another.

The ribaldry dispensed with, a man in white draped skirt and heavy copper jewelry, presumably the slave master, freed the serving girls. The girls took the trays of wine set on a sideboard and circulated. They smiled and answered the men's pats and pinches with saucy comments. They skipped past grasping hands and seeking mouths. A woman had to be sober and quick-minded to elude some of the men present tonight. So, girls of the house.

Mrs. Cratchitt clapped, like a schoolmistress calling a class to order. The audience indulged her. Probably because they were looking forward to the treat.

"First on the block we have Vivi, a beauty from the far East!"

A lovely Indian girl was led forward to a podium that looked too much like an executioner's block for Alex's liking.

Years ago his father had taken him to see the execution of Lord Lovat, after the 'forty-five. He'd never forgotten the horror of seeing an eighty-year-old man beheaded. Alex had avoided public executions ever since, as far as he could. The sight of this woman standing on the block brought those memories roaring back.

Tension knotted his stomach and he only pretended to sip the wine one of the slave girls had handed him.

He remained languidly draped over his chair, handkerchief held elegantly, every muscle, every nerve under rigid control.

The girl stared out at the audience but because her eyes were so dark, he couldn't tell if sheer terror or drugs kept her rooted to the spot. She swallowed as the half-naked man playing the slave master sold her for three hundred guineas. Bidding was brisk and the girl went to Lord Tyrone, who would at least treat her with kindness. His for the night. She was not announced as a virgin.

Next, came the first declared virgin, a fresh-faced girl who probably came straight off the coach. She was definitely drugged. Her eyelids drooped and she staggered.

Cratchitt caught and straightened her once more.

Alex held his fire and she sold to a man for five hundred.

The trouble with watching something like this was that he wanted to buy them all, or at least the drugged ones, and set them free. Someone had lured them into this. That would play perfectly into Dankworth's hands. But he feared the man planned more.

Some 'slave auctions' were good-natured, lascivious fun, the girls willing, the virgins of the mock-maiden variety. This was certainly not one of those. It was disgusting, the girls drugged or scared.

Cratchitt hadn't even tried to hide that some of the girls were drugged. They were here for dangerous play, the kind that could kill them.

Dankworth would not win.

The next girl on the block was definitely drugged, her steps sluggish, her eyes half-closed, and she was not advertised as a virgin. Had Cratchitt checked? Of course she had, the bitch.

She'd probably examined Connie, too. Infuriated, Alex shifted in his chair. He could only wait, get Connie out of here and then put events in train. The girl wore a shift, which drooped over her chest. She was skinny, with tiny breasts, her bones protruding, her skin stretched over them. If Cratchitt had any sense she'd have looked after the stock better than this. A servant girl, maybe, looking for honest work and finding this instead.

"What do I have for this handsome wench?" The slave master tucked his whip under the girl's chin, forcing her head up. "Jest lookit her hair, gentlemen. Down to her backside. Your own personal harness to control her with!"

The room fell silent. Cratchitt nudged the girl and she yelped. Probably less of a nudge and more a pinch. "All scrubbed this morning. All the girls here are guaranteed clean inside and out!"

At last, Alex raised his hand. Costly lace fell back from his wrist. The auctioneer saw him immediately. "A hundred, sir?"

Alex shook his head. "Fifty," he suggested. "And I'm being generous." He couldn't bear it. This girl would die before too many days were out if she wasn't attended to. He couldn't let that happen.

Nobody else bid. The girls that had gone before had at least a chance and he would have a quiet word with their 'owners,' if he thought it necessary. He memorized the name of every man in the room. Alex let his lip curl in a sneer. Why not tell them what he thought of them?

Cratchitt brought the girl over.

Alex gestured a nearby chair. "Sit her there. I've not finished yet."

The girl shot him a disinterested look then closed her eyes. Alex poked her. She was dangerously close to falling into a deep, dreamless sleep, the kind people rarely woke from. She came to with a start and sat upright.

A buxom blonde followed, alert and chirpy, giving back what they sent her. A willing slave. She fetched a good price.

Then a woman, honey-colored hair trailing over her face in bedraggled tails. She wore a shift and a pair of blue brocade stays, cinched so tight that her ample bosom swelled with every breath.

Connie.

Normally Alex would find the quivering of such sweet flesh enticing. Not tonight. He felt every pinch of that tight lacing, every short breath she took as if it was his own. *Look at me. I'm here. I won't let them hurt you anymore.*

The slave master grabbed a handful of hair and jerked up her head. Connie's chin jutted out and her eyes, red-rimmed and watery, stared sightlessly into the room. All Alex's muscles tightened as he resisted the urge to leap onto that damned block and grab her, cover her with his coat, hide her from the leering eyes of the crowd. Fury and sense warred and sense won. Barely and only for her sake. He had to get her out of here and if he tried violence, the room, rendered volatile by excitement and strong drink, would erupt.

The wine had its effect and the audience was yelling and hooting their approval. "That's better!" someone cried. "I'll give her something to wake her up!"

Alex would kill him.

Again, she wasn't introduced as a virgin and Alex gritted his teeth, adding to the mental tally of what this Cratchitt bitch owed him. She'd had her hands all over Connie's sweet skin. The slave master began his chat but calls from the audience almost drowned him out. They liked her.

Connie swayed as if she'd fall off the block. A tiny thread of drool slid out of the corner of her mouth but Mrs. Cratchitt took care of it with a rough swipe from a cloth. Connie flinched.

If Alex had ever felt like hitting a woman, now was the time.

"Three hundred for Rattigan!" Dankworth cried.

Fury rose to choke Alex. How could he bandy her name like that? The bastard was making sure everybody knew her name. Alex gritted his teeth and forced his temper down. He needed all his wits about him now. Alex held his fire and let them bid. Occasionally Dankworth sent him a triumphant grin but Alex remained grimly silent, a supercilious smile firmly planted on his lips. He yawned again and shifted in his chair. Let them fight it out.

When the bidding had reached a pitch of intensity, but only in the hundreds he opened his mouth. "Five thousand."

The room fell silent and the audience turned as a man and gaped at him.

He shrugged. "If we only have them for one night, we'd best get on with it, hadn't we? With her, I'll have my two."

Murmurs followed his remark and a few "Hear hears," too. Maybe they'd come straight from the debating chamber. But he'd made his point.

Nobody else wanted to pay more than five thousand guineas for the woman. After all, she was no virgin. They had Cratchitt's word for that. When Lord Spinder opened his mouth and made a move with his hand, Alex met his gaze and let the smile drop. Gratifyingly, he received a shame-faced shrug and one man, standing at the back, nod in approval. An ally.

This wasn't right and some of them knew it.

Thanks to Mother Cratchitt, no doubt coached by Jasper Dankworth, everyone in this room knew the name of the woman here tonight. Alex didn't know if it was possible to recover from that. But she was barely recognizable from the woman he'd met at the Downhollands'. That could work in his favor.

Two bullies half-carried, half-dragged Connie off the block toward Alex. She staggered and stumbled, more asleep than awake.

He stood as they approached and swept her up, one arm under her knees and the other around her back, pillowing her head on his shoulder.

Her hair straggled over the fine red velvet of his coat. The last time he'd seen it, she'd swept it up into a glossy knot, leaving a few curls to tease her shoulders saucily. He'd wanted her then. He wanted her now, God help him.

He nodded towards the other girl he'd bought. "Bring her," he said curtly.

He strode from room, Mrs. Cratchitt abandoning her auction to chase him. The bully who'd shown him to his seat picked up the skinny girl as if she weighed nothing, which was probably not too far from the truth and followed him.

"This way, my lord," the doxy crooned, gesturing to the stairs.

Alex spared her a scornful glance. "I think not."

"Sir, you can't take the girls out of this house. I bought them girls good and proper. You only get a night."

Alex ignored her and headed down the stairs. Connie groaned and he took a moment to tuck her head more securely in the crook between his neck and shoulder.

"Sir, I'm warnin' you—" Cratchitt's accent grew less refined by the second.

He got to the bottom of the stairs and swung around, putting all his aristocratic hauteur into play. "I'll warn *you*. Ask about me and who my friends are. Then try to make trouble."

He was taking a risk because someone with influence and money had helped Cratchitt set this place up. "One peep from you and I'll visit my lawyers. Abducting a respectable female could get you into more trouble than you want. And the other one?" He nodded at the skinny maid in the other man's arms. "She'll die if she isn't cared for, I can see the signs. Do you want her dying here, or shall I take her to a hospital?"

"You can't leave!"

"Watch me."

He strode to the door and stood before it. The bully stationed there took a position before him and crossed his arms over his chest. Alex stared him out, his chin up, his eyelids lowered, looking down his nose at the man as if he meant nothing. Aristocratic hauteur often worked where swords wouldn't. "Open the door," he said quietly.

"Do it," said the bully behind him. "This girl must have come in by accident, or somefink. She shouldn't be here."

At last, a man of sense.

The man in front of the door glanced over Alex's shoulder. He must have received permission because he stepped back and flung the door wide. "And don't come back!" Cratchitt shrieked after him.

Alex left the house with the other man at his heels, ignoring the madam's shrieks that he should leave the other one behind. They raced down the steps and straight to the house next door.

The man stationed in front of it let them in without hesitation and slammed it in the faces of the pursuers.

The large figure of Mrs. Dawkins waited. She took one look at the girls and swore long and lavishly. "Take yours upstairs. Third floor, second door on the right. I'm taking this one to the doctor right now. I ain't havin' no girls dyin' in my house."

"Much appreciated, ma'am."

She grinned, displaying an alarming set of gleaming teeth, not all of them hers. "Like I said. You do me a favor, I'll do you one."

She nodded to the man carrying the skinny girl. "I'll see her right." She raised her voice. "Get a warm cloak and bring it 'ere!"

"Eh, Mother, is the girl for sale?" cried a raucous male voice.

"Not in this house," came the rejoinder. "You want 'em drugged and 'elpless, you go elsewhere."

Alex trusted the girl with Dawkins, because they'd made a deal. Despite his burden, he mounted the stairs two at a time.

The room assigned to them was dominated by a large, well-furnished bed, like most in this house. He laid Connie gently on top of the covers and examined her, touching her brow and finding it clammy and overheated. The pulse in her throat fluttered like a bird's wings, unsteadily and far too frantic.

She was still conscious but only just. He forced a smile. "You can relax now, Connie. You're with me."

"Bought me," she murmured, her voice thready and hoarse. "You bought me."

"I couldn't get you out of there any other way." He'd considered laying information at Bow Street and forcing them to raid the premises but that would have taken longer and they would have locked her up and forced her into the public eye. She might have had to stand in the courtroom at Bow Street before he could get her free. Unthinkable. As it was, he'd made this deal with Dawkins. Bow Street would hear about tonight's travesty, just not from him. And he'd got Connie free of the mess.

Lynne Connolly

A can of hot water was set just inside the door and a substantial washstand stood on the far wall, its basin ready for use. At least he could clean her face. And loosen those damned stays.

He'd have to sit her up to get to the laces at the back. Better still—ignoring her flinch when he touched her, he rolled her on her stomach. Someone had laced her up so tightly she could hardly breathe. She gasped and panted, then moaned and tilted her head to one side, staring at him, her pupils pin-points of blank darkness. Strands of hair lay over her cheeks and he pushed them aside.

"I need to get you out of this thing, Connie." He spoke slowly and clearly, using her name to keep her with him.

She nodded, a tiny movement against the pillow. "Hurts."

After fighting with the knots for a few minutes, he realized they weren't meant to be undone. Most women fastened their stays with slipknots or bows, something they could undo later. Whoever trussed her into this thing hadn't bothered with such niceties. The fancy blue brocade that covered the instrument of torture mocked him with its appearance of sumptuousness. Underneath, it was as hard as steel.

Connie panted for air. He'd made the situation worse.

He plunged his hand into his pocket. Julius Winterton had given him a couple of the fine, razor-sharp knives he liked to carry with him and these days Alex usually carried one in a decorative sheath. He sliced through the knot and when the laces wouldn't give, he cut them too.

She gasped and he stopped work. "What was that?"

"Don't hurt me," she whimpered.

His heart stuttered. What had they done to her? He swore to God he'd never allow such a thing to happen to her ever again. "Never, I swear it. I'll never hurt you, Connie. Let me care for you now. When I get this thing off, I'll help you to drink something."

He peeled the stays away, wincing at the sight of the red welts where the bones had bitten into her skin. She should have a shift on underneath, which would have helped.

He lifted her gently and propped her against the pillows. "Now you can drink and then sleep."

Food wasn't wise just yet. She might vomit and he had no idea what drugs she'd ingested although laudanum played a large part. He knew the signs. Her drowsiness and her inability to concentrate, together with the red-rimmed pupils. People could choke to death in an opiate-induced sleep.

His hostess had left some clean clothes. He picked up the clean linen shift and helped her into the shapeless garment, manipulating her arms as if she was a marionette. It whispered over her poor, abused flesh.

He removed the stopper and sniffed the contents of the carafe on the small table next to the bed. It held barley water flavored with lemon and honey. He gave a grim smile at the reminder of nursery fare and the incongruity of finding it here but he poured a glass and gave it to her.

She was watching him. He sat on the bed, wrapped one arm around her shoulders and leaned her against him to hold the glass to her lips.

"No!" She jerked away. Some of the drink spilled but he held her firmly and talked to her. "This is Alex, sweetheart. Remember me? Would I give you anything you couldn't trust? Drink the barley water and then sleep."

"Sleep," she murmured. He held the glass while she drank. She felt warm against him but after undoing her garters and rolling the stockings off her legs, he left her in the shift. It was too transparent for his liking, misting her fine, pearly skin with a glow that in other circumstances he'd find seductive.

The stays had hidden nothing and he'd had to sit in that damnable room, biding his time, while those bastards ogled her and bid on her as if she were a horse on the selling block.

He wanted to blind all of them, bury a blades in their eyes, one by one, just for looking at her, degraded as she never should be. Cold fury simmered under his skin but he couldn't set it free for her sake.

He wouldn't let his violent thoughts mar the way he treated her. When she'd drunk, he lifted her, settled the pillows and threw back the covers before laying her back down on the sheets.

He was gently covering her when someone knocked on the door. He left her in the bed and opened the door cautiously.

Mother Dawkins stood there. "She all right?"

"Come and see for yourself." He opened the door wider.

The madam had removed the cloak, hat and gloves she'd worn for her journey, revealing her glorious gown for tonight. She specialized in finery to the edge of irony and tonight was no exception. Scarlet gown and yellow petticoat, both fabrics the finest silk, neither the right shade for the other. Her cap was a profusion of lace, the lappets touching her shoulders. She handled Connie gently, putting her hand over her forehead and then tucking her hair away from her face. "She'll be fine. A day or two and she'll be just like new. A big sleep and she'll feel much better, more herself. After that, a good meal. Do you want her to stay here?"

Her accent had turned more natural, less heavily accented and Alex wondered, not for the first time, where the lady's origins lay. A respectable man's daughter, perhaps, making the best of what she had, like many of the whores in the Garden. This one had risen high, ran her own establishment, which proudly proclaimed it owned the reputation of being the best whorehouse in London. He respected that ambition in a woman and he never made the mistake of underestimating the redoubtable Mother Dawkins. "If it's convenient."

Dawkins gave a wry grin. "Hardly. You're taking up a good bedroom here. I could rent this by the hour. But I'm only charging you two night's rent. For the favor you're doing me, I'd like to give it you but business is business." Plus the extra incentive.

Alex smiled, the first one since he couldn't remember when, relief washing through him. He'd achieved the first part of his plan. Now to decide what to do next. "I know. I'm only too glad to pay. When she wakes I'll send for her maid, then we'll go."

Mrs. Dawkins nodded. "She needs somebody to sit with her. Best it's someone she knows."

"Where's the other girl I bought?"

She shrugged. "I took her to Bow Street, since my doctor's not available right now. Magistrate Fielding kept her and promised he'd look after her." The doxy chuckled. "He was outraged when he saw who was at his door. You know how he feels about us harlots. Wants to reform the lot of us."

Most people knew the Fieldings' opinion on the harlots who thronged the area where they held sway. Magistrates at Bow Street, just around the corner, they dealt with a lot of people from the trade.

Alex shrugged off his heavy evening coat and laid it across the back of the only comfortable chair in the room, then helped Mrs. Dawkins sit, using his best courtly style. She loved what she called gentlemanly behavior and it wouldn't do any harm to butter her up a bit.

He took the hard, wooden chair. He didn't much care which one he used. "I'd have paid good money to see you and Fielding go at each other." Mother Dawkins lifted a penciled brow. "Not like that. The verbal exchange would be enough."

He didn't like to think of anything else. The ample Mrs. Dawkins and the equally ample magistrate would make a formidable coupling. Perhaps it was just as well that they were on opposite sides of the legal fence. "So what did he say?"

"He got the gist when 'e saw the girl in Gosset's arms. She was out cold by then. I told him the truth. There was an auction going on and they were drugging the girls near to death. Appealed to his chivalry. Told him that I was laying information because I didn't want no trouble on my side of the Square. A law-abiding bawdy-house, we are. He laughed, damn his eyes. But he knows if he raids my establishment, he'll find nothing he shouldn't.'"

And wasn't that the truth. Not that her house had been raided for a long time now. She paid her dues and the officers left her alone. But Fielding was as near incorruptible as a magistrate could be, so he was the right man to go to in this case.

"So I said to 'im I want that woman out of that house. Sooner or later somebody's going to die there. He asked me how I found out and I said you was passing my house with the skinny maid in your arms and I took charge. I told him your name, since you said you wanted me to." She scratched her upper arm and grinned at him, perfect pearly whites gleaming in the low light of the two candles Alex had left burning in their ornate silver holders.

Alex nodded. "I'll confirm your story if he asks. Hopefully, he'll think it was just the one girl I saved."

"What about the other gentlemen there?"

"I know their names. I'll deal with them." How, he didn't yet know, but a plan was slowly forming in his mind.

He got rid of Mother Dawkins's thorn in her side, or rather, thorn next door. That was his bargain. She would give Connie sanctuary if he helped her get rid of Cratchitt and her unsavory practices. And her competition.

But for now, all his concentration was on Connie.

"Fielding kept the girl but he got one of his maids to put her to bed and watch her. After getting a man in to bear witness about her condition. I told him I don't hold with abducting respectable girls for the trade. He said he thought we were all evil but he'd fight one battle at a time. There's going to be a hell of a row next door. This room's at the front of the house. You can watch it from the window. Do you think the auction'll go on much longer?"

"I doubt it. But there'll be fun and games after. Enough for the authorities to find."

She made a sound of disgust. "I can't understand 'ow she got a house like that. I mean, the rougher trade's on the other side of the square and by the piazza, in the smaller places and the shacks. These establishments cost a fortune. I only employ the best here and I'm barely holding on. But the gentlemen who come to these houses want a bit of class. Not just a roll in the 'ay."

Alex loved listening to her. To the customers she was the madam who arranged the fun and games, who ruled her kingdom with an iron rod. But her girls were never anything but lively and the doctor visited every week to ensure they were clean. "When does your doctor come?"

"The pox man?" She waved a beringed hand, the multi-colored jewels glittering in the candlelight. "You shouldn't need 'im. Your young woman'll come round on her own."

"You know I'll go after the man who had this done to her, don't you?"

She nodded. "Just keep the trouble away from my house."

"Oh I mean to," he said grimly. "It won't happen here. I owe him, and it won't be easy and it won't be fast. And he won't do this to anyone else, ever again."

"Good to know," she said. "I'll try to find out who sponsored Cratchitt. Of course, she could have had a nest egg saved up but she didn't come from anywhere I know." She shrugged. "Which more or less rules out London. Could be a country madam come to try her hand in the city. In any case, the extra money your mark gave her wouldn't have come amiss. He might have paid for tonight's fun and games. Though I'd like to know what he's going to those lengths for." She yawned hugely but didn't cover her mouth.

"Connie was inconvenient to his plans but he didn't want to kill her. That could catch up with him one day. So he tried to disgrace her. He'd made sure enough members of society were there tonight for the word to get around."

Jasper Dankworth didn't have the money to pay for a venture like this. Barely enough to take advantage of it. Alex had a sneaking suspicion that he knew who was funding this venture. He needed to speak to his cousin. Julius knew much more than Alex did about the Dankworth factory.

"So he's won the first round," the madam said.

His determination firmed. Jasper Dankworth wouldn't win any more. "And thanks to your help, I've won the second. If Fielding can get Mrs. Cratchitt to lay evidence against him, I might even help her."

Mrs. Dawkins gave a harsh laugh. "Don't bank on it. She'll be in Bridewell before the week's out."

"Not if Fielding gets her."

Connie stirred and moaned.

Immediately Alex tended to her, soothing her with soft murmurs of, "I'm here, you're in safe hands now," and she settled down again. Once he was sure she was fine, he returned to his conversation with the madam.

"Fielding doesn't believe in sending doxies to Bridewell. A whore's academy, he calls it."

She gave a grim smile. "He might have a point."

A commotion erupted outside the window. Covent Garden was never quiet but this cacophony overtopped the usual sounds of revelry. Alex got to his feet and went to the window. And smiled.

Several burly men were hammering on the door of the house next door. If Alex stood to one side of the window, he could see them very clearly. The sound of their pounding echoed off the buildings ringing the piazza, attracting the attention of the roués and whores lounging around. Their raucous cries added to the row.

If it were he, Alex would have people around the back of the house. Since Mother Dawkins had a vested interest in seeing the house taken down, she'd willingly provide access if they needed it.

The door opened from the inside and the men poured in, shouting.

The powerful scent of lily-of-the-valley indicated his hostess had come to stand by his side, "I'm surprised you're not downstairs supervising," he said.

"I'm here with you. You can vouch for that, right?"

He might have known it wasn't his scintillating company or concern for Connie that moved Dawkins to linger here. She wanted a witness to confirm she had nothing to do with this raid. Mother Cratchitt might have friends who would object to another of their kind peaching.

Out of the front of the house streamed half-dressed doxies and clients but none that he'd seen in the large saloon on the first floor. They'd pay to leave by the back door, too influential to become involved in this. Or they'd stay where they were and leave when the fuss died down.

The crowd jeered as the doxies left, formed a column to stop the officers taking the whores away but so far, they kept the proceedings in good heart. No trouble. The mob could change its mind in a flash, turn from good natured to vicious killers, rampaging through houses and streets.

Alex addressed Mrs. Dawkins. "You have your bullies ready?"

She waved a hand, vaguely indicating the door. "Oh yes. All but two downstairs and a few hired chair carriers to bulk them up. We're well protected here."

He nodded. Safer than trying to leave this house with Connie in the middle of this rabble. If necessary they would barricade the door but he doubted anyone would get this far. "We have a good view from here. Do you know any of the girls?"

Lynne Connolly

Mrs. Dawkins peered closer. "Some. One or two single workers with their own lodgings. Probably looking for a bit more work where somebody else pays for the wine and the food. One or two new girls. I might look into them once they get out but they've got to be good to work here."

One of the house bullies from next door left carrying a woman. Her pale skin gleamed with sweat and she stirred weakly in the man's arms. He held her closer and glanced, grim-faced at one of the officers who indicated a vehicle drawn up by the house.

The crowd fell relatively silent, with individual catcalls and not yells. Several women were carried out and loaded into the waiting carriages. At least two women weren't moving and lay limp in the arms of the men who carried them. They could be dead. Alex feared for them, then, struck by a new thought, he spun around. Connie had taken the same drugs.

He turned to the figure in the bed and didn't return to the scene outside until the covers moved when Connie breathed. "Are you sure she'll be all right?" he asked Mrs. Dawkins.

"Yes. I wouldn't be surprised if she hadn't puked some of it up. They don't know what they're doin'. It's criminal."

She didn't realize the irony of her worlds. He didn't feel up to arguing the point at the moment. He'd rather watch the activity in the square and keep an eye on Connie.

With the house empty, even Cratchitt carried away and marched around the corner in the direction of Bow Street, the officers left. And didn't bother to close the door behind them.

The mob shrieked and surged in.

Alex turned away, not interested in watching the windows smash and the valuables destroyed or stolen, or the scared customers flushed out from hiding. If it didn't find what it wanted there, the rabble might turn on other houses. A few night watchmen's kiosks would be destroyed tonight unless their owners fortified them.

"They're not in a bad case," said the madam. "I've seen enough riots to sense the mood. They won't go running tonight." Once roused, a London mob could destroy houses, shops, each other, anything that got in its way.

He had to accept her word because he was effectively locked in here, at least until the morning. He could only wait and hope that Mrs. Dawkins was right, both about the mob and about Connie. She slept now but she might never wake up.

If that happened, he'd kill Dankworth and to hell with the consequences.

Chapter 9

Connie blinked and light pierced her eyes but it wasn't as painful as the dagger someone was repeatedly stabbing through her head. She wished they'd stop doing it. Nausea roiled through her belly and she took a deep breath, then another.

She heard a voice, so soft she couldn't be sure it existed outside her head. "Connie?"

Soft bedamned. The echoes revolved around her. She groaned. "Not so loud."

A chuckle. It *was* him. Either that or her imagination had taken wings. Cautiously, she turned her head, glad to find a soft pillow supporting it.

Alex sat on a chair next to the bed, his face illuminated by the flickering light of a branch of candles. Grey dawn filtering through the narrow window. She opened her mouth. "I dreamed about you." She was mildly surprised that speech emerged.

He placed a damp cloth on her forehead. Her headache receded a tiny bit under the blessed coolness. "I trust they weren't too disturbing. I came as soon as I could."

"What happened to me?" Visions shot through her mind. Arriving at the inn, then flashes of memory, or dreams, she didn't know which.

"You were abducted from the Belle Sauvage." He kept his voice low but emotion throbbed in the low tones.

"I remember arriving at the inn then something happened." She spoke slowly, drawing out her words, trying to dispel the sick, floating dizziness. "Then a woman told me to drink something, that it would do me good. She said I was ill. Then little bits of memory." She waved a hand, glad she could still do so. "That's not right. Dreams, visions, drinking again. Wine and something else, sweet and sickly. I was sick and somebody brought a fresh pot, then I was sick again. Someone undressed me and said they'd bring me fresh clothes. Then noise and people. And I thought I saw you, in red but I couldn't have, could I?" Her voice tailed off.

"Look over there."

A figured velvet coat in a rich red color was draped carelessly over a chair.

"I couldn't stop what they did to you. I'm sorry, Connie."

"What did they do?" It was real. Her dreams were real. What did that mean? Connie felt anchorless, plunged into a place she didn't understand so that even as the clouds in her mind cleared she entered another world. "I came to London to see Jasper. He said we were to be married."

A pause, then, "I know."

She sat upright. The room spun around her once more. Putting her elbows on her upraised knees, she planted her hands either side of her head, holding it steady. "My maid came with me. Did they hurt her?"

"I have her safe."

"Oh thank God!" A surge of relief filled her she felt a little better sitting up. Either that, or she'd left some of the headache behind. She dared to release her head, relieved when it stayed on her shoulders.

The mattress depressed when he came to sit on the bed by her side. He put his arm around her shoulders. Shamelessly she leaned against him, his hard-packed body a place of strength in her shifting universe.

He stacked pillows behind her and leaned her against them. "Can you drink something?"

She shuddered. "That's what they did. Kept making me drink."

He waited until she turned her head and met his gaze. "Do you trust me?"

"Of course." She said it before her mind processed the question but it was true.

"Then drink this." He held a glass to her lips and obediently, she swallowed. Lemon and honey barley water, a nursery drink. But thirst-quenching and so welcome. A tang of the sickly sweet drug they must have fed her remained on her tongue but the fresh taste helped to wash it away. She sipped then gulped. When she'd emptied the glass, she demanded more.

He laughed softly. "Not yet. Let your body absorb it first."

She wanted to find her anchor again, reconnect with the flow of her life. "I arrived in London on Thursday. What day is it today?"

"Tuesday."

"Oh." Exhausted, she leaned against his shoulder instead of the pillows and he didn't move away. He only wore a shirt and waistcoat and she became aware of his body as she rarely did of any man's, warm, and firm under her cheek. A refuge when she needed one.

"They took you on Thursday and kept you drugged until last night. They gave you a mixture of substances. You weren't the only woman they took." Abruptly, he stopped.

"Tell me everything."

He nodded. "You deserve to know. They took other girls as well. Madams and bullies sometimes meet unaccompanied women off the stages. The girls think they're going to a respectable house to be maids but they're introduced to houses of ill repute instead. Some take to it, some do not. Sometimes they're drugged. It's a regular occurrence but not for respectable women of some substance. Someone paid them to put you in the latest house."

"A…" She knew the word but she couldn't say it.

He could. "A brothel. Like this one."

With a stifled exclamation, she jerked away and then wished she hadn't because her head throbbed anew.

He drew her back against him. He smelled good, a faint trace of the citrus scent she remembered from their time at the Downholland's, plus a stronger aroma of soap and pure, clean male.

She drew deep, cleansing breaths.

"We're safe here, I swear it. The madam here never takes anyone unwilling. If I'd taken you anywhere respectable, the world would chatter and you'd be no better off. I've been sitting here, watching you and I've had a few ideas."

She thought he might have pressed his lips against her hair but she wasn't sure. Her heart fluttered.

"Don't think about it now," he murmured. "Just get better. The drug is out of your system, so you can eat, drink and feel better. Much of your light-headedness will be lack of food. We managed to give you a little but you need to eat properly now. You'll feel better in no time."

"In that house did anyone—did I—"

He hugged her closer then relaxed his hold. "No. At least I got there in time to stop any of the men molesting you."

She echoed a vague memory. "They took away my clothes and didn't bring me any more. Just underthings."

He sighed and stroked her hair, the motion soothing. "I was hoping you wouldn't remember that part."

"Tell me everything. Please." She stared out of the window opposite the bed. The tops of a few buildings and some church spires were all she could see. This room must be high up. "I need to know, don't I? All the truth, please."

"I fear you do. Well then, these houses have something called a slave auction."

She shuddered and hoped he hadn't noticed but that would be too much. He rubbed her upper arm with gentle strokes. "So I was naked?"

"No, you weren't. But close."

"And I'm still here?"

"We're not in that house, we're next door. It's a brothel and gaming house. The best in London, the madam claims. Honest, or as honest as these places ever are."

"So some of the fashionable world, I'm assuming the male part, has seen me all-but naked. Would they know me again?"

"Probably."

"Thank you."

"For what?"

"For answering my questions directly." Her world disintegrated around her, as if made of pastry. Everything she'd considered solid and real proved to be nothing.

This time she felt a gentle kiss against her hair. "You're welcome. You deserve the truth."

Now it started to make sense. "So someone abducted me, sold me to a brothel and saw to it that people saw me half naked."

"I'm afraid so. But you can't do anything about it. Sleep for a while."

Held close and safe in his arms, she drifted away.

* * * *

When she awoke, the light outside had changed to the full light of day. This time she felt immeasurably better, her headache almost gone.

He filled her glass and although she was capable of holding it herself now, she let him help her drink. Afterward he put the glass down and stayed with her and when she leaned against him, he put his arm around her again. "Don't think about anything now. Just get well. I have you here and safe."

She could forget everything, here in his arms. Dangerous to think like that, because she'd have to leave this place and face whatever mess waited for her outside.

Someone knocked on the door. Alex left her and answered the summons, returning with a tray holding food. She eyed the viands cautiously.

"Don't worry. There are no drugs in this. You're safe."

He was so gentle and understanding. If she felt less fragile, it might annoy her but as it was, she welcomed it, too weak to fight or even think properly. Her world had changed so profoundly. Once she'd thought through the events and their possible consequences, she'd deal with the problem. She'd been solving problems all her life. This wouldn't be any different. Porcelain was like that. Tough when whole but so easy to shatter into a million pieces.

He placed the tray on her lap and let down the little legs at each corner which meant it rested on the bed, not on her. "There's bread, cheese and a stew. Mother Dawkins serves hearty food. She says her girls like it."

She'd picked up the spoon but it rattled against the dish and she nearly dropped it. "Maybe I should count myself amongst them."

"No. And you won't. I promise."

She couldn't think now. She picked up the spoon again, gripped it firmly and began to eat.

Alex had a tray of his own delivered and he sat in the upholstered chair. It gave her a chance to take stock of her surroundings. The bed faced the window, and as well as the buildings and church spires, it gave a view of the roof of some grand building across a large space. She guessed a square, because it was wider than any street she knew. Either that, or lower houses sat between them.

He glanced up and followed her gaze. "This is Covent Garden and that's the theatre across the way. Between us is the piazza, a grand square. The builders wanted to encourage the rich to live here and built good houses but the polite world had already begun to move west, closer to the park, away from the crowds in town. So the houses are now shops, coffee houses and—"

"Brothels," she finished with a grin. Surprisingly, her appetite had returned with a vengeance. The first few spoonfuls of the soup had stopped her stomach churning and set it to processing what she was giving it and now the stew smelled appetizing. She ripped off a chunk of bread. Fresh and soft, as good as anything she could get at home. She chewed, enjoying the flavor and feeling it chase the last of that other, unpleasant taste from her mouth. "I thought London bread was supposed to be poor and adulterated."

"It depends where you buy it." He took a mouthful himself. "The lady here employs a full kitchen of staff. She serves food to her customers, should they wish it." He chuckled. "This is also a gaming house, remember. And the play here can be deep. Men need sustenance on the road to losing their shirts."

She ate in silence for a while, concentrating on her swiftly recovering body, giving it the fuel it obviously needed. The barley water, though bland, proved excellent for rejuvenation. She drank a lot of it.

When she finally put down her spoon, she was surprised at how much she'd eaten.

"Four days' near abstinence will make you hungry." He took their plates, stacked them on the tray and put them outside the room. "You should be feeling better now."

He closed the door and stood in the middle of the room, gazing at her, his eyes tender. "Perhaps you should rest a little. You'll feel much better when you wake up."

"Not immediately." She shifted uncomfortably. She might be in a whorehouse but she didn't have their ways. She still had her modesty.

"Ah." He nodded. "There's a powder room through that door. You'll find what you need in there."

She was only wearing a shift. Heat flowed under her cheeks.

Alex smiled and picked something up from the bottom of the bed. A substantial wrap. She breathed a sigh of relief, even more when he averted his eyes. She folded back the covers and stepped out of the bed. Luckily, it wasn't too high.

Without looking at her, he held the wrap so she could slip her arms into the sleeves, and then she drew the fine, yellow silken fabric around her. "Thank you," she murmured and took her first steps since she'd arrived here.

She stumbled and immediately, he banded his arms around her waist, steadying her.

His body pressed against hers, his chest to her back, his groin to her buttocks and it felt so good. His strong, masculine hardness surrounded her, giving her the illusion that nothing bad would happen to her while she stood like this. She wanted more of it, in a way that heated her cheeks even more. And the rest of her.

Before she could feel any more of him, or do something rash like lean back against him, she drew away and headed for the door he'd indicated.

It led to a blind room, with no way out other than the door she'd come in by. She suspected it might once have been part of the bedroom but it now contained toiletry materials. After lighting the candle she used the pot and then poured some water into the basin and rinsed her hands. After pouring that away in the slop basin by the washstand, she was too tempted not to put herself to rights.

She poured more water, stripped and washed. The relief was almost as good as using the necessary. She hated being dirty, always had, but she might never wash away the experience she'd just gone through.

When she poured her washing water away, she let herself imagine that all her experience in the house next door went with it. Discarded. That all went in the basin and then she poured it in the slop bucket. Gone, done with. She dusted her hands together, as she did when she'd completed an onerous task at home.

Although she might think about it, might even relive it some lonely nights, she would never let it become part of her. She swore it, even though only her reflection could bear witness to her oath.

She found a brush and cleaned her teeth, freshening her mouth. Even better. Now all trace of the drugs they'd given her had gone. She'd ask if someone could help her wash her hair later, perhaps wash again to make doubly sure any trace of her ordeal had gone.

Now she had to face the music, whatever that turned out to be. She still didn't know why Jasper would do this to her. When she'd last seen him, they'd signed a contract for something that would never happen now. And that night, the night before he'd left so precipitately, she'd given him permission to come to her room. She shuddered. A narrow escape, as it had turned out.

She put the shift and robe back on then went back into the bedroom.

Alex was sitting in the chair, his head leaning against the back, his feet up on a small table. He hurriedly restored his feet to the floor.

She shook her head and climbed back into bed as quickly as she could. Wearing only a shift and wrap made her vulnerable and she kept the wrap on until the sheet covered most of her, although part of her, the wanton part she'd never known what to do with, urged her to let it drop and flaunt herself. "How did you find out where I was?"

"Your maid came to me and told me you'd gone missing on your arrival in London. I retraced your steps, found out that Dankworth was involved and hunted him down. That was how I heard of the auction. He has no idea that I had anything to do with the raid. I suspect he heard of the auction and decided to make use of it." He frowned. "Either that, or someone gave him the money. Setting up a new brothel in Covent Garden doesn't come cheap." He glanced at her and his face cleared. "The authorities raided the house and took everyone away after we left. That was my doing. I wanted you out of there first, but the audience saw you."

"They knew me?"

His chest heaved. "Yes. Dankworth made sure of it."

She blinked her tears away. No time for them now. "What can I do?"

He stared at her, face stark and serious. He'd had a twinkle in his eyes before, at the Downholland's, but now those dark pools were completely serious. They held a gravity and concern she badly wanted to see more of, but knew she had no right to demand. He had helped her, and that was that. He'd saved her from a fate she shuddered to consider but consider it she must. Connie had never shirked from the truth. Raped, maybe hurt worse, maybe even dead from the drugs they were feeding her.

"I have a plan," he said. "Saxton and I are the only people apart from Dankworth who know you're in London. Know for sure, that is. You may quietly and discreetly return from whence you came. Then I will tell everyone that I know you well and Dankworth was mistaken, that you never came to London. The woman might have looked like you but she certainly wasn't you. Since I bought your lookalike and bore you off, they'd probably believe that I wanted some illicit fantasies brought to life."

Clever. Yes, that would work. So why did she feel so deflated? Just a natural reaction to the horror she'd suffered, her body's reaction to her ordeal, was all. "If I go home and tell them I fell ill on the road, nobody will know I reached London. I can write to my godfather and tell him I don't wish to marry Jasper."

Slowly, this nightmare began to make sense. Why Jasper would put such a terrible series of events in train. In short, money.

"I'll give him a full accounting of Dankworth's activities recently. That will ensure you receive none of his lordship's opprobrium. He might even decide to name another heir."

She nodded and met his gaze for a fraught moment. Without him, she'd be completely ruined. He deserved the truth. "I know why Jasper did this."

"So do I. The morality clause. You had one, isn't that right?"

She nodded. Many marriage contracts had them, so she hadn't thought it too unusual. If she was proved of unsound mind, or if her behavior was proved immoral in some way, then her estate would be forfeit to Jasper in default of a court case. Of course, the clause only went one way. Jasper could keep a string of whores and nobody would call him for it.

"We can't afford to lose much time," he said. "As soon as you're well enough to travel, you must go. I'll hire a chaise for you." He filled this room with his powerful presence. Not that she'd see him again. Thus the reason for her lingering sadness.

"Not all the way home," she said quickly. "Chaises are remarked on in my village. I'll go to York and then claim I fell ill there and stayed at the coaching inn until I felt better. I'll return home on the stagecoach." She lifted her knees and dropped her chin on them, feeling unaccountably sad. She couldn't deny that she'd been looking forward to her visit to London with more than a little excitement but the only part of it she was destined to see was the view from her window. The wedding, yes, but also getting out of the place where she'd spent most of her life and outgrown a long time ago.

He shook his head. "It goes against the grain for me to do it. I want to keep you close, ensure you come to no more harm."

She wanted it too. But it was not to be.

He forced a smile, one that didn't reach as far as his eyes. "But the plan is a sound one. Society will forget. I can, at least, ensure you're comfortable on the road and send a man to bespeak good rooms for you." He leaned forward. "Let me go out and arrange a few matters."

He crossed the room to where his coat still lay, thrown over the chair. "I wish I could accompany you but perhaps I should not. I will, however, come to see you as soon as I've assured myself that matters are as they should be in town." He turned to face her, his expression grave. "I promise you that, Connie." He hesitated, gazing at her. "I want more for us."

She met his gaze frankly. "So do I."

Neither said any more, but her mind went back to those kisses they'd shared once and the promise of so much more, now destroyed forever. There was no future here. She was lucky if she had any kind of future, but certainly, it didn't lie with this man.

With her relentlessly realistic view on life, she couldn't see it happening. She'd realized what he was and how important his position in society was when she'd seen that caricature in Leicester. She didn't belong to that world.

After he left Connie gave in to her overpowering urge to weep.

* * * *

After stopping at his house to wash, shave and change, Alex walked to the Cocoa Tree coffee house, a place of commerce and superlative gossip.

On his entrance, he gained several furtive looks. Hell, the bastard had been busy already. Alex had chosen dark brown today, sober and industrious, except it was in the best cloth money could buy and the merchants here would recognize that. And his waistcoat was a riot of twining vines and glittering cut steel buttons, a reference to his frivolous side. Julius Winterton had taught him the value of dressing well *in extremis*.

Dankworth couldn't hope to compete with Alex's wardrobe, or, for that matter, his contacts but he could make a hell of a stink and make it impossible to restore Connie's good name. That was what Alex had come to scotch and that was why he couldn't escort Connie on her journey north.

"Alex, just the man!"

Devereaux was sitting at one of the long tables in the center of the room. Around and in front of the windows ranged smaller booths, benches facing large tables but the center held two large tables where men could conduct their business and there was his cousin, Maximilian, the Marquess of Devereaux.

Not the person he wanted to see most in the world but one he had to face, since Devereaux was as influential as the rest of their family and at the moment Alex needed all the allies he could muster.

Alex strolled across the room, taking his time, nodding to people and then sat in the space Devereaux had indicated. The bastard slapped his back. Hard. "I heard you made a fine purchase last night, my man. How was she? Still a virgin?"

Alex shrugged. "The evening turned out not as I expected. It was deeply unsavory. I merely got the woman away from Dankworth. The man annoyed me and I decided to pay him back for it."

"How did he annoy you?" Devereaux's green eyes narrowed but his face remained mildly amused, his mouth quirked in a smile. "Apart from being a Dankworth of course."

"Just by being alive." Better he gave no details in public.

Devereaux's mouth flattened into a straight line and his expression sharpened, creases appearing between his brows. "The Dankworths have caused me more than a little trouble recently. I never considered Jasper more than an irritation. He's from a minor branch of the clan." He raised a brow and Alex nodded in comprehension. Devereaux shrugged and went on. "I saw him at Lady Wren's last night. He seemed in good spirits, said he was on his way to a new bawdyhouse. When I saw him later, he was damned put out. Bow Street raided the house, apparently and spoiled his fun. Did you see any of that?"

"It must have happened after I left." Devereaux would understand some of what Alex wasn't saying. "I bought two girls and left. They were both drugged. I didn't use either of them." He paused. "I'm not so desperate that I need to render my women insensible."

Devereaux tsked. He moved closer but didn't lower his voice. Everyone in the coffee house would hear and then everyone in London. That was the point of coming here today. "Poor show. I like my girls willing. Vicious practice, that."

Alex lifted a finger and ordered a coffee from the pretty girl serving the table. "The waiters here are a damn sight better than the ones at White's." He got an approving nod from the woman sitting at the cash desk just inside the door and a laugh from the other people at the large table. Good, they were listening.

"Alex, tell me if this is true. Was one of the women Dankworth's previous fiancée?"

He'd known this question had to come but Devereaux did him a favor by asking, giving the opportunity to explain. He thought he'd prepared himself to answer but rage rose inside him all over again. Only Devereaux would see the spark of fury. Alex fought to keep his sangfroid, his languid air of aristocratic hauteur. "Where did you hear that?"

"It's all over town, dear boy." The green eyes flashed a warning now and Devereaux—Max—had used Alex's Christian name, not his title, something he rarely did in public. That was a warning, too. Devereux's father had died young and consequently Max, elevated to marquess at a young age, had more formality about him than his cousins. And probably a harder edge, though that would be difficult to assess, with a family packed, as theirs was, with influence and wealth. Max had fought for his, after his father had left him all-but bankrupt.

Alex leaned back and forced a bored yawn, covering his mouth as he did so. "How many fiancées does one man need before he settles on one? I had always thought one at a time was good ton but Dankworth seems to be trying to set a new fashion. He will not. He's not good ton."

The girl leaned over more than she needed to when she placed the fragrant coffee in front of him. He gave her the smile that made people call him charming. He'd even practiced it before the mirror in his youth, another weapon for his armory, as potent as any sword in certain situations.

Her bosom came a little closer and the fichu covering it wasn't quite as well tucked in as it could have been. Although she didn't interest him, he handed her a shilling for her pains. She made a point of pushing it down her cleavage. "You should be careful," he murmured. "Respectable businessmen don't like that kind of display."

She flushed. "Are you respectable, then, sir?"

"Completely." His firm words gained him sniggers from the other occupants of the table, a mixture of society gentlemen and City businessmen. They all came here for one reason—to facilitate the making of money. They made deals, bought and sold, and picked up the gossip that proved so lucrative. Around the corner, the men frequenting Lloyd's coffeehouse sold insurance to cover the deals made here. The scent of pipe tobacco wreathed around them and the buzz of a place where something important was happening tingled his fingertips.

The hum of conversation hushed, as he turned back to Devereaux. "Tell me, my dear cousin. Would it be considered good form to dispose of one fiancée before taking another or can a man have more than one at a time?"

Devereaux leaned back but not too far, as the benches in this part of the house had no backs. His eyes gleamed. "Taking one after another is close to the line, two at the same time is definitely crossing it. You know Fox and his friends are taking an interest in Dankworth?"

Fox and his cronies took people up and dropped them again with ruthless efficiency. But while in favor a man would be advised to use them as fast and hard as he could. But their interest could also prove very expensive. No doubt about it, Dankworth was running in circles he couldn't afford.

Alex shrugged, as if their interest meant little. "I met him at the house of a friend of my father's. You know Lord Downholland?"

Devereaux shrugged. "I've met him once or twice. Prefers to live in the country, doesn't he? Moderate fortune, pleasant man, as I recall, even if he does talk to you like he's delivering a lecture."

"That's the man. I came to town from his place in Yorkshire. Devilish tedious journey. His goddaughter was visiting and Downholland was brokering her marriage contract to Dankworth. Then I came to London and discovered he's courting another lady." Alex laughed carelessly, as if the news he was imparting was mere amusing gossip and not a matter of vital importance to someone very dear to him. "He has a complete lack of staying power. I understood they signed the contract in Yorkshire but I did not stand witness, so perhaps I was mistaken. Or perhaps Dankworth is merely amusing himself with the lovely Miss Stobart until the lovelier Mrs. Rattigan arrives."

Devereaux took a great deal of not-so-innocent amusement from the doings of others but more than that, he'd built his family fortunes from near ruin to formidable by listening and acting on his discoveries.

That last hint, said carelessly, would interest him, especially if—"Has Dankworth been in here recently?" Alex asked.

"Last week. He seems interested in one of the ships setting out for India. But you need a good stake for that one."

"The *Caroline*?" He hoped not. He had a share in that one himself. He'd hate to scupper his own investment but he refused to allow Dankworth to profit from it. He'd buy the ship and sink it himself, rather than let that happen.

"No." Devereux frowned then his expression lightened. "The *Spirit of Adventure*."

"Ah." Alex knew the vessel but didn't hold great hopes for the proposed cargo, because the *Caroline* would get there first and take its pick of the spices available. And being faster, it would return the cargo in better time. He could say that aloud but that would give information the men sitting at this table might not have. "A hefty stake required, then."

"He has expressed interest in my new delivery of wine from France," a man said. Alex exchanged a friendly greeting. This City man was a shrewd investor. And of a puritan cast of mind, despite his business. "Would you recommend him as an investor?"

Alex shook his head pursing his lips as if doubtful. "Truly sir, I can't say. But he was dipping deep in the hells last week. He must be made of juice. I'd say make sure of it but I know you'd do that with any new investor. Trust is earned, is it not?"

"Indeed it is." The man made a note in his account book. Every man of business carried his account book, which he took back for his clerks to transcribe but his word meant more than the scratches of a pen on a piece of paper. Signing was often a mere formality. Once the word of a man was lost, it took a lot to get it back. Most never managed.

Dropping a hint here was as good as standing in the middle of the marketplace and shouting, "Don't trust this man!" Alex took the risk that the gentlemen who frequented the coffeehouses of the City would take his word and not Dankworth's. After all, Dankworth had attracted the attention of Fox and his cronies, so he wouldn't collapse like a house of cards. And gamblers didn't lose all the time.

Alex drank his coffee, exchanged the time of day as if he had all the time in the world. Then he took his leave and crossed the floor to speak to another man, one he'd done business with in the past.

He made sure he asked if Dankworth was another principal in the investment. When the man said he couldn't possibly comment, Alex said that if Dankworth was involved, he might have to think again. When his contact asked him what he knew, Alex shrugged and said he just didn't like the man. That there was something about him he didn't trust, so he'd set a few enquiries in train. Once he had the results, he'd make a more permanent decisions.

He left the coffee house well pleased with his work.

Chapter 10

The day after she'd woken up in a second house of ill repute, Connie leaned her hands on the sill of her room and gave herself time to think. The square below had a canopied section in the middle. The remains of the morning market lay on the cobbles, bits of green vegetation, a flash of orange, and some crushed flowers. From what she'd read, Covent Garden was the most important market for fresh fruit and vegetables in London. Perhaps she'd see it in full swing before she left this place. Take one sight of London home to amuse her during the long, lonely nights. An arched passage stretched on one side of the square where men walked and chatted. They looked perfectly respectable but she'd already learned that appearances could deceive.

She'd always enjoyed watching life. That was one reason she'd gained a reputation for bookishness. She would pretend to read and watch instead, glory in the variety of human nature.

These buildings were part of the reconstruction of London after the Great Fire of nearly a hundred years ago. It was difficult to imagine the vice that went on behind the stately and imposing facades, although some of the buildings were admittedly not in the greatest state of health.

Although she regretted the way she'd arrived, it was still London and she still thrilled to be here. She'd dreamed of a visit to the metropolis for years but never thought it would happen. Her father had no wish for it and her husband had less.

She shed the garish yellow robe and slid into bed, thinking about the rescuer, the man who had aroused her with one kiss, who'd walked away because she belonged to someone else. But she didn't anymore. Whatever happened next, she wouldn't be marrying Jasper Dankworth.

She refused to lie to herself.

She wanted Alex. Badly, with a yearning that racked her body. Before she went home, she would compound her sins. If he was willing. She would have that much of him, at least. After all, what did she have to lose? Her reputation? She laughed scornfully.

The sharp knock on the door took her by surprise. Had a customer decided to explore the building? She leaped out of bed, grabbed the robe and shrugged it on, cinching it tightly around her before she called out, "This room is private."

"I know," came his voice. "May I come in?"

"Of course."

Her fingers trembling, she removed the robe and dropped it on the chair before climbing back into bed. She wouldn't seduce anyone in that.

He walked in, dropping the latch behind him. She found herself gazing into the dark depths. He didn't look away and neither did she.

After a moment of frozen awareness, he strode to the bed, and sat close to her. They still didn't look away. When he reached for her, she went willingly into his arms, where she wanted to be.

He touched his lips to her forehead, her cheek and finally, with a kiss that was barely a whisper, to her mouth. Eagerly, she strained up, urging him to come closer.

Instead, he drew back. "This is wrong, Connie."

"Why?" she dared to demand. "Here I'm nobody, nothing. Soon I'll be gone, with people none the wiser. And if you hadn't noticed I'm no shrinking virgin."

He shook his head and would have drawn back but she caught his face between her hands, making him look at her. His beard stubble abraded her palms. "For once in my life I want to know how good it can be. I want to know what a real man can do, what he can make me feel. And I want that man to be you. Please, Alex. If you desire me, take me. If you don't want me, if you're just being kind, say so now."

She'd been used and insulted enough. Now she wanted to take something for herself. Him. If—

"Of course I desire you." His breath heated her lips. "How can you ever doubt it? But I want to care for you, not use you."

She held tight to him, wouldn't let him move away. "I'll make a bargain with you. We'll use each other. That makes it fair, doesn't it?"

He groaned low. "God help me, I can't resist you. Connie." He said her name like a prayer, then he covered her mouth with his, taking her in a deep, possessive kiss, one she couldn't escape even if she wanted. She sucked gently on his tongue, stroked it with hers.

Alex wrenched himself away and held her firmly, his hands on her shoulders. "Connie, are you sure?"

"I'm sure about only one thing. Make love to me, Alex. Give us what we both want."

She melted into him, nestling her body against his, pressing her breasts against his chest and wishing there was nothing between them so she could feel his hot flesh on hers, his muscles massaging her, surrounding her.

He kissed her again, made a small sound into her mouth, vibrating against her tongue, making her open her mouth wider.

He banded his arms around her, holding her close but not safe, not this time. She tasted danger in his kiss, peril in that strong body and she wanted it all. Wanted every part of him.

She set her hands to his sides and tugged his shirt, trying to free it from the waistband of his breeches.

He drew back, his eyes slumberous with desire. "Allow me, sweet lady." He dragged his shirt free and pulled it over his head, tossing it over the chair he'd recently slept in.

Connie caught her breath. "So strong, so beautifully shaped."

He flashed a grin. "More?"

She nodded eagerly. She might not have the seduction skills of a courtesan but she'd persuaded him of her sincerity. He undid the fall of his breeches, slid down to stand on the floor. He discarded his breeches, underwear and stockings in one move, dropping the discarded garments on top of his shirt. His sideways twist to put the clothes down revealed the curve of his buttocks. They enhanced his slim hips, the muscles flexing with an unconscious strength she'd never get enough of. All his movements enthralled her. Especially when he turned back to her unashamedly naked.

His erection rose from a nest of black curls. He was already hard and straining, the tip of his shaft damp and shiny.

He smiled but the side of his mouth twitched. He wanted her and it looked as if he wanted her very much. Just as she wanted him.

She could only honor his honesty. So she undid the buttons on her cuffs and pulled the linen shift over her head. Leaning back on her haunches, she took her visual fill. Or did until he groaned and came back.

"You would tempt a saint, my lady. Beautiful, you're so beautiful." He leaned her back until she lay down. "I want to feel all of you against all of me."

So did she. So much that the place between her legs was damp with her need. She'd felt such arousal before but only when Alex looked at her that way. And she'd never felt so blatant about her body. She wanted to display it for his enjoyment, not just undress.

He lay by her side, propped up on one elbow and smoothed his hand down her body from her arms to her knees. "That curve of a woman's body is so delectable and yours is the most luscious imaginable."

She smiled up at him, suddenly light-hearted. "So you're not pretending to be a virgin?"

"No more than you are." He kissed her, their lips separating reluctantly. "I shouldn't be doing this."

"Too late for your conscience. Put it to sleep. You want me to feel better, don't you? I can't think of a better way." She wanted him so much she could hardly breathe. Her words came in small, breathy pants, because it was all she could manage. If he stopped now, she'd die.

She recognized her own desperation reflected back at her when he kissed her and went on to taste her lips, her neck, her throat. Stretching up, she gave him better access. He palmed her breast. As if it were meant for him to do that, had no other purpose his touch made her moan, arch her body towards him.

"Hush," he said. "Let me please you."

She melted, flowed into him, put her arms around him and slid her palms up and down his strong, smooth back. He explored her, touched her, made her mad with longing but at the same time she didn't want to stop. Didn't want him to stop. Didn't want him—

When he slid his fingers between her legs and slipped them along the dampness there her breath expelled in one long sigh "Ohhh."

Smiling tenderly, he took his time, explored her, touched her, always sliding past that part of her she'd barely been aware of before, the little knot of flesh at the front. She'd noticed its sensitivity before, when she'd washed but never like this. She'd tended to avoid it, thinking it too tender.

Now it had become even more sensitive under his ministrations but it felt so good, sending pulses of heat through her whole body. She opened her eyes, not having been aware of closing them and stared up at him. He was watching her and he smiled. "Good?"

"I—I think so."

His smile faded a little. "You didn't know about this?"

Swallowing back her nervousness, she shook her head. "I never—"

"It's called the clitoris and it will bring you great pleasure. Has nobody…?" He stopped, smiled tenderly down at her. "Obviously not. Lie back, sweeting, let it happen."

Listening to his voice, she lay back while his fingers increased and intensified their activity. She hid nothing of her reaction, letting him see her pleasure while he played with her, smiling into his eyes until the sensation increased, shivers rippling through her. She twisted under him, but he guided her back into position and relentlessly continued. Gradually, heat spread, sensitivity washing in its wake. She bit her lip, not sure how to react, but he kissed her.

"Don't hold back. Let me hear you. I want to know, I want to hear."

She moaned and he gave her an encouraging smile. "Now forget everything else, just concentrate on this, what's happening to you. Trust me."

She had from the first moment she'd seen him, which was ridiculous but just the way she was. If she couldn't trust him, she couldn't trust herself.

The next minute she didn't care. Every sense she possessed came together in a crescendo. The intimate wetness of his actions should have embarrassed her. It didn't.

She cried out, arched her body towards him and he pushed a finger, maybe two deep inside her. He murmured words of encouragement she couldn't hear properly but that didn't matter because they reassured her, reminded her who was doing this to her. She was his, all his.

In a series of jerks, she exploded, convulsed around his fingers, staring up at him in helpless, delighted confusion.

Before she could find her voice to ask him what exactly was happening, he rose up, removed his hand and eased her thighs wider, settling between them. She lifted her knees, hugged his body between them. His shaft, hot and wet, slid down to her opening.

She knew this part. It had happened before. But for what he'd just brought her she'd give him all he wanted. It was his turn now.

When he kissed her she opened her mouth for him and tasted his tongue in sheer delight as he worked his way inside her, mouth and—that part she had no name for apart from the vague 'erection' or 'shaft.' He lodged the tip inside her then pushed further.

That was different. He waited for her to open for him instead of forging straight in and pumping away like an automaton. She opened her thighs wider to give him better access and her hands glided down his back to rest on his beautifully rounded backside.

He moaned into her mouth and pushed in further. He wasn't backward in expressing the pleasure she was giving to him and that warmed her almost as much as his heated body. He'd responded to something she'd done.

Gripping his buttocks, she felt the strong muscles clench as he thrust in and out of her, small movements at first, getting stronger as his passage became easier, as she opened more to him and her body became wetter.

He tore his mouth from hers and gazed down at her as he worked. Flecks of lighter brown, almost gold, lightened the dark brown of his eyes. There was a ring around his iris, a black one, defining the circle and adding stark contrast between it and the white. "Beautiful," she gasped, unable to censor the journey between mind and mouth.

"Just what I was thinking. You feel so good, you define the word. But if you need me to stop, I think I can. Just ask me."

He moved with more purpose, drove in deeper and she gasped as sensation began anew.

Different from the last time, deeper, more pervasive. "Don't—stop."

"As you wish." Gritting his fine, white teeth, he lifted his head, driving harder and faster, increasing the pace of his strokes. She'd felt that heat before but it had faded before it had come to anything, leaving her to assume that was all there was.

This time it didn't fade. At this angle, every thrust grazed that knot of flesh and increased the heat. Tingles crept along her spine, up to her head and to the ends of her fingers. She arched under his weight. He gave a strangled laugh and lifted off her. Cool air swept between them, hardening her nipples even more, making her aware that he was watching her, as she responded to him.

Momentary embarrassment swept over her but he forced it away as he pounded inside her harder, faster. A long, strangled moan came from between his teeth. Their flesh pounded together and she pushed her lower body up to meet his every stroke.

Something caught inside her and the warmth flowing out to encompass every part of her. She cried out, cried his name as her world coalesced, heated and blossomed.

In one powerful movement, he plunged deep. Warmth pumped into her, as he held his body rigid above her and moaned his pleasure.

He dropped to lay beside her again. They lay next to each other, panting as if they'd run a mile. Connie tried to come to terms with the sense of wonder suffusing her.

She didn't realize he'd found a damp cloth until he swept it between her legs. Yet another new experience, having a man care for her afterwards.

She turned towards him, half expecting him to roll over and leave her now he'd had his way but he didn't. He folded his arms around her and took her mouth in a long, drugging kiss.

For a few minutes, they lay in contented silence then she found her voice. "Thank you."

"Entirely mutual I assure you, dear lady."

He kissed her again, the warmth in his gaze belying his cool tones, which she recognized as ironic. He didn't want to reveal how much what they'd just done had affected him. "Now we may make our plans. Work out what we do next."

Our plans? She caught her breath then remembered to let it out. It appeared as if he wanted this to continue, that they had some kind of future. That was impossible. Everything had changed. "You mustn't do too much. I appreciate what you're trying to do but Jasper is my problem. Once I've returned home and established myself there I will approach my godfather and have the contract canceled."

He held her close as if he hadn't heard her words. "I thought Dankworth wanted to kill you when Saxton first came to me but I refused to believe that you were dead. If he had done away with you, he wouldn't have gone unpunished."

He breathed a little deeper and took a moment before he spoke again. "But he knew your disappearance wouldn't go unnoticed, and the murderer go unpunished. What's more, if you'd disappeared, he'd have had to wait seven years before the authorities would declare you dead and he could hope to inherit your estate."

He growled low and she recognized his anger. "You're not an unknown. You have friends and he knows that. Lord Downholland, me, your friends at home. We wouldn't have rested until we brought him to justice. The way he planned, he'd have it all."

He murmured when she shivered and stroked her back, slowly, up and down in a soothing rhythm. "He has debts, sweetheart, not just from the tables, although he's been running with the crowd that plays deep. He's also been making unwise speculations on risky investments. By my reckoning, he has little left."

"He wants my money." Not her. Jasper had never wanted her. "Why wouldn't he just go with the original plan and marry me?"

He kissed her forehead. "Because you don't have enough for what he needs. So he wants what you have and then some more."

A question remained. "Why didn't he marry me and then kill me? He'd be able to marry someone else then."

His strokes stopped then restarted. "Because he needs the money quickly. And there's a bigger risk with that scheme. Your death would be a threat to him for the rest of his miserable life." His mouth flattened. "That will not happen, sweetheart. I will not allow it."

"Who is the heiress he's set his sights on?"

"He plans to marry Miss Stobart."

She hadn't liked Louisa Stobart but nobody deserved that fate. "Poor lady!"

He snorted. "Poor lady, my eye. She's showing every sign of welcoming his courtship. They're speaking of themselves as engaged."

"But he can't. He's engaged to me." A few facts settled in her mind, a fact that made sense of this plan. "Alex, we signed the marriage contract before I left Downholland Park. Lord Downholland offered to hold the marriage there but Jasper said no, he had business to conclude in London. He asked—he asked me privately if he could come to me that night."

He swore inventively and she listened with admiration. "I'm sorry, I shouldn't have said that."

"I enjoyed it. Genuine originality should be celebrated."

He gave a reluctant smile. "I like you, Connie. Oh yes, I know"—he stroked her body, making her arch toward him—"but it's more than that. You could twist me around your tiniest finger."

His frown returned. "You will not, however, charm me out of remembering what you just told me. He's worse than I thought and I didn't believe that possible. He must have met Miss Stobart at Downholland and decided to make a play for her. He was probably courting her while we were amusing ourselves in the library."

She snuggled closer. Whatever happened next she'd always remember that time fondly.

He continued his smoothing motion but the strokes didn't soothe her. She enjoyed them too much for that. His hand shook a little but his anger with Jasper probably caused that.

With a swift movement, she buried her face against his shoulder. A vision returned in full force, flashing into her mind in full, vivid color. "I can see it now. See him. I was shamefully dressed and he was leering at me. Sitting in a chair with red leather upholstery, a bit worn—" She broke off abruptly, fighting tears.

His fingers eased under her chin, forcing her to look at him.

She flushed. He responded by delivering a slow, sweet kiss. "I believe I could get addicted to you, my lady. Your job is to get better, do you hear me?"

"I feel perfectly well."

"Rest and I promise I'll take care of your interests. Mother Dawkins will look after you for the next day or two, while I put plans into action."

With an effort, she lifted up on one elbow. He stayed on his back and raised a brow. "Of course, if you're feeling adventurous…."

But she didn't smile. She had something important to say. "I won't let anyone leave me out. This is my life, Alex. I want to know what's going on. Don't do anything without telling me first. Promise me." Never again would she let someone else arrange her life for her.

He cupped her cheek. "You're a strong woman but nobody has let you demonstrate it yet. Now say it again."

"What?"

"Say my name."

"Alex?" She laughed as the darkness of desire filled his eyes. That she could do this to him astounded her. "Alex, Alex, Alex…"

He hooked his hand around the back of her neck and drew her down, ravishing her mouth with a kiss that spoke only of his desire for her.

She wasn't sure which amazed her the most—that he wanted her or she wanted him with a delicious hunger she'd never known before. And he took such care with her, too.

He explored her mouth with a gentle thoroughness that melted her. She moved closer, climbed over him and his erection pressed against the soft flesh of her stomach. Her nipples grazed his chest and she relished the soft hair rasping against her nipples. He finished the kiss only to return for more, taking her on a new journey, one where she knew what would happen. Taking his erection in hand, he guided it to her wet crease and she lifted her lower body. She wanted more and she wanted him now.

He chuckled into her mouth when he sensed her eagerness and finished the kiss. "Not so fast," he murmured, soft and low against her lips. "Let it happen, sweetheart. Like a flower growing from bud to blossom. You feel so lovely. Your nipples are driving me crazy. Feed one to me."

She could hardly believe what he'd just said, much less the rush of liquid desire that flooded her lower body when he said it. She lifted up on her hands, her breasts dangling before his face. Remembering what he'd said, she moved slowly and when he opened his mouth, she lowered one of her nipples into it. He closed his lips, feasting on her and she moaned, letting him hear her pleasure.

He rubbed the head of his shaft along her crease until her thighs were wet with her essence. She hadn't believed she could dampen so much for

a man, or how it eased his way into her, even a man as well endowed as
Alex.

He released her nipple with a wet sucking noise, not quite a pop and
kissed his way across one soft slope to the other, giving it the same
treatment. He held her steady, his hands on her waist and urged her down,
on to his hard and eager erection.

This time she felt him push her inner walls aside, fitting inside her as if
made for her. Her and her alone. She loved that notion, savored it, rolled
it around her head and tucked it away for another day.

She'd recall every second of this encounter and live and breathe it
again and again. Alex filled her in a way she hadn't believed possible and
when she thought she was full, he proved her wrong, by sliding the last
inch or two into her.

When she sank down on him, he breached her in the most delicious
way imaginable. With his hands on her hips, he urged her up, let her
nipple slowly slide out of his mouth as she obeyed his direction and sat.
Sat on him.

She'd never seen anything so wonderful in her life. Smiling up at
her, relaxed and happy, his eyes now filled with delight and a touch of
wickedness, Alex glanced down to where their bodies joined. "Look. Me
in you."

"You in me," she parroted and a modicum of sense back into her
wayward head. Their lower hair meshed, his dark as sin, hers lighter, with
a touch of pink between.

His hand left her hip and crept down, nudged the knot of flesh he'd
caressed to such magnificent effect. "Clitoris," he murmured. "Say it."

"Clitoris." At this rate, she'd lose her mind. He tweaked, stroked and
then pinched, making her leap at the flash of sheer pleasure that arrowed
deep into her body. That brought her partly off him and she lifted and
plunged, curious to explore what he was giving her. With his support, she
did it again and stared down into his eyes, warm and encouraging. He left
his thumb resting against the crux of their joined bodies, so every time she
came down, her clitoris grazed his thumb.

"Do it yourself," he said. "Take it. Take me."

With newfound power, Connie did. She lifted up, found that spot inside
her that delivered a shot of extra sensation and worked it, pushed in hard,
ground down on him until he moaned and begged for mercy. She gave
none, nor did she think he really wanted any.

Exhilarated by the control he was ceding to her, she worked him and at
the same time, herself, watching his muscles stretch as he held her firmly.

He only steadied her, didn't urge her to do one thing or another. He left it entirely up to her.

And she loved it. This time she brought herself close, right to the precipice, but however hard she pounded, she couldn't move over the top. Remaining hanging was sweet torture in itself, more than she'd ever experienced before but she yearned, ached and now she knew why, knew what was waiting for her.

The next time she descended, he caught her clitoris and pinched it hard, then pulled and pinched again. That knowing touch proved enough.

Connie threw back her head, opened her mouth and cried to the heavens, as every sensation built and exploded inside her, fireworks and waterfalls, starbursts and throbbing heat.

With a suddenness that shocked her, he pushed her hard on his shaft as he achieved his own climax, his essence jetting into her. His strong features convulsed in pleasure, pleasure that she'd given him and it brought her to climax again.

She stared down at him in complete delight, gasping for breath, feeling more alive than she could ever remember. He gazed up at her, smiling broadly. Neither of them spoke.

In a few moments, she came to herself.

When she looked for the cloth, she noticed lascivious design on the bedhead. It reminded her where they were but that couldn't dampen the joy and wonder of what had just happened.

After grabbing the cloth, she wiped herself, then climbed off him and cleaned him. He took the cloth from her and laid it aside, then drew her down to lie next to him. "Witch," he murmured, his voice seductively low. "I meant you to sleep." He kissed her with that leisurely thoroughness she was coming to crave.

She lay on him then he rolled so they lay on their sides, with his arms wrapped possessively around her. He drew away, smiling then said something she'd never in a million years have imagined. "Connie, will you marry me?"

He'd startled her enough for her to sit bolt upright. "What?"

He reached up, touched the underside of her breast and drew her back down. "If you married me, nobody would dare traduce you. I have influence and so does my family. If you lose your fortune, no matter. I have enough for us both. Nobody will notice the omission."

But what of love? She liked him, wanted his body with a desperation that shocked her but she didn't know him well enough for anything else. After making one mistake, she had no intention of doing it again. The marriage to Jasper was to have been a business arrangement with a little liking on both sides but this… "It's not an easy solution. We'd have many years to regret a rash decision."

His expression hardened. "Are you saying no?"

She knew she was doing the right thing. "Yes, Alex, I am. I've had time to think today." His eyes flashed but she continued, undaunted. "Are you in any mood to listen? I signed the contract, Alex. I'm officially betrothed to Jasper Dankworth."

"Not for long," he growled. "You're not marrying that man. That is one thing I am totally certain of. Marry me, Connie. I'll make a trip to Yorkshire to visit the Downhollands before they come to London and have that damned contract torn up. Then we may marry quickly, may we not?

"No, Alex." She dropped her gaze, resting her forehead against his shoulder. There were so many reasons she wouldn't marry him. Yet if she refused him now, he might not ask her again. "I will not let you risk everything you are. If you marry a woman society deems unsuitable, you won't just lose the chance of attending parties, you'll be shunned. You're a wealthy man, from a powerful family and you could all be brought down if one link proves weak."

Shock limned his face, in the lines at the corners of his mouth and the crease between his brows. Had he imagined she might not have understood what he could lose? She could never live with that.

"I will come to you with my name cleared, or not at all." And that wasn't going to happen. Society would condemn her. She remembered enough about that dreadful night to recall a large audience. They would know her, and reject her. And with her, him. Rather than that, she'd give him up.

"You are different, what you do matters. This is a difficult time for our country, isn't it?"

He choked a laugh of disbelief. "You'll refuse to marry me for the sake of the country? Connie, please."

"But your fate is bound up with your family. What taints one taints them all. Weakens them all."

"No. We may live quietly in the country. But I want to brazen them down. After I've made Jasper Dankworth pay."

"I won't be part of your revenge, Alex." She traced a line along the center of his chest, savoring him while she still could. "Too many inequalities lie between us."

He cinched her close while she continued to talk. Get it out now, while she could, before she collapsed in a self-pitying heap. "My standing, my influence—I have none outside a small area of Cumbria. None at all. I don't have the social skills you need for a wife." The word sounded so sweet on her tongue she nearly lingered on it, but aware of the trap, she hastened on. "So it's not just Jasper and what he did to me. But that is the main thing. Half society has seen me naked, or near it, on a slave block in a whorehouse. Barefaced. They'll know me. I can't let you do that. The results would fester and worsen until it was all we had." She knew about festering wounds in a marriage. Nobody better.

"You might fall pregnant after what we've just done." He was moving on, trying another tack.

She'd been married for five years and only fallen pregnant once. That had ended in disaster and she doubted she would conceive again. But a slight possibility remained. Enough for her to make him a promise with a clear conscience. "If I find I'm with child, then I'll marry you."

"You realize I wouldn't have made love to you if I'd known you meant to decline my offer."

His soft tones held menace, or maybe it was anger. She had to take care. "I just wanted you and for the next couple of days I'm nobody and nothing. I'll go back to Cumbria and if I promise to let you know, then you can be sure I will."

She bit her lip, tasting him on her skin. Alex had been there, touched her lips, kissed them.

He touched her mouth, stroked her skin reverently. "Sleep. I've exhausted you. We'll talk about this later."

Sleeping in his arms sounded like heaven. Exhaustion took her in a great wave, and she had no choice. Securely tucked in his arms, she let herself drift into a dreamless slumber.

* * * *

Alex hadn't meant to sleep, but it couldn't have been more than an hour or two. When she tried to move, he awoke immediately, alerted by the tension in her muscles. He drew her closer, spread his hand over that addictive satin skin, indulged himself in a caress before he urged her to roll on to her back and rose on one elbow above her. Perhaps he could catch her unaware, while she was still fuddled with sleep and his lovemaking.

"Marry me, Connie."

"No."

He pushed away, rolling to the edge of the bed and sitting up. "I won't let you go and I won't give in."

He grimaced, his head hanging before he lifted it and turned and faced her once more. He would make it right for her. "I'm starting the campaign today. I mean to ruin Dankworth for what he did to you. Half society saw me buy you and bear you off last night but what else could I do? I couldn't leave you there. He wanted someone to take you and boast about it. Think of this. Another idea. I shall say that we secretly married and that last night was nothing more than a prank gone wrong. A prank between a married couple."

"No, Alex. What couple would do something like that? Her parading in front of a room full of men to be sold?"

He raised a sardonic brow. "You'd be surprised. It happens. If we thought we'd appeared at a private club, it would be acceptable, if not approved of."

"I cannot."

"You're probably right." She wasn't, but he didn't want her to push him so far away that he couldn't come back. Anger simmered inside him, with her for refusing to let him help her, for himself for not moving against Dankworth earlier, against the man who would have destroyed everything this lovely woman deserved, and would have, if he had anything to do with it.

He grabbed his clothes and began to dress rapidly. He sat on the side of the bed to pull up his stockings and fasten the buckles at his knees. The sunlight glanced over the cut steel with dazzling sparks of light. "Meantime, think on this."

He bent to kiss her and cup one of her breasts. She returned his embrace eagerly, giving him ideas he should not have right now. He had matters to discuss, arrangements to set in place, plans to make. "We will find a way through this and I will not give up. I'll court you, Connie."

"No, you can't. I won't let you."

He ignored her protest and drew away to finish dressing. He grabbed his neckcloth, allowing himself a moment of violence against the man who had harmed her so badly. He would shock her into accepting his help if he couldn't do it any other way. God save him from a chivalrous woman.

He wrapped the cloth around his neck, tying it with a few swift, expert strokes without consulting the mirror hanging on the wall.

"You might not like to hear it, Connie, but you'll need protection at this time, or you'll find yourself with nothing. Dankworth will still try to discredit you. He's a desperate man. Do you want to know what it's like to live alone, without a good name or a penny to call your own?" He faced her, perfectly still. "Now is your chance to find out. This is a high-class brothel and many of the girls who work here are respectably born. Talk to them. Ask them questions. See if you can stomach the idea of what they do."

She picked up a silver brush. Before she could throw it at him, he grabbed his coat and left the room.

Chapter 11

If Alex did what every nerve in his body screamed at him to do, he'd go straight to White's, find Dankworth and force a confrontation right there. If he saw Dankworth now, he'd kill him.

Connie's unexpected rejection of his suit had infuriated him. But when he'd come to his senses he'd realized he had to be some kind of coxcomb, if he thought one bout of lovemaking would persuade her.

If they were married, he could act for her and his powerful family would protect her. He could ride out a storm. Instead of hunting Dankworth down like the dog he was, Alex decided to make a call on Julius. He needed someone with a cool head to stop him doing something rash.

He took a hackney to Brook Street and was relieved to discover the knocker gleaming brightly on the door. That meant they were in residence. Alex strode to the door and rapped on it.

"Is he in?" he demanded, striding into the hall as soon as the door opened.

The butler, Watson, bowed and took Alex's hat. "I will see if his lordship is at home, my lord."

Alex rolled his eyes but let Watson walk to Julius's book room at the back of the hall. After a brief consultation, he returned. "Would you go through, my lord?"

Julius glanced up from his place behind his desk and rose.

"Is it too early for brandy?" Alex demanded.

"Looking at your face, I'd say not. You're looking a trifle hagged, dear boy." He handed Alex a glass of fragrant brandy.

Alex took a seat in a wide leather chair and downed the contents of the glass thankfully, savoring the warmth it brought. Infinitesimally, he relaxed, partly the result of the spirit and partly the influence of this room, a strongly masculine one with leather chairs and dark mahogany furniture in a no-nonsense solid style. Dark green curtains hung at the window and a picture of the Kirkburton family seat on the wall above the fireplace, which was presently filled with a comfortably glowing fire.

"So what has put you in such an agitated frame of mind?" Julius raised an elegant brow. Many people made the mistake of thinking Julius Winterton's porcelain complexion and fine features, not to mention his extravagant taste in fashion, made him some kind of weakling but he disabused them of that notion with reasonable ease. If he wanted to.

"I came here instead of killing Jasper Dankworth."

Julius nodded. "The man is becoming a nuisance. More than a nuisance." He frowned. "What's this story about his fiancée from the country appearing in London?"

Alex's heart sank. Too late, too late. "How widespread is the news?"

"All over White's, which means it'll be all over town by nightfall. Scurrilous gossip, getting worse every time it's repeated. No matter that Mrs. Rattigan is a little-known lady, the story has caught the fancies of our most notable gossips. Walpole is making hay with it. His wit knows no bounds." He took a sip from his own glass. "None."

Alex swore, after which he brought Julius up to date, sparing him nothing except the intimacies he'd shared with Connie. He described the scene at the brothel well enough to make Julius toss the remainder of his drink down his throat and reach for the decanter.

When Julius was angry, his lips thinned and his face paled to porcelain white. He was angry now. Julius wasn't just Alex's cousin, he was his best friend and he would trust him with his life. If anyone could help, Julius could.

"I like your plan to send her home," he said. "Except it's too late now. The cat is well and truly out of the bag. If we don't do something about it, Constance Rattigan will have a reputation so black they'll even reject her in Cumbria. Do you have an alternative? You know I'll give you every support."

Whatever it cost him. Yes, Alex knew that and it was a measure of their friendship that he'd do the same, without hesitation. "I went to Lloyds yesterday and dropped the information that Dankworth was a bad risk. Or hinted at it. The gentlemen of the City prefer to discover information for themselves. Today I plan to visit to Doctor's Commons."

Julius raised his brows. "Rather extreme, Alex?"

"I want the lady and if I have a special license in hand, once I can persuade her, we may do the deed quickly and become man and wife before the week is out. No one will refuse her then." He would never have made love to her without being sure of his intention to marry her. It was her refusal that had thrown him off course.

"So you're getting wed because you compromised the lady by bearing her off?"

"Not entirely." Alex said no more. He didn't have to, with the perceptive Julius.

His cousin sipped his refilled brandy and put down the glass, never taking his attention from Alex's face. "You interest me strangely."

"She won't have me."

Julius's mouth curled in a slow smile. "You interest me even more. She sounds like a woman of character."

Alex grimaced. "You could say that. She's being naïve. It will take all the influence I can scare up to face this scandal down but I will do it."

Julius studied him in silence, a faint frown creasing the skin between his brows. Alex wished Julius's eyes weren't quite such a vivid blue. It made that perceptive stare all the worse to bear, but he'd had more practice than most. He bore it. His cousin was thinking.

"Bring her here," Julius said abruptly.

"What on earth are you talking about?"

"You'll be doing us a favor. I have my own problems, Alex." He pinched the bridge of his nose. "Yesterday we lost the chaperonage of Aunt Amelia. Aunt Frederica has fallen ill so Aunt Amelia rushed off to attend her, leaving Helena alone here." His fine features hardened. "Aunt Frederica has nothing too serious, I assure you."

Aunt Frederica took great pleasure in detailing her many and varied illnesses. "So she lured Aunt Amelia away from town?" And Helena, being single, could not live in her brother's household without a chaperone to escort her.

"I suspect it was a touch more sinister than that. My mother is determined to get Helena back. My esteemed parent has decided that Helena will attend her in her old age." She had done everything possible to deny Helena her rights in society until Julius had taken a hand and brought her to live with him.

"I will prevent it," Julius said smoothly. "I was about to look about for someone to act as a chaperone when you came visiting. Would Helena like your Constance?"

Alex didn't hesitate. "Yes, I'm sure she would. Mrs. Rattigan is a woman of good sense and she has a cheerful disposition."

"You make her sound like a candidate for housekeeper."

Perhaps he'd withdrawn his interest a little too much. "And damned beautiful. She's a widow, not straight out of the schoolroom, so a perfectly acceptable chaperone. And she has an unfortunate sense of humor," he said with feeling, remembering the incident at the Downhollands' with the dusty books.

"Helena would like that."

Yes, she would. Alex grinned. "Mrs. Rattigan might not be as well dressed as you might expect. Her luggage was lost at the inn when we arrived. I suspect the bawd took it and sold the contents, or they were dispersed when the mob wrecked the house."

"Then we'll ensure she's dressed appropriately. Does she have a maid?"

"I have the maid she brought with her in my house, using another name. When I thought Dankworth planned to kill Connie, I thought he might seek the maid out as the only witness to his intended perfidy."

Julius took another sip of his brandy and waved the decanter at Alex. Both men had extremely hard heads and it would take more than a couple of snifters of brandy to render either of them incapable in any way. Alex pushed his glass forward for a refill.

"Excellent," Julius said. "Then we have a plan. Put the maid and some luggage together—no matter if it's an empty trunk, just fill it with books or something and take her to the *Belle Sauvage*. That place is busy enough to cover your activities and the landlord owes you a favor. Connie has only been in London for, what, three days? It's easy to lose three days on the road, especially on such a long journey. She could have taken ill, or stopped her journey to visit a relative. Make sure you make a fuss, and that people know she's arrived."

Yes, he could do that. He had the landlord in his pocket. Then Connie could enter London respectably. "You would look after her?"

"Tell me something, Alex. Just to satisfy my rampant curiosity. You say you mean to marry her and intimate that she rejected you. That in itself is enough to excite my pique."

Alex gritted his teeth. Did his cousin have to be so damned clever with words? The double entendre was delicate but assuredly there.

"Are your interests in her more than mere expedience? Or revenge on Dankworth?"

"That, sir, is none of your business."

"I see." Julius took a long sip from his glass, watching Alex the whole time then a sudden smile split his features. "Damned Dankworths. They're playing Cupid now."

Alex ignored the Cupid comment. "You spoke to Devereaux? He has his own reasons to detest the Dankworths. He'll help you."

"Yes. We are at war with them, as always. Any reason they have resurfaced?" The Dankworths had been remarkably quiet recently, but maybe they were regrouping after their latest conspiratorial failure, the assassination attempt on the King a couple of years ago.

Julius frowned. "Not that I've discovered, but there's bound to be something. And they will strike at us, because our influence is wide-reaching and because we support the status quo. Or rather, we don't favor a return to absolute rule." He smiled thinly.

"Do you think this attack on Connie is anything to do with Jasper being a Dankworth?"

"I'm not sure. Let me make some enquires. If he noticed your interest in the beauteous Connie, he'd certainly see that as a way to weaken us." He put down his empty glass. It hardly made a sound against his desk. Then he pulled a piece of paper out of a drawer and dipped a pen in the standish.

"I won't tease you any further, until I discover more. Leave that side of the business to me." He scratched a note. "Back to your side of the business. We will say that Helena and I met your lady at a house party last year and she and Helena have been corresponding ever since, so that when Mrs. Rattigan declared her intention to visit the city, we naturally invited her. Plus, she's a respectable widow and she may chaperone Helena. That will add credence to your story, because I do not welcome riff-raff into this house."

"Only people who interest you."

"Precisely."

Alex sipped his drink thoughtfully. "I hope you weren't planning any extravagant entertainments. I thought she could live quietly for a while, and you'd give me a chance to court her."

"Oh no, we can do better than that," Julius said gently. He was at his most formidable when he was gentle. Alex's "We must ensure they are thwarted."

Alex smiled, the grim determination only a few close friends would have recognized. "Indeed we must."

* * * *

Waiting was driving Connie mad. She'd never had so much inactivity in her life but at least she'd had the opportunity to think.

The bawd provided her with clothes and a bath, both of which she received gratefully but she opted to remain upstairs and ate another hearty meal when a maid brought it up to her. The fewer people who saw her in this place, the better.

She spent some time observing the world from her bedroom window. While the house bustled downstairs, the occasional shout telling her they were cleaning and the girls preparing for the night's work, Covent Garden transformed from daytime market to evening center of revels. She thought about what happened within these walls every night.

When the house opened men began to gather in the square outside. Not many and some just wanted to stare at the wreck of the house next door. At least Connie assumed it was a wreck but she couldn't see it. Nobody had set fire to it.

She couldn't remember her sojourn there clearly, however hard she tried, except in flashes of memory, elusive snatches of visions that eluded her when she tried to chase them, like that vision of her on the auction block. It scared her to know that people like that existed and they could take control of her so completely.

With a scrape of bolts and a clang, the front door opened and the few men below, the early birds, began to enter the establishment. Mrs. Dawkins's house was open for business. A clock struck three. But Connie didn't see Alex.

She continued to watch, trying to fool herself that she wasn't on tenterhooks, not waiting for him.

Eventually a coach drew up and a man alighted. He turned and handed some money to the jarvey, who touched the brim of his hat. When he entered the house, the hackney remained outside.

The man was Alex. The way he moved told her it was he. Already she knew him so well. He made her heart ache, although she refused to allow it to affect her judgments. At least, she'd try her best.

But when he knocked on the door and called her name, softly, in case anyone heard, she flew across the room and turned the key in the lock. He entered with eagerness and then she was in his arms and he was kissing her. She opened her mouth to him eagerly and just as eagerly he took her invitation, holding her close enough that the hardness of his erection pressed through all their layers of clothing.

Losing her mind was so easy with him. She'd allow it once, this once.

"We can't take long," he muttered, "But by God, I need you, Connie." Already he was grabbing her skirts, lifting them and she helped him, hoisting them out of the way, tucking them under her arms and behind her. Getting him out of his breeches took less time. He lifted her.

She raised her legs and gripped his hips with her knees.

Fumbling a little, he guided his shaft to her entrance.

She took him in, gasping with relief as he breached the walls of her inner passage, opening them for his invasion. He thrust then thrust again, and she found the rhythm.

He sighed, a deep expulsion of tension. "Oh, Connie. How do you do this to me?"

"I—could—ask you the same thing," she managed, between his pounding. She caught her breath, sighed his name and he groaned, pulled her closer and kissed her.

How did he do it? Make her forget all her good intentions. Make her forget—everything except him. He drove inside her, each plunge pushing her further towards the peak he'd shown her before. Waves of hot ecstasy built and rose, taking her senses with them. She relaxed into them, let Alex take control and guide her to that special place he'd shown her before.

It would never be like that with anyone else. This pinnacle they reached belonged to them and them alone.

He growled as he thrust, as he kissed her, sounds of possession and she drank them in, took them as her own. As her right.

Then he opened his eyes, fixed her with a wild stare. "How close?"

"So close. You—always make me feel like that. Close, all the time. Alex, never before you. Never."

The light of triumph dawned in his eyes. She was his and he knew it.

With a gleam in his eyes, he told her, "Ladies should always come first."

They rattled the door with every stroke, the latch jangling on its stay, but she doubted anyone would complain about the noise. By now the party downstairs would be beginning.

Her party was here. Gripping his shoulders, driving her nails into the thick fabric of his coat like a kitten, Connie let him take her there. When she relaxed into him, she achieved that last soaring fall into ecstasy. She cried his name just once and to his muttered encouragement, she came around him, her inner passage fluttering. "Yes, that's it. Nobody else, just me and you and what we make together. Go, sweetheart. I'll follow."

He was as good as his word. When she cried his name and arched her back, her sex clenching around his shaft, he gave a strangled cry and then came, his member pulsing deep within her.

Chapter 12

Alex laid her on the bed, keeping her skirts clear of the wetness between her legs. Bidding her stay exactly where he'd put her, he fastened his breeches before he went into the powder room and brought back a couple of cloths. He wiped her carefully and then bent and dropped a kiss where he'd so lately been.

"It's a cock," she murmured.

He stilled, glanced up at her face, then finished his task, chuckling. "You're learning lascivious things, aren't you?"

"From you. But I like that word."

"It's also a prick and a pizzle. And a dozen other words. It would be my delight to teach you all of them." He looked forward to it. He fluffed her golden intimate curls and then smoothed down her skirts. "There. Good as new."

She smiled and held her arms out to him. He caught her hands and lifted her up, so she sat on the edge of the bed. Then he knelt.

Gazing into her beautiful blue eyes, he said, "Mrs. Rattigan, will you do me the honor of marrying me?"

"No." She answered with no hesitation.

"I warn you, Connie, I shall keep asking." He squeezed her hand. "May I ask my friends to wish me happy?"

She swallowed. "No." So she wasn't unaffected. That tiny swallow was her only giveaway, though.

If he asked her often enough, one day she might give in. And marrying Connie had become a challenge.

A jolt of recognition momentarily swamped him. He'd been in this situation before, but from the other side. He'd been the one rejecting. He remembered the pleas of his last mistress when he'd told her to take her time packing and leaving the house, that he'd give her the place if she wanted it. She'd said she didn't want a house, only him. He'd thought it

Lynne Connolly

a bargaining tactic at the time but now he was not so sure and a pang of guilt pierced him at the remembrance. He'd only felt relieved when he cut her out of his life. Now Connie was threatening to do it to him. He'd given her more than he'd given a woman before but that hadn't swayed her. She was walking away.

He couldn't think of a woman he'd ever wanted more than he wanted Connie.

All wasn't lost, not yet. Feeling more than a little self-conscious, he got to his feet. He might as well break the bad news. "Connie, you can't go home."

She stared at him, eyes wide, her pretty mouth slightly open. "Why not? Has Jasper claimed my home already?"

"No, not yet but he will if you run back to the country. He's moving faster than I thought he would. Town is talking and he's bruited it about that he saw you and recognized you. Just going home won't work any longer. We need you in town now to face your detractors. You won't do it alone."

He paused, considered his words and rephrased them. If he'd taken her to Julius's as his affianced bride, he could have put this differently, but he needed to ensure she went along with this part of the plan, for her own sweet sake. "Instead, I have an invitation for you from my cousin Julius Winterton and his lady sister. Helena has recently lost the good offices of our aunt as her chaperone, so you would be doing her a favor by staying. With Julius on your side, we won't fail. We'll restore your name and shame the devil."

She blinked at him. "You're giving up? You'll accept my decision to refuse your offer?"

"By no means," he said softly. "But I won't force you, my sweet lady. If you want time to know me better, you have it. If you want to live down this scandal, we will help you. But be warned, I won't leave you to the vultures."

He drew her to her feet but didn't let go, pulling her closer for a kiss. He kept it soft and gentle, fearing that if he let it, they would end on the bed again. And they didn't have time.

"Come now. We're going to the *Belle Sauvage*. Your maid is waiting with some luggage in a private room, so your name is on the register at the inn. I'll pick you up, after shouting your name through the inn, so people will hear. We'll climb into my coach and I'll take you to Julius's house in Brook Street. That will start our campaign."

"What do you mean?" Her bewildered expression rocked him to the core. He wanted nothing more than to carry her off to a place where nobody would traduce her, or hurt her. If he'd had his way and married, her, that was his original plan.

"What can you do?"

He sighed and bent to pick up his hat from the floor where it had fallen disregarded when he'd come in. "Your name was mentioned—hell, it was bruited about and Dankworth made sure people remembered it."

Her jaw trembled but she didn't break. He adored her for that bravery.

"That doesn't mean the deed cannot be undone. I belong to a family that has roots that run deep and wide in society. Few people wish to cross us. If we provide a reasonable alternative, then they may *choose* to believe that they saw someone else, maybe someone masquerading as you or someone who looked like you." He dusted off his hat, more to look at something rather than her stricken face, but he had to look up. He'd promised himself he'd tell her the truth, and he would. Every bit of it. "The Dankworths are old adversaries of ours, and this attack on you may well be an attack on us, since I've shown an interest in you. We will traduce Jasper Dankworth and elevate you. Sweetheart, there are houses that cater for such things, women who will pretend to be whoever you want for a few hours. Maybe this woman at Cratchitt's was one of those. But it couldn't be you, because you've only just arrived in town. It couldn't be you because you're close friends with a duke's daughter. We give them a chance to believe that, give them a story and they can believe it without losing face." At the top level, society thrived on public and private faces. Give them a reason to believe, and whatever the truth, they would. "You see?"

She did. Her heavenly eyes were alight with understanding. She wouldn't refuse that plan, would she?

She might. His Connie had a mind of her own. She pulled out of his arms, walked to the window and stared out. "So you're saying that if I'm to confound Jasper, then I must remain in town. And I have to confound him, because otherwise he'll have me declared morally incompetent and take everything I have to pay his wretched debts. These society people have to see me to assess my competence, do they not? They won't endorse someone they don't know, haven't met, someone who could be everything they believe. Please don't think I'm not grateful. I'm more grateful than I can say." She turned around to face him once more, tears shimmering in her eyes.

He stayed where he was, but he didn't need to get any closer to see her distress, her wide eyes, and the creases by the corners of her mouth. "Don't be. I told you, you'll do Helena a favor in return. Julius is the son of the Duke of Kirkburton. Their mother is a controlling woman who sees the only value in her daughters as pawns to further the family fortune. As such, she has raised her two daughters to be what she wanted them to be, not what they are. Helena, who the duchess labelled the ugly one, although I assure you she is far from that, was to become her companion. So her eldest daughter reached the age of five and twenty without entering society, but Julius bore her off to live in his household when he married. Now he is a widower he is determined to keep his sister, to prevent her mother getting her back. Helena is a strong woman, but she cannot set up her own household, not without declaring spinsterhood, and she cannot live respectably without a woman to chaperone her. Julius will do anything to prevent her return back to her mother's embrace. The woman will bury her."

Her eyes met his, wide and grave. "I find that treatment shocking in the extreme. My father never did that. I lost my mother early but my father never dreamed of holding me back to act as his housekeeper, or keeping me for his service. He offered to bring me out in society, and I said no. A York debut was good enough for me." She nibbled at her lip, the gesture that he'd already learned meant she was fighting to retain her serenity. "I'll come, if I can be of use to Lady Helena."

"And to my family. It goes beyond familial vendetta. The Dankworths have been plotting for the return of the Stuarts for years. Any victory, however small, goes toward that."

Alex wisely held his tongue, but he yearned to urge her to let him take care of her, to give her more than she'd imagined she could have. The desire to pour diamonds into her lap wouldn't go down well with her in this mood. "Come, madam. Your carriage awaits." He led her down to the hackney, taking the backstairs so none of the clientele would see her.

* * * *

An hour later, Alex's town carriage deposited them outside a neat looking house in a fashionable part of London. As soon as Connie alighted, the door opened and Alex led her up the four shallow steps and into the hall.

Connie's first impression was of superb taste and yet a sense of welcome. Since this house belonged to a leader of fashionable society she expected all taste, no warmth but she couldn't have been more wrong. A vase of narcissi rested on a table by the entrance and the black and white tiled floor was dappled with light form the skylight high above.

She stood blinking, resisting a desire to move closer to Alex. After a happy reunion at the *Belle Sauvage*, Saxton had helped her into a cloak and hat. She handed them to the footman.

She presented a respectable appearance and felt more comfortable for it, even if the clothes weren't hers. Hers had disappeared along with her respectability, even her mother's pearls and her amethysts, something Connie regretted but refused to dwell upon. She had other mementoes of her parents at home in Cumbria.

A superior man not in livery, therefore probably a butler, stood at the bottom of the stairs. When she turned her attention to him, he addressed her. "If you will come this way, madam, my lady is waiting on your arrival."

"Is anyone else there, Watson?" Alex asked.

"No, my lord. Only my lady and my lord."

Intimidated by the perfectly superior manservant, Connie did what she always did in these situations. She put up her chin and lifted her skirts enough to climb the stairs without tripping.

Upstairs the butler led the way to a room at the back of the house and opened the door. Connie half expected him to announce her, like a town crier but of course he did not. Alex caught up with her and grinned. "Come and meet my dearest friends," he said.

She stiffened her spine and did just that. Alex's dearest friends were some of the most important people in society. She took a deep breath and pasted on her best smile.

Lady Helena welcomed her with smiling pleasure that Connie thought was for the benefit of the manservant and the maid who followed on his heels with a tray of tea.

The maid laid the precious china reverently on a table by the side of a large, comfortable sofa that retained the air of elegance Connie'd sensed the minute she'd walked through the doors.

Lady Helena was tall for a woman, deep bosomed with unpowdered fair hair, which gleamed in the light streaming through the large bay windows. She smiled with genuine warmth.

"But what a lovely room!" Oh no, her unruly tongue got the better of her again. The trouble was, she rarely did it when she felt comfortable, which meant she did it in company, or when it mattered. And she'd just done it again. Personal remarks might not be welcome.

"Thank you," said Lady Helena. "It was the first room I'd had a free hand decorating."

Connie wondered at that, because most women lucky enough to have their own bedchambers usually started there. Surely as the daughter of a duke, she'd had her own bedroom.

"Then she agonized over the expense," said a cultured male voice. "She tends to do that. Always the provincial."

Her ladyship's laugh indicated that this wasn't a bone of contention. More like good-natured teasing.

The exquisite in sapphire blue standing to greet her took Connie's breath away.

Everyone had heard of Julius, Earl of Winterton, even people immured in the country. He featured in the gossip-sheets, the regular newspapers and sometimes in the more scurrilous literature Connie wasn't supposed to know about. Someone who set fashion but who had also killed more than one man, if rumor had it correctly. The fascinating thing seemed to be that the more he exposed himself to the public eye, the less there was to see.

He glanced at his sister as if exchanging a joke with her, then performed the most beautiful bow imaginable, Alex excepted of course. "Madam, you are welcome. What do you say we dispose of all the titles and formality and resort to our first names? It's a family joke, that we are all named after emperors and empresses."

Helena laughed merrily. "We have such wonders as Marcus Aurelius and Nicephorus among our cousins."

"Marcus and Nic," her brother said. "I drew the line at Jule or Jules, so pray, do call me Julius when we're *en famille*."

Connie found him utterly charming. Also utterly terrifying, a sense of danger lurking below the urbane exterior.

Connie bowed. "If you wish it, of course. I'm Constance. Connie."

"Then sit down, Connie and have a dish of tea. I think we have macaroons as well." Helena inspected the plates the maid had brought. "Ah yes, so we do. We put back dinner for an hour, awaiting your arrival but you might be faint with hunger after your long journey."

They exchanged a smile.

Alex escorted her to a sofa and sat her down.

Julius cocked his head at Alex. "Any news to impart?"

"Just that we're here and thank you for helping," Alex said. "I made sure the footmen positively yelled Connie's name across the main tap room of the inn and then again when a fresh coachload of passengers arrived. I fussed about the disposition of her trunk and gathered quite a crowd before we were finally off. They will know that Helena's dearest friend has arrived from the country. Today."

Julius sat next to his sister on the other sofa and crossed one leg over the other. He wore breeches to match his coat and a waistcoat decorated with such delicacy Connie wanted a closer look. But she didn't stare.

Helena wore a gown of darker blue, simpler but just as elegant.

Such an expensive air of fashion intimidated Connie, but she tried not to show how much this situation overwhelmed her, particularly after her recent adventures.

"How would you like us to help you, Connie?" Julius said.

She appreciated being consulted on the matter. "I'd like to clear my name, if I can and lift any stain before I—before I move on." She doubted Alex would propose again. He was being the perfect chivalric knight, as well as acting on the attraction that undoubtedly flared between them but she didn't want to be beholden to him forever, or put him under an unbearable burden of debt. "I want the choice, even if I never take advantage of it. And I want Jasper to suffer for what he's done. He shouldn't marry Miss Stobart."

"That is the main crux of my interest," Julius said. When Alex threw him a fulminating look, he spread his hands in a gesture of apology. "I'm sorry but it is. I won't have anyone of that nature running amok when I can prevent it. Of course I want to help you too, Connie but I do feel that you could help yourself to a great extent. Dankworth has to be stopped."

He leaned back, supremely at ease in these opulent surroundings. "We have two aims. To destroy Jasper Dankworth, or at the least to let people know what he's capable of and to ensure you are accepted in society, Connie. As a person in your own right. I think we'll achieve this best by attacking on several fronts at the same time." His voice hardened. "We'll ruin him."

It sounded like a promise. One Connie could wholeheartedly agree with.

Chapter 13

Waking in yet another strange bed seemed almost normal to Connie. All those inn beds on the road, then the strange one at Cratchitt's, then at Mother Dawkins's. Now here.

This was by far the most luxurious. After meeting Julius and Helena yesterday, Helena had taken her to her room and called her own formidable maid, Marsden. Together with Saxton, they measured her and decided what colors she should order. Her protests that the gowns would be too costly, that she couldn't take this fell on deaf ears. Saxton was thrilled and Helena told her she needed them if she was to take her proper part in society, so she succumbed and settled to enjoying the experience.

That night, at dinner, it was only Helena, Julius and Connie. "I've sent Alex away," Julius said. "I want to get to know you, Connie, and with him acting the perfect knight, that's hard to do."

A civilized conversation later and they understood each other much better. They enjoyed similar books, and Julius kept the conversation ranging widely over subjects that had Connie believing that at least one of her dreams would come true, and she'd get to see some of the sights before she went home.

However one matter raised contention. After the footmen had brought in some delicacies to complete the meal, Julius dismissed the servants.

As Julius helped Connie to a slice of almond tart, he commented, "You must get your wardrobe in train. I believe the bawd stole what you had?"

"Indeed, but I am here as myself, so I need not spend too much on replacements." She wanted no further subterfuge, no pretending she was more than a country widow come to visit friends in town.

"We must make a splash," Helena put in. "Everybody must know you're my dear friend and our protégée. You need the support of our family."

"Alex is rallying them as we speak, letting them know you're here. I'll join him later to support what he's saying. We won't tell them everything, only that you came to town to visit us and the Downhollands are your godparents. And that Jasper Dankworth has betrayed you by affiancing himself to another woman. Do not concern yourself, Connie, he won't tell them the other secrets."

Connie wasn't sure she wanted anyone to know even that much, but she was learning just how close the Emperors were. "But I thought I just had to show myself—"

"We plan to take you to some of the most exclusive affairs in London," Julius said calmly, evidently unaware of the terror he was evoking in his guest. "You must have the wardrobe to suit."

Helena clapped her hands. "I have had the most delicious idea! I will sort the gowns that I have bought and not worn and my maid will make some of them over for you."

"Oh, I couldn't possibly—"

"Connie, please," Julius said. He gave Connie such a pathetic look that she burst out laughing. "The house is crammed with my sister's gowns, many of them unsuitable for her, bought on a whim. I have begged her to sort them out, but she will not have it."

Connie bit her lip. Of course, the allure of new clothes appealed to her, but she couldn't possibly take them. On the other hand, they were right. She needed something to stand out in the highest of society. An idea struck her. "We are of similar build. I could purchase them from you." Even second hand, the kind of gowns Lady Helena wore, and so far, today she'd seen two exquisite ones, would ruin her. So be it. Better to be ruined buying gowns than have her reputation shredded. At least she'd get something from them.

"If you insist, we'll call them a loan," Helena said, her eyes dancing, "but in truth, it means I can go shopping for more. Your coloring will suit the colors much better than I do. I am somewhat of a magpie. If it's shiny, I buy it. I'll send my maid to you with a selection after dinner. Better still, come to my room and we'll decide together."

"Don't you have a ball or something to attend?"

Helena waved her concerns away with a careless wave of her hand. "Pooh, this is much more fun!"

Later, in Helena's bedroom, Connie surveyed the plethora of gowns thrown carelessly on the bed and nearly passed out from shock. She couldn't possibly take even half of these.

"Aren't they too grand for a poor country widow?" she protested.

"Not if you want to make a splash," Helena picked up a dark green gown that flashed as she moved the fabric. The dull satin background only served to emphasize the decoration. "This never suited me. I look like a dowd because this green is too dark for me. It would become you admirably." Ignoring Connie's protests that she had more than sufficient, Helena added the gown to the growing pile.

"You won't find much occasion to wear fine gowns in Cumbria, I suppose. But you'll need them here." Connie smiled. She liked Helena. Perhaps they could remain friends once this sorry episode was over and Jasper no longer a threat in her life.

So at the end of the day Connie found herself with two new friends and a new, dazzling, wardrobe, most of which she'd persuaded Lady Helena to loan her. And far fewer than the ones her ladyship wanted to give her in the first place.

She went to bed and slept the sleep of the just, waking in the morning to a brand new world.

Connie folded her hands behind her head and stared at the embroidered canopy above her. Goose feathers made for better sleep than a rope bed and a thin feather mattress. That was for sure. But she suspected that a certain relief also added to her dreamless sleep last night. She was doing something. At last, she could act instead of being the recipient of acts committed against her.

And strange though it might seem, she missed her bed partner. Missed rolling over straight into Alex's arms. Foolish in the extreme, considering their brief, though glorious history. And she'd turned him down? Sheer madness but necessary madness. If he came to her again, which she very much doubted, it had to be as a man wanting a woman, not as a man *rescuing* a woman. What she'd shared with Alex had been inevitable, rare and sweet. Even if she'd only had the one kiss, the one in the library at the Dankworth's, that would have sufficed for some time. But she had so much more now.

A knock on the door preceded the entrance of her maid bearing a large tray, which introduced the scent of food and tea into the room. Connie hadn't realized how hungry she was until she smelled that heavenly aroma.

"If'n it please you, missus but Lady Helena says if you feel up to it would you like to accompany her to the mantua-maker this morning? And she'd like to stop at the Exchange and visit a toyshop she's fond of."

Toyshops sold expensive trinkets. Connie doubted she could afford any of the goods on offer but she guessed this was her first test in society.

Today's gown was a lovely green silk, cut in the latest mode, with a petticoat of palest pink. She'd sent a fine cap, barely a wisp of lace and double ruffles. Unfortunately, Connie took a larger shoe size than Helena but her outdoor shoes would, if not match the gown, at least not offend if she wore them. And the day was fine enough to wear a shawl and leave off a cloak. A straw bergére hat, with a bunch of ribbon sewn on to the brim would go with it.

After eating, she got out of bed, stripped and Saxton helped her wash. She put on her shift and a pair of stays before she sat at the dressing table for Saxton to pin up her hair.

Then came the gown. So light, so pretty, Connie caught her breath when she stood before the mirror and viewed herself, turning in delight to view the deep box pleats at the back, which flowed nearly to the floor. She was surprised that Saxton didn't have to take the gown up a little but the maid explained that she'd already done so.

Thinking no more about it, she had Saxton pin her hat in place and found her gloves and fan.

Her heart beating hard in anticipation, she went downstairs to find her hostess similarly attired but in blue. Helena had an effortless elegance Connie admired, because it was something all her own and either bred into her or developed so long ago she didn't have to think about it. Connie should develop something similar, something that belonged to her alone. If the next few days had their required effect, she might have the time to do so. But she had a fight on her hands, ladylike though it would be.

Helena led the way to an open landau outside, two gorgeous grey horses champing at the bit, a smartly attired coachman at the front and two liveried footmen behind. They climbed into the low-bodied, open topped carriage and set off.

Despite her worries, Connie enjoyed the drive into the city. Even if no one had told her they were travelling through the fashionable part of London, she'd have known from the general air of prosperity and cleanliness, although the streets and squares weren't devoid of the shabbier element. Boys darted from one person to another, begging, selling, probably picking pockets and street sellers bawled their wares in none-too-tuneful voices. Somehow, the combined effect of street sellers, horses and chat sounded like sweet harmony. The deep bass tones of a chair mender combined with the high-pitched call of a milkmaid to provide something Connie had rarely heard. Of course, she'd visited big towns before but London was in a position of its own and she began to believe what she'd heard—nothing like it existed anywhere else.

Helena was smiling. "You remind me of the time I first visited London. It was after I came to live with Julius, so I had a somewhat interesting introduction. I had to attend court. It's beastly hot and the clothes you have to wear are simply hideous. London astounded me. I truly believe there's nothing like it anywhere else."

"Not as big, certainly." Connie would dearly love to travel, to see more of the world but she'd always assumed she'd have to content herself by reading about it. "I need to write to my godfather to tell him the state of affairs, when I can do so, although I believe Alex is writing, or has already done so. He will be distressed that Jasper has done his best to ruin me." She frowned. "I don't know if Lord Downholland will believe me, though. Jasper is his nephew and my godfather's designated heir."

Helena touched her hand. "I'm sure he'll know who is telling the truth. You must hide nothing from him and be completely honest."

They rode in silence until they turned a corner so smoothly that Connie hardly felt the movement. "This landau has marvelous suspension."

Helena smiled. "Yes it does. Julius never buys anything except the best."

"I feel the same way. If I can't afford the best, then I do without it. I don't have as much, that's all." She and Helena shared a smile before the carriage arrived at the Royal Exchange.

A place for business, where men stood in small groups together on the ground floor making deals that could affect hundreds of people and cost thousands of pounds but, as Connie soon discovered, a place that also held some beautiful shops. The Exchange was built around an open courtyard and although historically placed, this edifice was relatively new. Something she felt glad of, because the open cloister-like corridors needed good support.

She forgot her fears when she saw the shops. She'd have been happy window-shopping but Helena led her to several places where the goods were affordable and of excellent quality. Connie had a small sum of money she'd allowed Alex to lend her, a sum she would make up when she returned home, so she could afford a fan at one place and some new silk stockings at another, not much higher priced than she would have paid in York or Lancaster. With a sturdy footman following to hold the packages for them, they had little concern about overburdening themselves.

Helena proved a discerning buyer but did select a breathtaking porcelain snuffbox for her brother, with a painting of a beautiful house on the porcelain lid and pearls studded around the gold frame containing it. "That looks very much like his house in Berkshire," she remarked, "And

Julius collects snuffboxes. He says he takes snuff, though a small quantity lasts him an inordinate amount of time. It gives him something elegant to do with his hands."

They left the shop and Helena handed the small package to the footman. She stilled and watched someone approach. "Oh lord," she muttered but kept her mask of perfect contentment. A very small woman of around fifty-five or sixty, thin as a rake and with a face set into hard lines but she had blue eyes that seemed familiar. Julius and Helena had eyes of that startling bright blue. Was this the formidable Duchess of Kirkburton?

Helena swept a curtsey. The newcomer gave Helena a sharp nod and then turned enquiringly to her. "We have a houseguest," Helena murmured. "Mother, may I introduce you to Mrs. Constance Rattigan?"

The gaze snapped away, the woman glanced back at Helena, gave her a curt, "Good day," and swept off, holding her skirts to one side so she would not come into contact with Connie.

Tears sprang to Connie's eyes but she determinedly blinked them away. Her anger grew as what the duchess had done to her sank in, surging deep and hot in her veins. "I'm assuming that was the cut direct."

"It was indeed." Helena was tight-lipped, her eyes sparkling. "She's insufferable. Absolutely insufferable. You're fortunate that you only have to encounter her once or twice." She stared ahead, her bosom rising and falling as she breathed deeply. "I will make this right and she will acknowledge you. I swear it."

"No, you said I might have to expect…" Connie tailed off as Alex's dark figure vividly clad in scarlet heading her direction. *Alex, it was Alex.* Like a child, her excitement flooded her whole being.

Alex smiled affably and bowed over her hand. He had to take it, because she forgot to hold it out to him. His lips grazed the back of her hand like a healing touch, warming her whole body and bringing it back to life. He bowed to Helena then but stayed by Connie's side and crooked his arm for her to take.

Helena gave a low, hardly audible whistle. The sound startled Connie. Helena looked so respectable and she could have sworn Helena's lips hadn't moved. "Very partial, Alex."

"I mean it that way."

Connie followed their reasoning a little while after. "You should have greeted Helena first, shouldn't you? She's higher ranking than I am."

"What he did," Helena said calmly, "Is declare his intent. Done in a place like this, there's no mistaking it."

"No, you must not!" Connie would have snatched her hand away but he put his free hand on top of it, stopping her. To anyone watching it would appear a fond gesture but he held her securely.

"I don't want you to do this," she protested.

He guided her past a couple too busy conversing to notice anyone approaching them. "Too late. I intend to court you publicly and unmistakably. You may refuse me if you wish but I will do it."

Helena outlined the duchess's social cut and Alex's lips thinned. "Speak to Julius. He'll handle her. By God, if he does not, I will."

He smiled as he strolled, his feet clumping over the wooden boards that made up the walkways. "My mother was a kind, gentle soul. I would have loved her to know you, Connie."

Alex escorted them for the rest of their shopping trip and everyone else they met gave Connie a civil bow and made polite conversation. She knew how to play that game. She was less sure how to deter Alex's gallantry and his evident attraction to her, an attraction he made clear to everyone they met, merely by a glance or a touch.

Matters were getting out of hand but moving away might give the message that she didn't want him and she couldn't do that, either. Because that would be a lie.

In one shop, Alex bought an exceptionally pretty fan and presented it to Connie with a bow. "I'd be honored if you'd accept this."

Her first instinct was to refuse such a costly gift but that would have been churlish. She smiled and took the package, holding it herself instead of passing it on to the footman. "Th-thank you. You should not."

"Yes I should. It will give me pleasure to see you use it. It's a mere token."

She was so weak where he was concerned. When he touched her, she wanted to move closer and her eyes at least must be betraying her emotions. She tried to keep every other reaction to herself but she wasn't as accomplished as her new friend.

They completed their purchases and took another tour of the second floor of the Exchange, before Alex took them back to their carriage. He paid particular attention to Connie, murmuring society secrets, explaining who people were and how they fit into London society.

They were people, not just caricatures, as she'd tended to think of them before. She'd read about them in gossip sheets and newspapers but now, thanks to Alex, they became living, breathing people, just like her.

Back at the house, in the privacy of her bedroom, she unwrapped her gift. The fan was perfectly lovely, a design of lovers painted onto its fragile surface, the sticks made of pierced ivory. Brilliants sparkled on the outer sticks and at places in the design. So pretty, she dreaded to think of the cost. But that, she was learning, would be provincial thinking. If she rejected his suit, she could send back his gifts but he probably wouldn't take them.

She couldn't understand why she was doing this, playing with fire. Last night she'd ached for him and now she longed to see him again. Tomorrow night, he'd said, if they attended the ball at Lady Tremayne's. Helena had said of course they would, that it was one of the highlights of the season.

If she were to re-establish her good name and put an end to any claim Jasper might make on her estate she had to go through with this. But she shouldn't encourage Alex. He wanted her, he'd shown that in those glorious two days at the whorehouse but she couldn't let him. She couldn't bring him what he had the right to expect as a bride. She had little influence, no powerful relatives and only a modest fortune.

Status and influence were important to this class. They ruled the country. They had to be strong. But none of the common sense she prided herself on came to her aid.

She still wanted him.

Chapter 14

After spending an agreeable hour with Connie and Helena, Alex took his leave and went to White's to join Julius in a positively sunny frame of mind.

At last he'd found a woman who didn't bore him and who he found exciting in bed. He hadn't planned to test that last part, though. He smiled at the memory of the way she'd seduced him. He wanted her again and again. His cock rose and it took a lot of hasty thinking about the practicalities of their dilemma to will it back into sleep again.

As far as he was concerned, he'd claimed her. She'd already promised to marry him if she should prove with child, so she was half his already. It was tempting to take her away and keep making love to her until she agreed to marry him. Certainly, that would be less painful than this nonsense.

Julius hailed him from across the room with a negligent wave of one white, perfectly manicured hand. Everything about Julius was always perfect.

Alex took his time crossing the large space, pausing to nod or exchange a word or two with acquaintances and friends. By the time he reached Julius, they owned the room. They'd played this trick before and could perform it to a nicety. They were fully aware of the value of their looks, their attraction and their position in society and perfectly prepared to use it to their advantage.

He dropped into a chair next to Julius, one of the deep winged armchairs the club had made especially for their clients' use. The club was full and apart from the chair next to Julius, every other one was occupied.

"Seen him today, coz?" He didn't have to say whom.

Julius shrugged. "Carefully absent, dear boy. But that might be because he dipped rather deep last night after you went home. He might need time to come around."

"When I last saw the Downhollands her ladyship said that she wanted to hold a ball in Mrs. Rattigan's honor," Alex said, dropping the information casually. "While it was to celebrate her betrothal to their nephew, perhaps they might be interested in helping us host it for their goddaughter." Now he was turning the possibility into reality. "I thought we might allow them to host it at Kirkburton House, since they have a ballroom. Your parents hold a ball every year, so why shouldn't Connie be one of the guests of honor?"

Julius brightened, sapphire eyes sparkling. After the way his mother had cut Connie, that would be sweet revenge, something Alex knew only too well. Julius clapped his hands together. "Capital idea. I'll talk to my father. He's bound to agree."

Which meant Julius had a lever to persuade him. He hardly spoke to his mother these days and addressed her with careful formality when he had no other choice. However, his relationship with his father had rarely been less than cordial.

The ball would happen and Alex had chosen White's to announce it because he wanted the news spread. By tomorrow, people would be angling for invitations. They'd be lucky to get them.

Alex agreed to walk with Julius in the direction of Piccadilly where Julius would call on his father. Nobody would overhear them while they walked. "I want her," he said bluntly.

"I rather thought you'd had her, old man," Julius replied, equally brisk.

He glanced at a man heading straight for them, who gave no sign of stepping aside. He also wore a sword, something only aristocrats were allowed to do in London. Not a good sign. At the last minute, the man took a step to the side. Alex breathed more freely and addressed Julius bluntly.

"I want her for good, and not because of any plan to restore her reputation."

Julius halted and swung around, glaring at Alex. "You're serious. Do you love her?"

"What kind of sentiment is that from the son of a duke?" He wasn't ready to admit his feelings, or how deep they might go, even to himself.

Julius paused, and then gave Alex a perfectly sincere but melancholy smile. "You forget. I loved, once."

Alex grimaced. He didn't want to remind Julius of that time, or of his determination to exert revenge on society for what it did to his wife. "Look how well that turned out."

"We had some experiences I wouldn't have given up for anyone or anything." Julius's voice was softer than his usual tones.

Considering the times Alex knew about, that had to be profound. "So the next time, you'll marry for love again?"

Julius shook his head. "Once was enough. The next time, if there is a next time, I want a mother for Caroline and heirs for the dukedom." He sounded not the least bit regretful or yearning but Alex knew Julius felt both those things. Considering he had a small daughter in an otherwise empty nursery, Julius's decision to look for someone sensible and wellborn seemed appropriate. Not for Alex, though.

Alex's immense attraction proved only one factor in his reasoning. He found himself watching absurd sights, like a monkey dancing on his owner's head in the street that he'd seen just that morning and he'd longed to have her with him because knew she'd share his amusement. That was what he wanted. Sharing a life with someone as a partner and a loving companion. Plus the passion in bed. The less he thought about that the better. He didn't seem to be able to control his baser urges when he was around her.

He strolled down the well-appointed street, the broad pavement indicative that this was a prosperous area. "My father keeps throwing seventeen year olds my way and I haven't found one to interest me. I can only presume that an older woman would prove more attractive. Connie certainly does. She's of an age that interests me, she's lovely, she conducts herself with grace without simpering and she's a constant delight to talk to." That sounded reasonable from a reasoned perspective. None of the wild urge to slam her against the nearest wall when she smiled at him and lift her skirts.

"I'm glad to hear it. We must ensure that nothing gets in the way of your laudable ambition. Your father will be pleased."

"I'm not doing it to please my damned father." But yes, the old man would be pleased. Up to a point. Connie was older than he would have liked but he'd have to live with it.

They turned into the next street and confronted a group of boys having a loud dispute that would undoubtedly end in a fight. And, no doubt, copious picking of pockets. They elected to cross the road, tossing the sweeper a coin when he'd done his duty and cleared the inevitable horse manure out of their way.

This side of the road was relatively clear. Until a man stepped in front of them, deliberately blocking their path. Another stood behind them, preventing people from walking in front of him. And damn him to hell and back, he was the man who passed them earlier, the one with the sword.

Alex bowed to the inevitable. They wanted to cause trouble.

"Your purses, gentlemen." The ruffian stood full-square, one hand in the pocket of a ragged rust-colored coat, the other on the hilt of his sword.

Julius raised a brow. "You jest," he suggested mildly. "You have steel, Alex?"

Only his small sword and a knife in his pocket but they would serve. Unfortunately two more men stepped up, one before, one behind, both armed, their attention fixed on their targets.

Alex's blood rose to the challenge and he forced back a grin. He'd wanted to fight somebody for some time now and since Dankworth was as yet out of his reach, these vagabonds would do. "Your preference, Winterton?" He kept his tones low and silky.

"I'll go fore, you aft."

Alex raised his voice. "You want more than our purses, I think."

"We have a message," the one in front said, his country burr evident against the harsher accents of the London native. "We're warning you to leave the business of Mr. Dankworth alone."

"I think not," Julius said. He sighed theatrically, his shoulders moving up and down again. Alex had seen that move before. He was loosening his muscles in preparation for the fight. "You're not going to listen, are you? Your sort rarely do."

The man's lip curled. "Our sort?"

"The sort that prefers violence to words. As if that ever cured anything."

The man tipped his cocked hat and laughed. "It's an answer. And against niminy-piminy little bastard lords like you, it usually works."

"You must tell me if you meet any." With a smooth metallic slide, Alex drew his sword. It was a pretty weapon but made of strong, flexible Spanish steel, so useful too. The gems in the hilt glittered coldly in the sunshine. He heard the scrape as Julius followed suit with his own weapon. No doubt, his sword was prettier but it would be just as deadly.

Their opponents grinned, a ghastly sight, blackened and missing teeth decorating their mouths. When they moved, they brought the odor of the rookeries with them. Never pleasant. No night soil men ever ventured into Seven Dials.

One lifted a sabre and the other had a pistol.

Alex disarmed the man with the pistol first, taking him with a lightning slash across his wrist that made his opponent curse and draw back. Alex kicked the weapon away and ducked, narrowly avoiding the sabre sweep from the other man. From the clash of steel and the pained yells, he guessed Julius was dispatching his opponents but he didn't pause to look.

The man with the sabre had expected to chop the thinner blade of Alex's small sword in half but Alex slid his blade down the sabre in a deadly glissando and closed in on his man, enough to bring his knee up. It found satisfying contact with soft flesh, hopefully the bottom of the man's ball sack.

They weren't fighting amateurs. The second man was already back on his feet and came at Alex swinging his sabre expertly, the weapon gleaming dully in the spring sunshine. Alex waited until the man had put enough power behind his blade to commit himself then used his foot again but this time as a feint.

The man dodged aside to avoid it and found Alex waiting, his blade already heading for its mark. All Alex had needed was a moment's inattention and he'd won. He pierced the bully's shoulder and withdrew immediately, blood welling satisfactorily over the man's grubby coat. The dark stain spread, not deadly but enough to slow him down.

The other man had gone behind. but Julius and he had fought this way before and when Alex's back found another's he knew it was Julius's.

He took the second man with another slash to his wrist and then brought his weapon over the man's hand. His opponent dropped the sword, howling in pain. Alex didn't hesitate. He tossed his small sword to his left hand, bent and swept up the sabre, baring his teeth at the other man as he straightened up. "You want more?"

Some people never learned. His opponent came at him but with a sabre and a small sword to beat down, he didn't stand a chance. Alex had him. He advanced, knocking his opponent's sabre aside with the larger weapon and going in with the smaller. He ducked as his opponent's sword came down, whirled and found himself on the man's blind side. He brought the sabre down but edged it aside at the last moment so he delivered a hopefully painful flesh wound.

Julius didn't need any help. He'd brought one man down with a neat thrust to the upper thigh and the other ran off, yelling insults and threats.

Around them stood the men who'd left White's and others who'd been strolling down Piccadilly when the fight began. The yells Alex had blocked out when he'd started to fight returned now and he grinned.

"Fifty, I only wagered fifty on Winterton. I should have made it a thousand."

"Did you see what that fop just did?"

"Have you been taking lessons on the sly, Ripley?"

To which he grinned and replied, "No, I've always been this good."

Alex dropped the sabre and shook Julius's proffered hand. "We have been warned," Julius said with a broad smile. "Just when I thought London was growing tedious."

"So our enemies come out into the open," Alex murmured.

"I know," Julius replied, equally quietly. Of course he did.

He sheathed his sword and reviewed his appearance ruefully. "I can hardly call on my father in all my dirt. I'll have to change. Will you walk along with me?"

"Willingly."

To the sound of soft applause and coins chinking as they changed hands amongst their audience, Alex and Julius strolled in the direction of Bond Street.

Julius studied the wide cuff of his coat and tutted. "The man marked me. Blood's the very devil to get out of broadcloth."

Alex grimaced in companionable agreement. "My sympathies. Dankworth must be desperate to try something like that."

"Which Dankworth? Do you think the duke is taking matters into his own hands?"

"Not overtly," said Julius. "He'll keep his distance. Operate at arms' length so he can deny anything if he wishes. This is merely an opportunity. I suspect he couldn't refuse the opportunity of attacking us. He knows of your interest in Connie, he also knows of his relative's contract, and he sees a lever."

Alex recalled something Connie had told him. "Jasper Dankworth said he'd visited the duke in London."

"Then Northwich has offered Jasper something he can't turn down. Wealth, most likely. If Jasper becomes the Downholland heir, then he is more useful to Northwich, who sees a man as a tool, no more. He will do anything, sell anyone, for the opportunity to bring the Stuarts back. More power for him and less for us. His first objective, as always, is to bring the Emperors down. You played into his hands, dear boy, or he will see it as such. Word has travelled exceedingly fast that Connie is in town and people have seen you paying her particular attention."

Alex sighed. "I need to set a guard on her, don't I?"

"Consider it done. The footmen who accompany Helena are large and capable. They have orders not to leave your lady alone."

"It's not enough." Alex waved a hand, trying to scrub away what he'd just said. "Oh, I don't mean that precisely, I know you have a care and some great hulking footmen. Just that it should be me. I should be the one who cares for her. I will have a special license tomorrow. If I can find a man of the cloth and Connie agrees we can marry within the day."

"You do want her badly." Julius's indulgent smile told Alex he'd been in that situation.

"Is it that obvious?"

"Only to people who know you well. Have you told your father?"

"I'll put him in the way of it later today," Alex told him. "I'm hoping he comes to the ball we're attending tonight and meets her there. He'll like her, I'm sure."

His father could do nothing to deter him and his own concerns about the matter weren't in question. He didn't give a damn. "It's her or no one, Julius."

"Exactly the way I felt about Caroline. I said the same thing to my mother when she protested my choice. Don't worry about my mother's compliance. I'll speak to my father and point out that it will do someone she hates a bad turn. I'm sure I can find someone; at one time or another she hates everyone in London."

Alex kicked a loose stone and watched it skitter over the pavement. "Are you inviting Dankworth?"

"Of course. I'll tell my mother I particularly don't want him to come. That should do the trick." While the feud between the Dankworths and the Emperors simmered below the surface, they tolerated each other at big society events.

Alex chuckled. "It should indeed."

"Do you want to kill him?"

"Lord, no!" he said in revulsion. "Too clean, too quick for Dankworth and what he tried to do to Connie. I want him to suffer. I need him at my mercy and penniless, so Stobart will cry off and he knows the real meaning of despair. He's in debt, and I'd wager Northwich has refused to settle them until he gets his pound of flesh. If Jasper's creditors come for him, they'll kill him. He'll be punting on the expectation."

They commenced walking once more. Alex paused at the window of a gentleman's tailor shop and gazed at the particularly vivid shade of blue satin displayed there, tossed over a chair set in the window as if it cost nothing. "I'll wear my new dark green velvet to the ball next week, I think."

Julius gave him a surprised glance. "Why would I want to know that?"

"Because I don't want to clash with what Connie chooses to wear. I'll make my intentions unmistakable. You could always send word of the gown she'll wear."

"Will you tell her where they're coming from?"

"Knowing Connie, she'll work it out eventually. Connie is shorter than Helena and fuller of figure. And the garments are new." He sighed resignedly. "She'll work out who's paying for them, too. I just hope there's time for her to enjoy them."

"She will." They walked a short distance in silence. "I like your Connie, you know. She'll suit you."

Alex glowed. "Yes. So you'll either persuade her to choose something that goes with dark green, or send me word of the color she's wearing."

Julius grunted his assent. "But she isn't choosing them. When they visited the mantua-maker and then the draper, Helena took careful note of the fabrics and colors she liked and we've been working off that. We'll pay another visit. She did show a fondness for a shade of lilac that would become her with the right accessories. Will that do?"

"Perfect."

They continued to Brook Street in perfect harmony and then Alex passed on to his own house to let his own valet tut and frown over his bloodstained coat and waistcoat.

* * * *

Lady Tremayne's house was a relatively large establishment on Grosvenor Square. The servants had stripped the first floor saloon of furniture, except for a few sofas and chairs for chaperones and people resting between dances and the drawing room next door held a long table, which would hold a variety of refreshments in due course.

Connie had attended events like this at home, only not half so elegant and with less exalted guests. Still, they had enjoyed themselves and made the necessary connections. Balls, assemblies and the like were essential for maintaining local networks.

This appeared exactly the same. She guessed that men would be discussing business as well as playing cards in the smaller salon and the women were arranging matches, estate matters and politics. In her case, she'd have talked to the local member of Parliament, discussed the upcoming assizes, whose fields were most fertile, whose son was making up to whose daughter and the highwayman they couldn't catch.

Not very different, after all. Except that at home she belonged in the inner circle. Here she was most distinctly an outsider. Nobody would trust her to discuss their intimate secrets and she didn't imagine the covert glances people shot her from time to time.

Nerves seized her, bile rising in her throat. What if they all ignored her?

For the first time since Mother Cratchitt's, she and Jasper Dankworth would share the same space. Alex had met them outside and exchanged a warning look with Julius.

She sucked in a cooling breath and lifted her chin. Jasper was strolling around the perimeter of the ballroom, a lady leaning on his arm. Miss Louisa Stobart. Would Miss Stobart ignore her? Would they cut her? She tensed, readying herself for the ordeal.

But they didn't approach her, they turned and walked in the opposite direction without seemingly seeing her. Bad but not disastrous. A cut but not a direct one.

Helena ignored them and introduced Connie to more of her friends. Helena was a popular person and people greeted her with genuine warmth.

Julius had disappeared in the direction of the card room, to, as he quietly informed her, reconnoiter the terrain.

In the swift appraisal she'd allowed herself, Connie noted Jasper's new finery, his air of prosperity and she'd wondered who he owed for it. And pitied them, because the chances of getting their money must be slim. Honest tradesmen came bottom of the list when it came to paying debts.

"*Not* the cut direct," Alex murmured. "They can hardly act in a friendly way toward us when he's trying to have you declared unfit but they will acknowledge you before the evening is out."

Connie forgot all her intentions to hide her emotions and turned to him, distressed. "Has he started the process?"

"Hush, my—Mrs. Rattigan. It's what he planned, so he's going ahead with it. My informants tell me he has filed the action, but he has a long way to go before anything is resolved. And my friends and I have ways of delaying the case for long enough. Once society has seen you and spoken to you, his claims will go away."

Connie wasn't so sure about that.

"Mrs. Rattigan."

Turning too suddenly, Connie nearly overbalanced but Helena reached out to steady her, beating Alex by a whisker. He cleared his throat and drew back.

"Lord Downholland, what a surprise!" Alex said but he didn't appear surprised. He made an elegant leg, bowing low, his arm sweeping up in an extravagant gesture.

To her mortification, heat rose under Connie's skin. At least they had chosen to acknowledge her. She forced a smile and sank into a curtsey. "I thought you fixed in Yorkshire for the next few weeks, sir."

"So did I." Lord Downholland glanced around at the glittering throng and grimaced. "I prefer the country but I heard some disturbing news last weekend." He fixed Alex with a considering stare and eventually greeted him. "Ripley. I wonder, Connie, would it be possible for you to call on us in the morning?"

"Of course."

Lady Downholland gave her a fond smile. "I had no idea you knew Lady Helena, Connie."

She didn't want to lie to them. "Lady Helena kindly invited me to stay with her."

Helena stepped in to the breach. "Lady Downholland, Constance has kindly agreed to keep me company while my Aunt Amelia is out of town. I'd be heartbroken to lose her so soon. I would love her to stay." Her mouth turned down at each corner. "Otherwise, without a respectable companion, I must return to my parents' house."

"Oh." Lady Downholland looked from Connie to Helena and back. Her plump face creased with concern, a frown marking her forehead. Lady Downholland must be aware that staying with the Vernons gave Connie more opportunities to enter the inner sanctum of society's hallowed portals. While the Downhollands were perfectly acceptable to society, they didn't visit London very often and they had never penetrated the inner circles. "It's extremely generous of you, Lady Helena."

"Indeed not. If I may, I'll accompany her when she visits you tomorrow."

"I'd be honored." Lady Downholland curtseyed and Helena responded. Both used the exact depth required of each other's rank and Connie felt overwhelmingly glad that her godmother had taught her the niceties of behavior. Her father had preferred to remain in the country. John had left her in the background, running his house. Especially after she'd disappointed him.

After chat about more general matters, they separated and walked on. "Do we come clean and tell them the whole?" Connie murmured to Alex.

In the background, a quartet tuned up, ready to begin the dancing for the evening, giving them a better opportunity to exchange confidences, although she knew better than to discuss the matter unadorned.

"I think so," Alex said. "They are your allies. We have to trust them. But we can't tell them everything."

She knew which part he meant.

* * * *

So far, Alex would count the ball a relative success but only relative. He wanted more for Connie. People met her, smiled and moved on. He wanted her position in society inviolate and if she refused his proposal until that time, then he'd expedite proceedings. He needed a scheme. Something showy and flashy but not vulgar. While nobody exactly cut Connie, a few avoided her. She wasn't yet clear of scandal.

After touching her exquisite skin, kissing her ripe mouth, he wanted her badly. He ached for her when he allowed himself to slow down enough to think. Which didn't happen often.

He had a thought. Julius had returned from the card room and the small orchestra was taking a break from playing dance music. "Want to liven this affair up a little?" Alex asked.

Julius raised a querying brow.

"You wouldn't think of disrupting this assembly would you, Alex?" Helena's voice held hidden laughter but also a challenge.

"Not for a minute. I don't dare, with the duchess standing there watching us."

"Glaring at us." Julius didn't sound in the least discomposed but he had grown out of fearing his mother a long time ago. "So what's your proposition, Alex?"

"Connie, would you be game?"

"That depends what you want," she said cautiously.

Julius chuckled. "You're learning. We cannot trust Alex when he has that gleam in his eye."

Alex turned a serious glare onto his cousin. "Connie, if you go and stand at the bottom of the room, by the dance floor but in front of the doors, then flick out your fan when one of us reaches you, that's all you have to do for your part. Helena will perform the role of arbiter."

Julius laughed. "Hardly neutral."

Helena flicked open her fan in an elegant gesture. "You think I'll cheat?" She lifted her chin. "I am not so paltry."

A gentleman passing by drew closer. "Did I hear you say a wager? That would enliven this tedious affair."

"The dowagers must not know," Alex warned. "Rotherham, you may spread the word but you must behave with discretion. Tell them that Lady Helena will take the bets or the notes of hand and distribute the winnings after the event. The bet is fifty-fifty, Julius against me, so all Helena has to do is keep the reckoning."

"I can do that," Helena said.

Alex made the bet. "Julius, I wager you that I can reach Mrs. Rattigan before you. We start here, at this end of the ballroom and make our way around the dancing area. It sounds simple but look at all the people here and think of how many you must converse with to get there. No ill manners, no deliberately informing participants."

Julius gave a low whistle. For the duration of the game, Connie would be the cynosure of all eyes, at least the ones taking part in the bet.

"When Helena opens her fan, we will begin. When Connie flicks hers open, the game is done," Julius said. "And make my wager a hundred pounds, not fifty."

"Done."

Alex had roused the family for the ball and most of them were present tonight. He went and roused Devereux from the card room and once he heard the purpose, he declared himself only too willing to take part in the game. After wagering a hundred on Alex, he offered Connie the support of his arm and chatted with her for the duration of the event.

The two participants stood by Helena and she flicked open her fan. They were off.

A minute later, he thought he was done for. The formidable Duchess of Northwood stood squarely in front of him, preventing him from passing by. For such a small woman, she blocked his way pretty much completely.

He forced an affable smile. "Good evening, your grace." He executed a full bow and bent over her hand. She wouldn't accept anything else. Time wasted.

"Good evening, Ripley. My daughter Georgiana wishes particularly to speak with you. We will be at home tomorrow at two."

Oh dear. That meant the duchess wanted him on the playing field as a suitor for Georgiana. Although he could think of a fate worse than allying himself to the pretty, laughing Georgiana, that described the problem in a nutshell—she was a girl. He'd never think of her any other way.

"Thank you for thinking of me."

"I am holding a small poetry salon. I believe Cowdrey will attend."

His heart sank even further. What Cowdrey called epic poetry, Alex called tedious rubbish. An hour should suffice to mollify the duchess. More than that and he might run mad. Perhaps he'd share the ordeal with Connie. A small gathering would further her acceptance by the ton.

At last, her grace withdrew her hand and as she opened her mouth to speak once more, Alex pretended not to notice, bowed and moved on.

Julius had gained a length on him. He'd banked on Julius's finesse proving his handicap; his social expertise and the fact that people avidly sought his attention, especially women. However, Alex had omitted to factor in his own recent activity in the feminine stables. He'd made himself available and they'd descended like wolves on the fold. Pretty, scented wolves but the instincts remained buried underneath. They didn't fool him.

The first few smiled and fluttered their fans and eyelashes. One flicked her wide skirt out so he nearly fell over her hem. Oh that was all he needed. Obviously, word had gone out about his unfortunate escapade with Miss Stobart and torn flounces had become the order of the day. So tricky to dodge them if a woman flung a few acres of silk in his way. But he managed it, hopping and dodging like a dancer.

A flash of green fabric across the room revealed where Julius bowed and nodded his way down the line. Was he gaining on his cousin? Alex made up the length, although Julius might still have a head on him. Maybe a nose.

"Lord Ripley, how delightful!"

Oh lord, he'd never have a chance, now, because Miss Stobart blocked his way, wafting her fan at him and smiling winsomely.

"I don't believe you were about to pass me without exchanging a civil word. Of course, after our recent adventures together, we need not stand on ceremony any longer." She fluttered her eyelashes. Actually *fluttered* them at him.

"Just so, ma'am." No, he couldn't say that. Couldn't agree with her, or it she'd spread it all over town in the morning that he had shown her particular attention. Before the night had fallen the book would be shortening on him in White's. He'd been chagrined to discover just how high the odds were on him marrying the woman, even though her betrothal to Dankworth was public knowledge. But until pen hit paper, she was free to entice whomever she pleased.

"I have such consideration for your reputation that I fear I can't linger."

Let her make what she wanted of that frankly ridiculous remark. At least it struck her into temporary silence.

He moved on, having to take a circuit around her. She tried the skirt flick but he had prepared for the maneuver and avoided it. Breathing a sigh of relief, he moved on and assessed the field before him. Since this was the beginning of the season, fashionable society packed the ballroom but he tried moving to the edge of the dance floor.

This being a converted large salon, there was no delineated floor but by general agreement, the guests had left the center of the room clear for dancing. He wanted to loosen his stock, tied far too tightly around his neck as today's mild weather, the hundreds of candles and the presence of so many bodies in one space had their cumulative effect and he started to sweat. Reminding himself that the game didn't matter so much as the result for Connie didn't do him any good at the moment. He wanted to win.

He nearly collided with a woman at the end of the room but nodded and danced around her, turning it into an improvised step until he left her behind. And carried on down, further down.

Damn, Julius had nearly arrived. He'd grabbed someone to help him, a small woman, one he vaguely recognized then he handed her off on someone else who tried to approach him. Tricky. Alex should have been more careful setting the rules.

Further down and one dowager later, Alex had a clear field.

One more hurdle and this one could be his downfall. His damned father. Could he, dare he, just walk past? Oh, yes. His father leaned forward, murmured, "I have two hundred on you. Go to it, my boy."

If his father understood nothing else, it was a bet. With a brief squeeze of his shoulder, his father stood back, rather sportingly blocking a dowager with two lovely daughters in tow. Actually, not so lovely, he amended.

"For the honor of the family," his father murmured and let Alex pass.

He threaded his way through the throng, smiling here, nodding there, exchanging a word or two and circumventing the gloved hands of rapacious ladies, soft and grasping. Nearly there, at the finishing post.

And then he had arrived, in the haven of Connie's lovely smile.

He looked up, across the dance floor. The dance floor was relatively clear, giving him a view all the way to Helena at the far end. Cicisbeos surrounded her, men who wanted her for herself, as well as her position. Not that either he or Julius had managed to persuade her of that fact, not yet. Years of constant insults and denigration by her mother had their inevitable result and his beautiful cousin didn't realize her effect on the opposite sex.

He sensed Connie's presence next to him; his skin prickled with awareness. He bowed. "Mrs. Rattigan."

With a flash of pink and green spangles, she flicked open her fan. The race had ended. Helena had decided to join them and was presently sweeping down the center of the dance floor, admirers in tow.

Before he could stop him, that idiot George Wyvern had wrung his hand. "Oh very well done! When I saw your father, I knew you'd won the day. Effective fielder swept away your last threats, didn't he?"

He might as well admit it, but hopefully, he could limit the damage. "The duchess nearly proved my downfall. How much did you have on me, George?"

George glanced around. "Only a couple of hundred, although if my darling Caroline asks, it was fifty, you hear?"

"Did you work up any odds?"

"No time for anything but evens, dear boy."

Alex frowned. "George, if you don't pipe down, we won't be able to do it again."

George put his finger to his lips. His protuberant blue eyes were a little rheumy, indicating he'd been drinking for some time. "Oh, ah, yes. See what you mean, old man."

"Well done, Alex, the best man won tonight," said a familiar voice, much softer than George.

Alex grinned at Julius. "The mamas did for you. You had more your side than I did on mine. They want you to attend their rout, Venetian breakfast, literary salon or music recital. Or something a little more private."

Julius glanced at Helena, a sharp gleam in his eye that only his closest acquaintances could interpret. "I choose where I go and where I do not. Keeps people wondering."

Win or lose, Alex had achieved his aim. Triumph rose, more intoxicating than brandy. They'd done it. Everyone in the room was watching them. From someone on the outskirts of society, he'd just turned Connie into someone of note.

Julius glanced at the men surrounding his sister and effortlessly forged a path to her side. "My dear, you have collected quite a court."

"I hold their markers."

Julius raised a brow. "I think it is more than filthy lucre that draws them, my dear."

Another of his cousins, Marcus Malton, cleared his throat. "I had fifty on you, Julius but I swear Ripley's father had a stake on, because his actions on the final stretch were masterly."

"Two hundred," said Lord Leverton, who just happened to be passing by. "Lady Helena?"

She nodded her confirmation. "He signaled me very effectively before the race began."

Lord Leverton paused in his perambulations. "Gentleman, if we are ever to repeat this enlivening experience, we must disperse. Lady Helena has your markers. Allow her time to sort out the winners and losers."

One of the gentlemen tapped the side of his nose. "White's tomorrow morning. We should enter this in the books. Make it a full season."

Julius nodded and a slow smile crept over his features. "That might be acceptable but I can't promise to act as your runner every time."

"But you're not averse to taking the role occasionally."

Julius shrugged. "Possibly."

"Julius, this was a momentary amusement," Helena protested. "We cannot do this all the time."

"And why not? Are we hurting anyone?" When the gentleman had mentioned White's the crowd had thinned somewhat, melting into the general crowd. "It will delight the matrons. It will bring more young men to their balls, eager to play."

She gave him what could only be described as an old-fashioned look. Skepticism overlaid with a reluctant twist of amusement. "I cannot consent to hold notes of mark all the time."

"Understood. My dear, I regret dragging you into this affair." Alex bowed over her hand, giving her an exaggerated flourish of one hand.

She hit him with her fan and he laughed and caught her wrist.

Julius winked at Alex and then led his sister onto the dance floor, as the quartet had returned to their places, ready to play once more.

Alex bowed to Connie. "Now I've made you the center of attention, would you care to dance?"

Chapter 15

On the day she planned to visit the Downhollands Connie decided to wear one of the plainer gowns she'd chosen for herself, since they wouldn't expect anything fancy, when Saxton entered her bedroom bearing yet another lovely gown.

"Another loan," she said gloomily. Connie supposed she'd grown tired of pricking her fingers taking the gowns up to fit her and adding ruffles to the sleeves of her shift.

She couldn't refuse it without upsetting Helena, so she let Saxton help her into the gown. This time it was pale blue, embroidered with tiny snowdrops around the hem and on the matching petticoat. She'd have thought the color not right for Helena but it suited Connie perfectly, the blue enhancing her eyes and contrasting with her dark gold hair.

Taking her cue from her hostess, she didn't powder her hair and wore the minimum of make-up. Helena said that powder made her sneeze and she only wore it when she had to but Connie suspected she didn't like it because her mother had made her wear it all the time. She'd have felt the same.

She went downstairs to meet Helena in the small parlor on the ground floor but she hadn't arrived downstairs yet.

Alex turned from contemplating the world outside the window and before she could mumble an excuse and leave, strode across the room and swept her into his arms. "This separation is driving me mad," he muttered before capturing her mouth and giving her one of the luscious kisses she'd been longing for in the last few days.

She couldn't push him away. She somehow lost the strength, once she found herself in his arms again. When he finally finished the kiss, he gazed down at her, his eyes soft, passion gleaming in their depths. "Connie, reconsider. Fight this battle at my side. Marry me."

"No." Though it cost her a lot to say it, she wouldn't do it, wouldn't drag him down with her, if that were what would happen.

They didn't speak again for some minutes as they made the most of their unaccustomed temporary privacy. Alex kissed her again, deep and passionate, his mouth working on hers like a man starved of sustenance, hungrily eating at her. Unable to hold herself inviolate, Connie responded, tucking her hands under his coat to spread over his back. As it was, his shirt and waistcoat were too thick, heavy barriers and only a hint of his delicious body warmth reached her questing palms.

Eventually he lifted his mouth from hers, their lips as close as they could get without touching. "I wanted to face the Downhollands with you. Since we're telling them all, I see no reason they shouldn't know—"

"About Mother Dawkins'?" She went cold.

He cinched her closer. "No, sweeting. That's our secret."

She wasn't a complete innocent. "Did you have to pay Mrs. Dawkins? You must give me an account of all the money you're spending on me."

He growled. "What do you take me for? A miser? No, I will not. I can't see the Downhollands bothering to check the story. Especially when I inform them I intend to seek your hand in marriage when this business is done. Before, if you'll have me."

She tried to pull away but he wouldn't let her. "Why? There's no need now. You made society accept me."

She wasn't sure the effect would last but she couldn't deny the extra attention and the invitations to select gatherings that now arrived at Brook Street and included her.

The race at the ball had completed their success. Most of society believed that Connie had arrived recently in London and gone straight to Julius's house. Or society *chose* to believe it, and what it believed had to be the truth.

"I want you. That's enough for me." He kissed her again and conquered her with passion.

This—he—was too dangerous. Every time he touched her, kissed her, she forgot everything else in a storm of need for him. And when he held her, she didn't want to be anywhere else, or do anything else. She found him too easy to talk to, too easy to share confidences with. It frightened her. The only person she had done that with in the past was her husband— and look where that had ended.

But for now, just for a little while, she'd let herself feel him and remember the bliss of having Alex's body deep inside hers.

His shaft rose and pressed against her. The light silk of her gown revealed more than the practical wools of her country wear. The curved shape of the head of *cock* sweetly against her belly. It had to be her imagination. She was wearing a hoop.

He thrust his tongue into her mouth, exploring and encouraging her and her whole body sighed in surrender. She stroked her tongue against his, shyly at first, then a little bolder and he rewarded her with a low groan.

Slowly, he finished the kiss and held her against him, his hands gently cherishing. She leaned her head against his chest. They were both breathing heavily.

He gave a shaky laugh. "Not the time, not the place. But Connie, I want to talk to you, really talk. Not about Dankworth, or your godparents, or any other damned issue. About us and what we want."

"Why not now?"

"Not enough time. Not nearly enough." He groaned and kissed her, this time briefly before he determinedly put her away from him, held her at arms' length and scanned her form in a way that made her feel stripped bare.

Not to mention wishing they were both naked and on the other side of a locked door. She must be mad to think of that when her reputation, her very existence as an independent woman lay at stake.

"I'll make sure you don't suffer. I swear it."

She shook her head in denial. "How can you promise that? It's still uncertain. You and Julius have enemies only too glad to pay you back for slights or imagined slights. Julius's brother has political opponents. They could all use me to drive a wedge between their desires and his."

Alex gave a low whistle. "Not only beautiful but clever, too."

She gave a derisive laugh. "I've played local politics for years. It doesn't take much to work out that the same thing happens here but at a larger scale with more at stake. Just the same games."

He dragged her back and held her tightly, their hearts beating against each other. "God but I want you. Connie. Say you'll marry me."

"No."

He sighed. "We could sleep in the same bed every night."

"Don't tempt me."

"At least you admit I'm tempting you."

A bustle in the hall alerted her to Helena's arrival downstairs. She suspected Helena had made more than necessary sound and hid her face against Alex's chest to cover her confusion when she realized the whole house knew she was in here alone with him. They shouldn't have allowed it but Alex ensorcelled people with his easy charm. She didn't doubt he did it with servants, too. Alex had probably had his own way his whole life. It would do him good to wait.

But what would it do to her? If he gave up his passion and moved on? She'd heard that about him that his affection was passionate but soon over.

She could bear it. She might have to.

Helena waited outside the parlor, clad in a rose-colored gown and wearing a necklace of pink stones she informed Connie were topazes. "Julius enjoys buying me jewelry and who am I to refuse?" she said, laughing, when Connie admired the stones. "Caroline broke a gold chain of mine the other day and Julius bought this as a replacement. It made me want to take the whole box to the nursery and tell her to go at 'em."

Since the day was drizzly and overcast, they took a closed carriage for the short journey to the Downhollands.

"I should like to see you in diamonds, Connie," Alex said almost diffidently.

"I had some," she said demurely. Her pearl necklace had also sported a few tiny diamonds. Very tiny. "I'd have worn them for you." Gone, together with her mother's pearls, stolen from her along with her good name. Recently she had purchased some pretty trinkets and used chokers of velvet and lace, which served as decoration when she needed them but she missed her mother's jewelry.

The way he looked at her made her flush. He didn't have to add, "And nothing else?" because she read it in his gaze. She'd spend all her life blushing if she stayed with him and she'd rarely had occasion to blush before. Alex made her hot with excitement, with teasing, with passion. Effortlessly.

Even when he wasn't there, when she thought of him and what they'd done together, she heated up, inside and out. Wanting him all over again.

Lady Downholland regarded her curiously when they finally stood in the saloon of the house she and his lordship had taken for the season. "You look very well, Connie," she said, "but I've been hearing disturbing news about you."

Connie wished she were alone, because although she didn't blame herself for her ordeal at Mother Cratchitt's, the more censorious in society would have it so. She'd already decided what she would say and she proceeded to do so, relating her story in dry, unemotional tones. Except the part where she succumbed to her baser nature and spent some time in bed with a most agreeable companion, lost in passion. She kept that part to herself and avoided Alex's eyes when she skipped past it, even though that was the only part of the discussion where she faltered a little, trying to cover that with something plausible.

Saxton had agreed to back her on that point and since the maid had spent the time in Alex's house under an assumed name, it was hardly likely anyone would discover that tiny deception.

Unless Connie looked at Alex now.

Jasper had lured her to London, had her abducted and put her up for auction in a house of ill repute. Lord Ripley had rescued her and taken her to his cousin's establishment. She also told them of the subterfuge, that she said she had been taken ill on the road, so her arrival was delayed. She confessed it all. The Downhollands had treated her with kindness and consideration. They deserved to know the truth, or as close as she dared get.

Alex sat next to her on a wide sofa, Helena on her other side. He sat with one leg negligently crossed over the other at the knee, his foot in its shiny black shoe and silver buckles swinging gently.

"I see," Lord Downholland said. "I appreciate your candor." He glanced at his wife. "Since we arrived in town we received a visit from your betrothed."

"You did?" she asked, at the same time Alex said, "That was quick."

"And how did you become involved in the matter, young man?"

"Her maid, Saxton, came to me after her mistress disappeared," Alex said unemotionally. "She suspected the involvement of Jasper Dankworth so she came to me, rather than to him. She knew nobody else in London. I had given Mrs. Rattigan my address because I wanted her to write to me."

Lord Downholland frowned.

Alex spread his hands in a gesture of submission. "What can I say? I was extremely attracted to her and I wanted to keep in touch. I couldn't approach her while she was engaged to another man but I enjoyed her company, so I would have pursued friendship, if she chose to give it to me."

They'd shared more than friendship. Connie hastily pushed the thought to the back of her mind.

Lord Downholland nodded gravely. "And you searched for her. Discreetly, for which you should be commended. What do you intend to do now?"

That was frank enough. So was Alex's answer. "I asked her to marry me but she refused."

His lordship's "What?" almost drowned out Lady Downholland's gasp.

That rejection seemed to turn the tide for Connie, because the tight lines at the corners of his lordship's mouth relaxed. "Quite right too. You cannot receive the attentions of one man while you are contracted to marry another."

Lady Downholland turned a beaming face to her. "Your father would have been proud of you," she said.

Tears sprang to Connie's eyes, so her godfather appeared through a fine mist. It was the best thing he could have said. And yes, the principles instilled in her by her father had made her decision inevitable.

"Your esteemed father encouraged you to be a person of good character," Lord Downholland said. "Be true to yourself, he said and often. One of his best sermons was on that very subject. Because of that, I believe you will come through this."

She swallowed her tears. Despite his bishopric, her father had never sought higher office or promoted his interests, preferring to minister to the parishes and clerics under his care. A truly good man. She owed him so much. "Thank you. I'm so glad you understand. It's because of that incident I must re-establish my good character, stand and confront my accusers."

Alex affected his society drawl. "We decided, my cousin Julius and I, to act quickly. So we have introduced Mrs. Rattigan to the highest circles and shown the people who might have gossiped and traduced her that she is a woman of principle. Although some people saw and identified her in lamentable circumstances, society may choose to believe itself mistaken and that Dankworth is not the man it took him for."

Lord Downholland cleared his throat and exchanged a speaking glance with his wife, who nodded. "We have not remained entirely ignorant of developments while we were not in town. Friends wrote to us. As a result, we came to town earlier than we'd planned to verify the events for ourselves.

"With your agreement, my dear, I will inform them of our decision." He covered his wife's hand with his, a tender moment that belied his formal words. "We've decided to investigate the matter further with a view to ending the betrothal and the contract."

His formal way of speaking obscured his meaning for a moment, and then relief swamped Connie on a wave of dizziness. That part of her nightmare was over.

She took a few deep breaths and then managed to speak. "That would be for the best. But will he not require compensation? Can he take you to court for breach of contract?"

Or indeed, her?

Downholland smiled grimly. "Yes he could. And since the inheritance is bound up with the marriage, we could lose everything."

"But he has declared his engagement to Miss Stobart," Connie protested.

"We have questioned him. He has confessed his admiration for the young lady, and that he was carried away by his passion for her. He's signed nothing."

Alex growled low. "The intention is enough. I have reason to believe he will bankrupt you and bring opprobrium on the title. He has notes of hand all over town."

His lordship sounded patient, as if he were holding in his ire. "I am making enquiries and I will discover the truth."

* * * *

"So you understand," Alex said to his cousin later, in the privacy of his study, "that I must supply them with something to convince them. Connie is free of the taint, but they haven't agreed to withdraw the inheritance from him. He is, after all, their only relative. Dankworth will ruin the Downholland title. He's borrowing on the expectation. Besides, I have a score to settle. When someone hurts someone I hold in great regard, then I take that insult personally."

He took a moment to quell his turbulent emotions. That sword fight the other day wasn't enough—not nearly enough to assuage his fury against the Dankworths, one in particular.

Julius stared at him, blue eyes glittering. "He's desperate. Without Connie's estate, he's lost. We must drive Dankworth to desperation, stop him borrowing on the expectation of the Downholland title and his marriage to Louisa Stobart and ensure he doesn't wed the heiress. I'm with you all the way."

Alex gave a terse nod. "Time to go in for the kill, Julius. I want him completely destroyed. I'll drive him out, back to whatever hole he came from."

"What do you plan?"

Alex tapped the side of his nose. "What say I take him into Hell at White's next week and rook him?"

Julius considered, not a flicker of surprise disturbing his features. "Not White's, I think. Mother Dawkins's. You can get a table to yourself and ensure nobody comes near it. I don't want to do it in White's. Too sacrosanct, too respectable."

"I take your point. Very well, I'll do it at Mother Dawkins's. I'll make the arrangements."

Julius leaned forward, his voice gaining a note of agitation. "Alex, are you sure? You know the risk you're taking?"

"Would you do it with me?" They had learned to cheat at cards from the best cardsharper they could find, did it for a joke one summer out of sheer devilry. Most of their acquaintances knew of their skills but they also knew neither of them cheated when money lay on the table. But doing it at one of the most notorious addresses in London would hold them up to the highest opprobrium if they were caught. Alex would do it and more for Connie but Julius had nothing to gain in this fight, except fulfilling his sense of justice.

Julius laughed. "Naturally. With a number of members of society looking on."

Alex wouldn't let his cousin take this risk. "No. I'll do it alone. If I suffer for this, Connie will need a powerful friend."

Julius nodded. "You're right. She's welcome to stay here as long as she wishes. And that will give me the distance to continue my very discreet enquiries into the Dankworths' involvement in this affair. Northwich in particular. So far, I've discovered nothing. Either they aren't involved, or they're playing a clever hand. Speaking of which, what game will you play with him?"

Alex frowned in thought. "Piquet." A two hander, a game nobody could ask to join.

"Dankworth made a serious mistake, bringing me directly into his dispute with you. He will live to regret it, whether his august relatives are involved or not."

Alex exchanged a look of perfect understanding with his best friend. "This is for me to do." He wanted to control the play and see Dankworth squirm. He would drive the bastard into the tightest corner he could contrive.

Julius didn't say more than, "Very well." He shrugged. He'd have done it and that was enough for Alex.

Chapter 16

"You're always welcome here, Lord Ripley," Mrs. Dawkins said to Alex. "You bring me custom." She smiled at another gentleman walking past her. "It's Lady's Academy night. Are you willin'?"

She never stopped asking. "Not tonight, ma'am. I'm looking for a quiet game of cards somewhere the ambitious mamas can't get at me."

She guffawed, her laugh echoing around the entrance hall. "They won't come 'ere, sir."

She was in her best London madam mood tonight. Later, she'd come over the schoolma'am. That was one of her talents; she became whatever the occasion called for. "Ever trod the boards, Mrs. D?"

"That'd be tellin'" she said with a mighty nudge and a wink as subtle as a sledgehammer. "My girls are clean, you know that. All in fun."

"You hardly need me to crowd out your room, do you?"

"Right enough. Meeting anyone tonight? There's a fair few gentlemen here you'll know."

"There always are. I'll take my chances." Although, he knew Dankworth planned to come to the house tonight. A mutual friend had arranged to meet him here, a friend who wouldn't be turning up. He'd merely done Alex a favor.

Julius had wanted to come as a witness but Alex remained adamant that he wouldn't allow Julius a part in his decidedly risky scheme. He didn't want anyone else involved. He saw tonight as a duel. One that didn't need seconds.

As he stood poised to climb the stairs, Dankworth entered the house. Instead of turning away, Alex confronted him. Right there, under the madam's jaundiced eyes. "Good evening," he offered.

Dankworth stared at him, pale blue eyes startled then he nodded. "Evening."

Alex could act when the occasion demanded it and now he put his best skills to use. "I must tell you that something I attributed to your offices has been discovered to be the act of someone else. My apologies."

Dankworth found his voice after a few seconds of pregnant silence. "You have?" He frowned, puzzled as well he might be because Alex hardly understood himself. However, he had the man under his gaze and he'd watch every twitch.

He addressed Mrs. Dawkins. "Have they found a new tenant for next door yet?"

"No and not likely to, the state they left that 'ouse in. I'm tempted to take it on myself but not at the price the landlord wants. I could knock through and make this house a bit bigger. But I want cheaper than he's arsking. And I want a lease, not rent."

Alex thought he could help there but he wasn't sure he wanted his name associated with the house. He'd look into it. In order to become independent of his father and the estate he was to inherit one day, he'd made a number of shrewd investments and was, as a result, well known in the City. And wealthy in his own right.

He addressed Dankworth again, forcing himself to affability. "I wanted to say that the slights I assumed you inflicted are, in fact, better placed at another's door." This had to be the best acting he'd ever done.

Alex offered his hand and Dankworth shook it, after a moment's hesitation. "It was an easy mistake to make," Dankworth said.

Alex let his anger evaporate for now, retaining his expression of lazy insouciance with an effort. "An understandable mistake, especially since we had a mutual interest. But it seems you don't want her, either."

Dankworth picked up on that quickly. "Either?"

Alex shrugged. "The world knows how fickle I am. I found the lady not as irresistible as I'd thought."

Dankworth didn't hide his surprise. His eyebrows rose and a slight smile quirked his lips. "The last time I saw you, you attended her with great care."

"That was yesterday." He kept Dankworth's gaze and then clapped him on the shoulder. "Did you come for the academy, or do you have time for a friendly game of piquet first and perhaps a bottle or two?"

Dankworth was no fool but this turn of events had to make him wonder. Alex wasn't unaware of his own worth and standing. If Dankworth made an ally of him, he could probably cozen a few more creditors into letting him punt on tick.

He gave a gracious nod. "Very well."

Alex had won the first round, even if Dankworth wasn't aware of it yet.

Alex led the way upstairs and took care to select a small table by the windows where few people would pass. He ordered a bottle of the house's best red, which was to say, a moderate wine rebottled to look better. Mother Dawkins was too canny to use really cheap wine and her discerning clients didn't mention her little subterfuge, which probably earned her a few hundred every year.

A woman had to make a living. One day she'd go too far with someone who cared enough to do something about it. Until then, she remained queen of Covent Garden.

They sat and a waiter brought them two sealed packs of cards and their wine. Alex allowed Dankworth to break the packs open and shuffle them. It wouldn't make any difference to the outcome. He poured the wine and while seeming not to watch, kept a close eye on Dankworth's actions.

Dankworth separated the packs, because in piquet they only wanted the higher cards. Then he dumped the rest on the floor instead of putting them aside. A prince of courtesy.

Alex lounged back and watched Dankworth deal. "Have you received your invitation for the Kirkburton ball?"

Dankworth smirked. "They can hardly leave me out. I'm the Downholland heir. I may get the title, you know. They're petitioning Parliament to allow a new creation when his lordship dies."

Alex wasn't supposed to know about the details in the contract. He feigned surprise. "So you may have that without the lady?"

"I can have a sweeter prize." Dankworth gave him a knowing leer that made Alex shudder for Louisa Stobart. It passed Alex's understanding how Jasper Dankworth could reject the gorgeous Connie Rattigan in favor of the rapacious Louisa Stobart. He'd take Connie with nothing.

With steady hands, Alex picked up his cards and fanned them out. He selected two to discard and took two from the *talon*, the pack in the center of the table. They played the first hand at a desultory pace, as if they had all the time in the world but they were gauging each other's capabilities, as good card players do.

Alex played in a casual way but used enough concentration to win that hand, because the person who had first choice of the *talon* generally won and to lose at this stage might look suspicious. He gave Dankworth an easy smile. "We are getting through the wine rather quickly. Another?"

Dankworth nodded his acceptance. Alex signaled the waiter who brought a fresh bottle promptly. Since Dankworth didn't offer, he paid for it, as he had for the first one. He preferred not to keep a tally tonight. He'd leave as soon as he'd finished his work.

Alex let his opponent win the first rubber. Dankworth won a hundred guineas, give or take a couple. The money should go to his tailor but it wouldn't, because Alex intended to have it back from him before the night ended. He won the next one and made sure he won less than Dankworth.

And he drank. Alex had chosen wine because he had a good tolerance for it and he'd heard that Dankworth did not. In fact, two things he could do better than his cousin were drink and play cards, although Julius was reasonably proficient at both.

While the occasional beau strolled over to exchange the time of day and several men glanced curiously in their direction, they couldn't deal anyone in. Which was just as well. Alex would have his work cut out explaining to his usual circle why he decided to play cards with a man like Jasper Dankworth. And cheat flagrantly.

When the rubber ended, they celebrated with a glass of wine and Dankworth became visibly more relaxed. He loosened his cravat and tucked his lace ruffles away up the sleeves of his coat.

Alex didn't bother. The only things he'd removed were his sword and his hat at the door.

"You're not pursuing Mrs. Rattigan any more, then?"

Bad show to name a lady in a place like this. Alex responded with a raised brow and a glance at his newly dealt hand. "Her virtue grew tedious. I prefer a widow who finally gives in. She gave every sign of doing so and then failed me. Will you take her back?" Over his dead body and that wasn't likely to happen before he had Dankworth dead at his feet.

Dankworth sniggered.

Fascinated, Alex observed the man's nose quivering in mirth. A rare sight and one he'd take care to recount to selected company in the near future, if they hadn't noticed it themselves already.

"Take her back? Not if she begged me but I intend to keep her dangling a while longer, just to teach her a lesson. She has little fortune to speak of and she's an unappealing piece, compared with the little morsel I have under my care at present."

Inwardly, Alex breathed a sigh of relief. Connie was safe, as long as Dankworth had the other girl on a string. "You know my father wanted me to court her?" He glanced up, smiled tightly. "She's a charming girl, but not for me."

In a few years, the empty-headed Louisa Stobart might have learned enough to make a man a tolerable wife. Not him, but it was only fair to give her those years.

"A tempting wench, you must admit. I'm surprised you didn't take her while she was willing. Took her into a private room, I heard."

Alex wanted to hit him. He had no love for Miss Stobart but disliked hearing the woman discussed as if she was meat. One day, he promised himself. His time would come. Now, if he didn't play Dankworth's game, he'd lose the bigger stake.

Alex played a card, retaining commendable control over his temper. "With a society woman, that's playing with fire. She is nominally pure, not a widow, so out of consideration. Whoever you are, if you upset enough members of society, you're finished."

"Society isn't the center of the universe."

You are about to find out how much it means to you, my bully. "It's the center of our world. You'd be surprised how many doors will close if society decides to turn its collective back on you. Not that it happens very often. After all, society isn't a homogenous whole but a collection of people. However, the highest and most exclusive part is a little more connected." He took the hand and gathered the cards to deal again. That was such a gentle threat he doubted Dankworth understood. Hoped not, because he probably shouldn't have said so much.

His father had influential relatives and his mother, God rest her soul, was one of five daughters to a duke and the sister of the present duke. Alex's tentacles spread wide. Take a few more families like the Cavendishes, Howards, and Lennoxes, remember that they were all twined in with each other and society went deep. Lose the approval of one and it might go very hard.

Dankworth took a noisy slurp of his wine and reached for the bottle.

Alex declined a refill but his opponent took one. Dankworth was unwinding. Alex told a few off-color jokes and Dankworth laughed uproariously, gaining a few glances from the others present in the far from quiet room.

The revelry in the main saloon was gaining in volume, which meant the academy must be in full swing. "You're very wise not to go in there yet. Do you plan to visit later?"

"I'm told it's one of the imperatives for a man visiting the city. But I don't want to appear too keen. In any case, I prefer the later events in the proceedings of these places."

He signaled the waiter for another bottle. Surprisingly, he'd only taken one glass from the last one. It was one glass more than he wanted in this company but it gave Dankworth a good head start. Alex might be able to conclude this earlier than he'd imagined. "You arrived at Mrs. Cratchitt's house in time for the whole of the auction."

"Capital fun. That's more in my line, truthfully. I prefer a little—danger with my females." He tutted. "No, that's not the right word." He glanced up and smiled brightly. "You know what I mean, though, don't you? If the girls in the salon were truly as young as they pretend to be, I might find some sport in that."

Sport in tearing young bodies, hurting them, frightening them? Alex thought not. He preferred his pleasures consensual and between adults. He couldn't live in London without knowing such practices went on but they didn't appeal to him or anyone he called friend. He avoided them, or combated them when he had the power to do so. After taking a sip of wine he dabbed the corner of his mouth with his handkerchief. Kept it in his hand, in the fashionable mode, to flourish. Although not many of the fashionable ones held a couple of aces. "You plan to return to the country after your marriage? How will you pursue your pleasures then?"

"York and the other larger cities have their own places." Dankworth glanced up, in the process of dealing. "But I see no reason to molder in the distant north. I like London life. My intended bride does, too."

Next to him, Alex felt as spotless as an angel. He let Dankworth win the rubber, exclaiming at his bad luck. Five hundred pounds this time. He yawned, delicately hiding his open mouth with his handkerchief. "Shall we add a little spice? How do you feel about doubled points?"

Dankworth shrugged carelessly. "If you wish."

Now the game really began. Although he didn't change his position, or his demeanor Alex played in earnest now.

The luck turned, or appeared to. Alex put his skills to work. Tired of conversation, tired of the company, he worked fast and skilfully, using every dirty trick he knew. Dealing from the bottom of the deck, bad shuffles, playing faster to give Dankworth little time to consider his play and he palmed several cards that weren't to his liking, adding them to the discards on the floor. He wanted a bath to wash away the memory of this venture. But he needed to do this to keep Connie safe. Needed to drive the man into such a deep hole of debt that he would be forced into action.

The points were moving faster and Dankworth's debt was steadily increasing.

Alex won the next rubber. And lost the next, leaving him evens. As the wine went down, the stakes went up. Alex had him.

At Dankworth's insistence, they broke out two new packs of cards.

It wouldn't make any difference. Alex could have told him that.

With the optimism of the compulsive gambler Dankworth raised the stakes again.

It was still relatively early in the evening when Alex decided he'd done enough. Unlike his opponent, he'd kept tally throughout. He'd been the scorer for the game but his own personal arithmetic left him well informed from point to point. Too wise to win anything substantial too early, he'd dangled the temptation of winning before the man, running it close a few times but he never let him win too much. Just enough to bait the hook. He yawned once more. "Don't know what I'm feeling tonight. Too many nights burning the candle at both ends and that's a fact. Well, old man, it was good to bury the hatchet. Very decent of you not to take umbrage. We'll put the events of the house next door behind us. Unless the lady involved has to give evidence, that is." He wanted to see Dankworth turn pale but unfortunately, the man was too far gone. He waved a careless hand. "You think she will?"

Dankworth shrugged. "What do you care? You've had your sport. I imagine she'll return to the wilds. I couldn't bear living in the back of beyond forever. Never could. I always looked for a way out and the visit to the Downhollands and meeting dear sweet Louisa provided the opening I needed." He glanced at the sheet of paper on which Alex was keeping tally of the points. "How much do I owe you?" The muscles in the man's face had hardened, the lines by the side of his mouth deepened.

"Let's see, shall we?" Just because he wanted to prolong the torture, Alex took his time adding up, failing to remember his figures once or twice, forcing himself to start again.

Dankworth's fingers clenched around the stem of his wineglass and fine lines tightened his mouth.

Alex enjoyed watching the increasing tension in the figure opposite him as he realized the enormity of the sums involved. Playing piquet involved putting a few pennies, or shillings, on each point but with thousands of points every game, it was easy to let the overall score slip.

At least, Dankworth had found it easy.

He tossed down the tally. "It appears you owe me twenty thousand, one hundred and sixty pounds—no, guineas." He glanced up with a bright smile, feigning lighthearted pleasure, covering his deep satisfaction with the result for entirely different reasons to those Dankworth might suppose. Connie was safe. "Rather more than I thought."

Dankworth swallowed and his eyes glazed. "Obviously I don't carry that amount around with me. But I will visit my bank tomorrow."

Alex should perhaps have stopped at ten thousand but it was too late now. His temper had driven him to it. "Call it twenty thousand. I never handle small change. Do take your time. Would next week suit you?" That would give him time to bolt, or to flush his powerful relative out of the bush and into full view. Bolting would prove enough for Alex, but Julius was after richer game, and Alex would gladly leave Northwich to his cousin's tender mercies.

"Perfectly."

If Alex was any judge, Dankworth would either urge Miss Stobart to marry him immediately, which her mother would never allow, because she wanted the ball and the gown and everything else, or he'd try to win the money back, either at White's or at the hells he'd taken to frequenting.

Alex would grind this man under his heel. He wanted him gone for good.

Chapter 17

Connie hadn't realized one prospective ball would make her so nervous but a lot lay at stake here. The Downhollands had taken her with them on various visits, she'd accompanied Helena to balls, literary salons and the shops and few people cut her these days. She had won. Nobody cut her any more.

The only time she'd seen Alex recently was in public. He'd made a point of seeking her out, dancing with her or conversing, escorting her generally but more intimate opportunities had, it seemed, gone. She longed to talk to him, *really* talk as they had in the library at Dankworth Park, touch him. He meant more to her than he should but she was long past denying it now.

Jasper often accompanied his newest fiancée and her mother but they never approached Julius, Helena and their set. "London has gone to Dankworth's head," Helena remarked on one occasion, when they were walking in the park, Caroline pattering by her father's side, her hand firmly in his. "I've seen it happen before. People come to town and go mad."

"You're too good, my dear," Julius murmured. "Maybe he always had those tendencies and London merely brought them into prominence. But he's been quieter the last few days."

He glanced at Alex, who had climbed down from his carriage and walked with them. "You did go a little too far, you know."

Alex shrugged. "I've sent him a note giving him more time. To be honest, I don't want the money, just the pressure the debt gives me."

Chills invaded her body, crawling up her spine. "What have you done?" Connie swiveled around to stare at him.

The expression in his dark eyes softened when he gazed at her and she reveled in it, her body yearning for his touch, although she did her best to suppress the feeling. "I merely played cards with him a few days ago and he lost quite a sum. It pushed him a little. I want him out of the city."

Her lips firmed into a thin line. At least she had a distraction from her increasing tension about the upcoming ball. Alex noticed her change of expression and his eyes turned wary, the lids dropping over the pupils a little more, his chin going up. "You have an objection, my lady?"

"You might say that."

Alex glanced at Julius and Helena, and decided not even these two should hear what came next. He sketched a bow. "Would you care to take a turn around the park, ma'am? My new phaeton is rather fine. I'd be glad of your opinion."

Fashionable strollers and drivers packed the park at this hour. It was perfectly acceptable for her to take a spin in an open carriage.

"I would love to, thank you."

She allowed him to hand her up into the carriage, lifting her skirts to prevent stumbling, flashing a glimpse of ankle and calf. On another day she might have teased him, might have thrilled at the touch of his gloved hand on hers but not now, not today. She was trembling with fury. But she would hear him out.

Once on the narrow wooden seat, she shook out her skirts and lingered to smooth a finger over the pattern of spring flowers she'd enjoyed so much when she'd dressed that morning. Helena hadn't asked for any of her gowns back yet and in truth, she wondered how her friend could take them back and wear them, because society had seen Connie in them now.

Alex swung up and sat beside her. He took the reins from the footman standing by the carriage then nodded to the man at the horses' heads. When the man would have swung up behind, Alex shook his head and the man stepped off without a word.

The matched greys went into high-stepping action but the carriage was so well sprung she only feel the slightest of motions. This beautiful vehicle wouldn't stand a chance on the rough roads around her home. It was all for show, all to display wealth, privilege and beauty. It did that superlatively well.

"You're well?"

"Well enough, thank you." She folded her hands in her lap, clasping them together tightly. An archly smiling lady she couldn't ignore was in a carriage about to pass them. She smiled back.

Alex negotiated a curve with great skill. Connie didn't even move her hands to retain her balance. She turned her head, keeping her expression calm with not inconsiderable effort. Even through the haze of anger she noted the strong line of his jaw, the capable hands and hated herself, that she wanted him even now. "What did you do?"

"I met him at Mother Dawkins's on academy night. We went into the card room and I won twenty thousand pounds from him. He'll leave town now."

"You did *what*?" She could hardly believe it. "You planned it, didn't you? It was no chance meeting, was it?"

He glanced at her and then took another look. "What's wrong? You wanted him gone, did you not?"

"Not like this."

He slowed his horses' pace from a trot to a walk. "What do you mean?" He didn't sound happy, his voice hard and slightly frightening. Lucky she wasn't easily frightened.

"You played him in a card game and won?"

He cleared his throat. "In a way, yes."

"Were you lucky?"

"Ah. Yes, very."

She sensed more than that. In some way, he'd manipulated that game. She could hardly ask him if he'd cheated. He could whip up the horses and throw her off for that. It was just too convenient. She could hardly get her understanding around the sum. "Twenty thousand?"

"It was piquet," he said, as if that explained it. Perhaps it did. The game involved thousands of points scored and if the bet was per point, it might happen like that. "Didn't you warn him?"

"Why should I? He's a grown man."

"You know why."

His dark gaze turned cold.

Despite the anger still coursing through her, she regretted his withdrawal. But she must make him understand she could not accept this.

"You still care for him?" Alex asked.

"Of course not. That's not the point. Alex, do you remember what I said to you?"

His voice softened infinitesimally. "Everything you've ever said. Every word."

She worked to control her voice, to keep it steady and reasonable. "Then why did you ignore me? Why listen and agree, if you have no intention of following my wishes?"

He frowned in genuine confusion. "I don't understand."

They swung around another corner, this time a little less steadily. Connie grasped the low rail at the side of the coach, clutched it hard, even though, once they rounded the bend, the carriage settled down once more. Fury welled up inside her. "I asked you to keep me informed. To let me make my own decisions, determine my own fate. You did this without consulting me, without asking me if I wanted you to do it."

He was staring straight ahead, his pose rigidly upright, his jaw set. "You would have me let him continue in town, lose that money to someone else?"

"You must know he doesn't have anywhere near that sum. And yet debts of honor must be paid, although respectable tradesmen can go hang. He'll grow desperate."

"That, my dear, is the idea. I have no intention of collecting that debt. I will visit Lord Downholland later today and give him the notes of hand as proof of Dankworth's perfidy. He may do as he wishes with them but I imagine he will call the man to account."

She made a sound of exasperation, a sharp "Tcha!" between her teeth. "And you think that will stop him? He has a wealthy fiancée. He'll bolt for the border."

"He won't." Alex twitched on one rein to control the horse that had threatened to veer off to one side. "I have a close watch set on his lodgings. If he is absent for more than half a day, I'll know about it."

"And that's that?" She could hold back no longer—her anger boiled over like a neglected kettle. "Alex, the great lord of Ripley and all he surveys has deemed it so? He made it happen? I don't want that. I don't want all my problems to melt away. I wanted to confront him, ensure he would understand what he's doing, to improve from his own nature. Otherwise, it will happen again and again. I don't want it ending like this, for him to end like this."

"How can you say that when he would have ruined you?" Alex jerked his head around and glared at her, heedless of the throngs of people around them, or that all of them would be watching them now. "I had the opportunity to put something right. I should have reached Mother Cratchitt's sooner, should have rescued you before half society saw you in a state of undress. I should have realized what nature of man he was long before I did."

She wanted him to get upset, wanted him to realize what he'd done. "What part of *I want to do this on my own* didn't you understand, Alex? I was about to visit Miss Stobart, to discuss Jasper with her. I would have done it. Hell on earth, I still will."

Ignoring the faces turned to the carriage, unashamedly watching them, Alex drew the carriage to a halt. "You nearly died, Connie. A man has to take the consequences of the decisions he makes and he should take his. I did it because I don't want you worried. I did it because I wanted nothing in the way of our marriage. Because I want you, Connie. Dammit, you're mine, you know you are!"

By now, she was in a fine temper. "I know nothing of the kind, you dolt! How could you have gone over my head and done this thing, without even informing me of what you'd planned?" She threw up her hands and dropped them into her lap where they landed with a soft slap, marking the moment she gave way to her anger. How dare he? "If I had come to you, it would have been on my own, for myself, not because you'd made me grateful or wanted me to do it from relief." She grabbed the rail and stood, swinging one foot out to find the tiny metal platform. A small surge of relief penetrated through the haze of rage when her foot landed squarely on it.

He sat stunned, his eyes blazing but the reins held still in his hands.

"I will attend the ball but after that I'm going home. You hear me?" She glanced down at the gown, and then back at him, making it clear she knew where they had come from. "And I'll be sending back everything you've bought for me." She paused. "Everything."

Her parting shot went home. He watched her but said nothing.

"Don't call, don't try because the last time I see you will be at that ball. You hear me, Alex? The very last." Having made her point, she swung down to the ground, almost stumbling when it turned out further away than she'd thought. She grabbed the side of the carriage and righted herself. She strode away, ignoring the people staring after her, uncaring of the fact that she was alone and unescorted.

"Connie!" Alex called after her, but she didn't slow down for a minute. He couldn't chase after her without losing control of his carriage, since he'd elected to drive her without a footman in attendance but if she didn't hurry, he'd turn that carriage and come after her.

In a moment, she'd reached the gates of the park. She walked quickly around a corner and then another, quickening her pace to one far faster than a fashionable lady should aspire to but one she was well used to in the country.

A child cannoned into her but by now she knew London ways and felt for her purse almost automatically, relieved to find it still there. She carried on walking, breathing deeply until she was more in control of her emotions. Breasts heaving under her fichu, she regained her breath and with it her composure.

She found herself near the house where the Stobarts were spending the season. Not that she'd have known it from the row of elegant, similar houses, brass knockers on the black painted doors gleaming in the sunshine, marble steps spotless, curtains carefully draped at the windows. Each house had a number and the name of the street was fastened to the upper story of the house opposite.

No time like the present. Although a little early in the day, it was still acceptable to pay a visit. Without allowing herself to reason against her decision, she ascended the steps and rapped on the door.

A superior personage answered it and reluctantly allowed her in, while he took her card to the Stobarts.

A pang went through Connie when she recognized her behavior wasn't dissimilar to Alex's, at least in intent. She wanted to control someone else's life. *No, no she didn't.* She wanted to ensure Miss Stobart understood what she was doing. Perhaps she shouldn't have come to this house in such a temper, because it was evaporating quickly and she realized how foolish she'd been. After all, she'd been abducted in a busy inn. A moment and the deed had been done. It could happen again to someone else. To her on the way here.

She'd call for a chair. Even then, chairmen weren't always trustworthy. Oh, hell. Too late now.

The superior person returned, with a deal more respect and asked her to follow him. After she'd disposed of her hat, gloves and shawl, she did just that, fished her fan out of her capacious pocket and held it loosely in the approved mode.

Mrs. Stobart was all graciousness and offered her tea, which she found most welcome. After talking about the Downhollands, how good it was to see them in London and what they would wear for the forthcoming ball, Connie finally worked her way around to the subject of marriage. At which Mrs. Stobart gave her an indulgent smile. "You and I know, Mrs. Rattigan, what a blessing marriage is. I can only wish that my darling Louisa finds such bliss."

Connie doubted Louisa would find Jasper blissful. "He is a man of decided temper and he does consider himself the master of his house." She might be here on a fool's errand but she had to inform them of their folly.

She smoothed away a piece of fluff on her skirt, enjoying the luxury of fine silk under her fingers. It would be a wrench to part with these lovely clothes but she'd promised, so she'd do it. In the carriage just now, she'd realized where all the gowns and trinkets had come from and she meant to task her hosts with their part in the deception later.

"He wouldn't do anything to upset me," Louisa said, pouting those dewy-fresh lips that had no doubt entranced her fiancé. "He said so."

"Love fades," said Connie, remembering how it had happened to her once. The remembered sadness was no more than a memory now, but at the time, she had been devastated. "And if there's nothing left when it's gone, then you have precisely that. Nothing. It's important to ensure your intended is a man of good character and steadfast intent."

"You speak with great good sense," Mrs. Stobart said. "But of course you know that dear Mr. Dankworth has just such qualities. He intends to remove to the country after the marriage, giving Louisa the time she needs to accustom herself to the married state."

To slake himself on her and then disappear back to London, more likely. Leave her pregnant and stranded. "I wanted to make sure you understood precisely what you were doing."

Mrs. Stobart handed her a dish of tea.

She refreshed herself with a sip. It was not particularly good tea, or perhaps her indulgence and Helena's excellent housekeeping had made her more discerning. "Jasper Dankworth must be fifteen years older than you."

Louisa beamed. "I prefer my men mature. He is *exactly* the right age for me. And so handsome, I can hardly stop looking at him."

Connie despaired. Maybe she could get Miss Stobart alone at the ball. Or somewhere else. "Do you plan to remain in London much longer?"

"Oh until the end of the season, at least. I'm enjoying myself prodigiously. Then I will marry my dear Jasper and we will go into the country. Do you have similar plans?"

"Something similar." Going back to the life she knew. Immuring herself in the country.

"I had no idea you knew such exalted people when I met you at the Downhollands'," Mrs. Stobart remarked. She picked up one of the small cakes from the spread on the small table at her elbow. From her ample collection of chins, Connie wasn't sure she needed it.

"The Vernons are leaders of society," Mrs. Stobart declared pompously.

"So they are."

Louisa shuddered. "Doesn't Lord Winterton frighten you sometimes? I've never seen anyone so haughty."

Julius spent time romping on the floor with his daughter and then, after she'd suffered a minor injury, cradled her in his arms with such tenderness she'd held her breath. And he hadn't been afraid of her seeing him so vulnerable. To her, that denoted real strength. "He is very kind, too. He adores his little girl."

"So gossip says," Mrs. Stobart said. "Of course, our dear Jasper will be a baron one day. We are assured the re-creation of the title will go ahead."

"And Lord Winterton will be a duke." Connie refrained from mentioning that there were variations without the ranks, some title holders rich, some moderately well off, and some plain misters as wealthy as any duke.

"Your suitor is a baron," Mrs. Stobart went on. "And he'll be an earl. I'm so glad you have found your admirers, instead of repining over Mr. Dankworth. Indeed, you were most gracious. I quite thought you'd cut us when we arrived in London."

Too close for comfort when Mrs. Stobart had cut her. Not the cut direct but she had pretended not to notice Connie's presence a time or three. Now, with Connie's reputation restored, she behaved with all graciousness. "Indeed not. My hosts introduced me to everyone they considered essential but I was already acquainted with you." *So you weren't important enough.* See how she liked that.

Mrs. Stobart wasn't stupid. She understood well enough. Despite her expression remaining the same, she gave a sharp breath. "Of course, with dear Jasper being the Downholland heir, we have excellent expectations. Otherwise, I would not have allowed my precious daughter to spend time with him. While I regret the way Jasper broke your relationship, he is a man violently in love. You do not seem too upset about it yourself, so we can say that no harm came of the situation." Her eyes gleamed.

At that moment, a discreet knock on the door indicated the presence of the footman, who entered and handed Mrs. Stobart a visiting card. She reddened and glanced up. "I'd be delighted to see them."

Had Alex followed her? Connie thought she had run fast enough but perhaps she had moved too slowly.

It wasn't Alex. Helena entered first, letting Julius take his time entering the room. "We've finished our errands, my dear, so we thought we'd bring the carriage around instead of putting you to the trouble of sending for it." Her perfunctory kiss on the cheek left Connie with the soft scent of lavender.

"Come and sit here my dear."

Her expression perfecty serene, Helena sat next to Mrs. Stobart.

Julius took his seat in a wide-armed chair, flicking the skirts of his pale blue coat into place before he sat down. He crossed his legs at the knee in the approved mode and accepted the dish of tea that would be past its best by now. But he made no comment, merely put the tea on a nearby table after a sip.

They spoke of nothing more noteworthy than society and the ball on Friday but subtle innuendo and the presence of two of the leaders of society here gave the Stobart presence more approval than they'd obtained all season. They might be received at the large occasions, but so far, the intimate gatherings Helena had taken Connie to had been unavailable to them. Connie didn't doubt that they had brought the crested carriage with liveried footmen and left them outside to wait. Society could take note.

Connie remained apprehensive that Alex would arrive but he did not and for that, she had to be grateful. He must have informed Julius that she'd left him so precipitately.

They didn't speak of him until they were in the carriage on the short journey back to Brook Street, a street Mrs. Stobart had heard was their private address with incredulity. She had heard, her great friend had said, that it was a street for musicians and artists and wealthy tradesmen.

"And politicians and earls," Julius had added smoothly. "I liked the house, so I took it. It has come into fashion recently." The gentle reminder that the Vernons set fashion, instead of following it, didn't fall on deaf ears.

Once in the carriage, Helena chuckled. "Brook Street is for the inferior sort, is it? She has a provincial turn of mind, does she not?"

"She can't help it." Connie subsided back into the comfortable squabs with a sigh. "Yes she can. But her daughter is so young. Too young for Jasper Dankworth."

"I made a point of leaving invitations for the ball, at the behest of Lady Downholland and I will ensure Dankworth gains admittance." While he kept his perfect poise, Julius dropped the superior manner. "I've told Alex to stay away from you. It's clear he distressed you in some way. He gave his word he would not visit unless invited."

Connie twisted her hands in her lap. "He did something I asked him not to do." Neither Julius or Helena had asked but she explained anyway. "He took the matter into his own hands. He did it without consulting me, or telling me what he planned and I specifically made him promise not to do that."

"Then I fear you have to be angry with me, also. Because I knew," Julius said.

Connie lost her temper all over again. "But it's *my* life, *my* fate. Don't you think I have some right to know what's happening?"

Helena put her hand over Connie's.

Connie shook it off. "Stop the carriage."

"So you can walk off? Connie, you'll find yourself abducted again. You really must control yourself." Julius met her gaze.

She flinched at the hard expression in his eyes.

"You must not run off like this. You will not see Alex again until you wish it."

She hadn't realized how the news would make her feel until tears misted her eyes.

Helena pressed a handkerchief into her hands.

"I don't know what I want any more. I want my life and I want Alex. Can't I have both?" Connie mopped her streaming eyes. "I'm so sorry. I don't behave like a watering pot, truly I don't."

"Women in love often behave out of character." Julius exchanged a sparkling glance with his sister.

The realization hit Connie with a jolt the like of which she hadn't experienced before. A bolt of lightning from a clear sky. "I'm in love?" She bit her lip, the sting of pain forcing her concentration. "What do I do now?"

It made sense. When she saw something she wanted to share, she immediately thought of Alex. The thrill she experienced in his arms was like nothing she'd ever known before, or imagined. It would hurt so much to separate, that she didn't know if she would survive the experience. If she didn't make a stand now, he might protect her into screaming frustration.

"You wait on events." Julius chuckled. "I believe my cousin is as deeply in love with you. I've never seen him behave in this way before. He's never cared about anyone enough to worry like this. After you left him in the park he was frantic but only because he feared for you. We sent for the carriage."

The coachman drew up outside the house in Brook Street with scarcely a disturbance. The disturbance inside Connie was enough to make her stomach churn and her limbs weak. She was in love?

She was in love.

Chapter 18

Alex stayed away.

Just as she expected, Connie missed him, more than she'd imagined. There were only two days and most of another day until the ball at Kirkburton House on Friday night, but she yearned to see him, to touch him. To kiss him. She wasn't even sure he'd come to the ball.

The day before the ball she received a visit from the Downhollands. Lord Downholland greeted her with a jutting chin and Lady Downholland with her usual, friendly demeanor.

"We wished to consult you on a matter," Lord Downholland began, "and to that end, we've requested that Lord Winterton attends you."

As if on cue, the door opened on a tap and Julius entered. The relative plainness of his clothes told Connie he'd been on business in the City.

He greeted them and they made small talk while the maid brought in a tray of tea and settled it at a table at Connie's elbow. Strange how many of the rituals of her life remained the same. Tea in the afternoon, for instance. True, the china and even the tea might be finer but the process was comfortingly the same. She made the tea and poured it out, Julius helping to offer it and the tiny cakes to their guests, dispensing with the need for a maid.

She liked the Downhollands enormously and disliked the expression of gravity that she discerned on both their countenances. It became clear when his lordship put down his empty dish and began to speak and, as usual, he spoke as if he were addressing a public meeting.

"As you know, Connie, my wife and I are childless and we have few relatives. It is fortunate that the estate does not have an entail associated with it, so I may leave the holdings where I will. I am most anxious that whoever inherits the property takes good care of it."

He cleared his throat and glanced at Julius. "Lord Ripley visited me yesterday and presented me with a number of notes that Jasper Dankworth signed over to him." He'd said he would. It was doing the deed without consulting her that had upset her, not his intention, so she'd let his actions pass.

"I have also received reports from other areas that claim a similar lack of regard for personal debts. I can no longer ignore the evidence and truthfully, that is the reason we are paying this visit today." He swallowed and took a deep breath. "I have taken steps to remove Jasper Dankworth as my heir and to withdraw my petition for him to inherit the title when I am gone. I am regretful but if I bestow the estate and title on him, he will fritter away the first and bring the second into disrepute. Better the title dies with me." He harrumphed and tugged the edges of his good country coat.

Connie smoothed hands suddenly gone clammy down the silk of her gown. "Are you enquiring for other relatives, perhaps more distant?"

His lordship shook his head regretfully. "I no longer have an interest in seeking out someone I do not know to inherit the estate I have worked so hard for. But there is a female who has proved her worth over the years, one who will treasure the heritage. You."

She heard her gasp at if from a distance but her head was swimming too distractingly for her to take much heed of it. She absently noticed that her fingers were shaking. She had expected the Downhollands to remove Jasper from the will but not to hand that fortune over to her. "I am but your godchild, sir, not a blood relative. I hope I never presumed on that relationship, even though you've always treated me with kindness."

"I know you didn't. But you have proved yourself constant over the years. You suffered a marriage that proved less than successful with dignity."

Connie felt Julius's perceptive gaze but didn't look in his direction. She hadn't discussed her first marriage and he was probably wondering.

"We can imagine nobody better to administer our estate and become our heir. We only stopped to inform you of our intentions and obtain your approval before we leave to finalize the business with my man of affairs. Although I may leave the estate where I wish, I do not wish to burden you with something you do not want."

"I don't know what to say," Connie murmured, stunned by the information, her mind dizzyingly spinning around the concept. She hadn't thought the Downhollands would take this step. Maybe insist that Jasper reform, even rusticate him but not cut him off so finally. "Of course, I'm deeply honored but—"

Julius said, "I suggest you leave Lady Downholland here, my lord, while you take care of business. It might help Connie to discuss the matter with her."

"Excellent idea." Lord Downholland got to his feet. "I'll collect you on my way back from the solicitor's office, my lady."

Lady Downholland agreed, smiling. Everyone was smiling except Connie. That made her an heiress. One with responsibilities.

* * * *

The next day, as Connie, still amazed by her change in fortune, was getting ready to leave for the ball, a nosegay arrived for her. It was a mixture of lilacs and lavender, with sprigs of tiny white blossoms and ferns, all wrapped in foil and put into a gold holder studded with amethysts. There was even room at the base of the container for a small vial of water, enough to keep the blossoms fresh for the evening.

Connie grinned. It was just as if someone had told the sender what she'd be wearing. Which, of course, they must have done. Because she wore a gown of ivory and lilac, the base color ivory, with a pattern of vines, grapes and here and there a small, colorful bird adding to the effect. The birds had brilliants for eyes but they were sprinkled randomly over the pattern, so when she moved, she glittered. A new amethyst necklace, bracelet and hair ornament made a modest parure but a pretty one. She had insisted on paying for her ensemble this time. She would stand before society tonight as her own woman with her own estate and expectations. They could snub her or accept her on those terms.

She took the flowers from her maid and buried her nose in them. Only to draw back with a sharp, "Ouch! These flowers are hard!"

Nestled in their depths was a brooch. Amethyst, surrounded by diamonds, glittering with the ferocity of the brilliant cut. The amethyst was magnificent, too, a deep, rich purple that meant it was a very fine stone indeed.

"Oh, Mrs. Rattigan, ma'am." Saxton's awed tones brought her back to the present. There was no note with the flowers, merely a card, one of Alex's embossed calling cards. Not even his initials scrawled carelessly at the bottom.

If she didn't wear it, he'd think she'd rejected him. If she wore it, then what? And if he'd told other people about it, they'd be looking for it, too. It could be a family piece. She turned it over. No, she didn't think so. It was too new, the gold gleaming, no sign of wear that would come with an older piece. She couldn't even say it wouldn't go with her dress, because it did, superbly.

Sighing, she gave in and let Saxton pin the brooch to the center of her neckline, where her cleavage swelled above the tight stays. She flicked the lace half over it, so it would flash and tease, rather than blaze. The diamonds on it outshone anything Connie owned.

At least, as the Dankworth heir, she could pay the Wintertons for the clothes. Or rather, Alex. When Helena admitted he'd paid for them, she'd asked Connie not to think too badly of him. For all the indignation Connie could muster, now her temper had subsided, she couldn't. Everything he'd done, everything had been for her. Which was the problem. She didn't want to be cared for so much that she never had to think for herself. To be an object, rather than doing.

Even though she'd powdered her hair tonight Connie looked well enough. Saxton had used a very pale grey-blue shade that suited her creamy coloring much better than stark white, which tended to make her appear sallow and left a few curls nestled teasingly against her neck.

She put on her long evening gloves and picked up the flowers and her fan. Flicking it open, she held it in front of her face as if flirting with an imaginary admirer. *Yes.*

She'd allowed Saxton to apply a tiny patch just above the corner of her left eye. She laughed at the effect, saucy and flirtatious. Clothes should never be deadly serious, Julius had told her and she found him proved right. Julius always had something on his person, a snuffbox with an odd design, something unusual in the embroidery of his waistcoats, or even just a quizzing glass that would make the observer smile.

Perhaps that was her problem. She took life too seriously. Until recently, she'd had no reason not to.

She'd smiled a lot more recently and that was despite the worry that had kept her awake at night. Life just seemed to have gone up a gear, like a cog moving to a larger cog, the same but more.

She was smiling when she went downstairs and met Helena in her ballroom glory. Helena wore blue, the moiré silk rippling over elegantly embroidered white silk and a sapphire and diamond parure.

Connie exclaimed, "Goodness, looking at those for too long could blind someone."

Helena laughed. "Julius bought them for me."

"A small apology," her brother remarked, coming out of the book room at the back of the house and joining them

His clothes never ceased to astound Connie. Tonight was no exception but he didn't linger to let her get more than an impression of rich, dark blue, enriched with crimson and rubies, before he led the way to the carriage.

Kirkburton House was, Julius told her, a remnant of an earlier time when the great London houses of the rich had lined the Thames. Few remained, the wealthy moving out to smaller houses near the park. Kirkburton had an elegant enfilade of staterooms and these were all open tonight.

Night had not yet fallen but once it did the elegant torchères set in holders by the double doors at the front and at intervals around the courtyard would be lit, flooding the area with golden light. Connie stepped out, awed by the great house, light streaming on to the flagstones of the courtyard, liveried footmen standing by every door and wondering if she could bear the thrill of it, or would die of excitement well before the ball opened at eight.

They would serve supper at eleven and the ball would end in the early hours of the morning. And yet most of the attendees would be up and attending church in the morning, probably at one of the fashionable churches, St George's or St. Martin's, although many people tended to use the bottom-achingly long sermons as a chance to catch up on their sleep. One vicar had asked a gentleman in a pew near the front to stop snoring, for fear he would wake the king. Or so Julius had told her and Connie wanted to believe the story, so she did.

Julius's parents greeted them, with Lord and Lady Downholland. Connie curtseyed to the formidable Duke and Duchess of Kirkburton, the duke a full-figured gentleman, the tiny duchess's waist so nipped-in Connie thought she could circle it with her hands. Not that she'd dream of doing such a thing.

She dropped a curtsey to Lady Lucinda, Julius's sister, younger than him by a good twelve years. She'd met pretty, lively Lady Lucinda before and enjoyed her company immensely. She embraced her godparents fondly, ignoring the duchess's indignant sniff. At least the lady didn't cut her again.

They went up to the drawing room, where the presence of at least thirty guests momentarily nonplussed her. She'd had no idea dinner would be so grand. Since this was Kirkburton House, they went in by rank, so although Connie got her first sight of Alex for days, she couldn't talk to him. Women surrounded him, cooing and batting their eyes and Alex looked deeply bored, at least he did to Connie's prejudiced eyes.

Why fight it? She loved him. She couldn't hide from that simple fact.

They exchanged one swift look and he smiled and bowed and even from across the room, his expression softened, the lines around his mouth easing. He wore green figured velvet, with a waistcoat embroidered with purple and green. Of course, he would. It was like a message, the way they complimented each other, his clothes echoing hers but not too close for anyone to remark on it.

She wanted to cross the room to him there and then, the reason for her anger with him, if not forgotten, then forgiven. Let the world go hang, let the ball go, too. She'd go with him now, if he asked her.

He turned away and addressed a woman to his left. He was seemingly uncaring of her presence. Perhaps the brooch was a farewell gift. Perhaps he didn't want her any longer.

* * * *

Alex couldn't look at Connie any longer. If he did, he'd cross the room and drag her out of it. She looked beautiful, ethereal, like she'd stepped out of a portrait, crisp and new. The way she looked at him, her heart in her eyes, killed him. Would she reject him tonight? But no, she carried his flowers. And the glint when she moved indicated the presence of his brooch.

She wouldn't reject him. At least she'd talk to him but he didn't know what else she'd do. Thinking about her was driving him mad. Last night he'd rolled over in bed, reaching for her and woken up when all he'd found was a cold pillow.

He wanted her so badly he couldn't think properly. Every time he set his mind to his plans for tonight or tomorrow, thoughts of Connie stopped him cold, hardened his cock and turned his mind into one aching mess of need. Eventually, he'd given up.

Turning his attention to the nearest person, he found Louisa Stobart gazing up at him with eyes as big as guineas. "You're enjoying the evening?" he asked.

"Yes indeed, sir, my lord. I'm surprised not to find my fiancé here."

"I believe he's attending the ball tonight." As he said the words, Dankworth strode through the door, like the proverbial bad penny. He wore crimson. Apt, or maybe black would have worked better. He just didn't know it yet.

Julius had informed Alex of the change in Connie's fortunes. Coldness crept into his veins when he realized the news would infuriate Dankworth, perhaps make him desperate enough to make another play for her, although if he came too close to Connie, Alex would kill him.

Lynne Connolly

For once Alex was glad of the women who had homed in on him, one of the unattached men in the room, because Dankworth couldn't get near him, especially when Miss Stobart slipped away to stand by his side. Dankworth greeted his godparents, who gave him a civilly cool reception and then the Kirkburtons.

Alex guessed why Jasper Dankworth was present at dinner. Dankworth must see it as an advance in his societal ambitions but he would discover exactly the opposite.

They went into dinner, Connie escorted by Sir Frederick Masters, a good enough chap but a widower with children, ostensibly an excellent match for Connie. Not that the man would get a chance, if Alex had his way. His partner was the daughter of an earl, a lady whose name escaped him until she reminded him, which she did volubly and often, just in case it slipped his mind again.

Being in Connie's presence again, however distantly, intoxicated him. Alex caught his father watching him at intervals through the meal. Lord Leverton had noticed his partiality. He had accepted Alex's decision to pursue Connie with reluctance but accepted it.

The dinner went on and on, three courses with at least a two dozen removes for each course, the plethora of dishes leaving Alex bored with having to choose. He partook of the food closest to his place, careless of what it was, so he found himself eating stuffed pigeon, which he disliked and steamed broccoli with a white sauce, which he liked only a tiny bit more.

Conversation he found tedious, although similar to the usual dinner table conversation and since the country was heading rapidly into war, more vital than usual. The table was abuzz with the Duke of Newcastle's failing hold on the Government and the consequent rise of rivals Fox and Pitt. Frankly, Alex didn't care much one way or the other, although a month ago he would have taken intense interest in the turmoil in which Parliament found itself.

Now the only thing he cared about was the well-being of one lovely woman, one he could watch but not touch or talk to. She looked so beautiful, that shade of lavender perfect on her. He'd dress her in satins and velvets, furs and fine silk but first, he'd undress her, because she was loveliest in nothing at all. If she ever let him close to her again. She must.

At last, after several hours and much spirited debate, some of which he forced himself to speak about, because otherwise, everyone would notice how moonstruck he was, the resplendently liveried footmen cleared the covers and set out the dessert.

The Kirkburtons owned a wonderful set of dessert dishes and figurines. Dishes that represented melons, pears, apples, bunches of celery and asparagus were placed on the table, interspersed with figurines, tonight a set of rural figures, shepherds and shepherdesses, fauns and nymphs, their shapes reflected in the polished gleam of mahogany. Every dish contained a fruit or a sweet, all counter to the containers, so the melon might contain candied lemon slices, the celery a rhubarb compote. Alex took some nuts, which he found in a dish depicting an artichoke and offered some to his companion, who smiled and accepted. The servants brought champagne instead of the usual dessert wine and Lord Downholland got to his feet to begin the toasts.

The bubbles in his glass foamed and sparkled as he lifted it, the candlelight turning it to a bright shimmer., Alex leaned back so he could keep Dankworth in the compass of his gaze while he listened to Lord Downholland. This should prove *very* enjoyable.

The guests fell silent, waiting for the toasts to begin. Usually the ladies would join in a couple, toast the king and their hosts then move to the drawing room. Alex guessed they would prolong that small ritual tonight to include an announcement.

Lord Downholland got to his feet. "My lords, ladies, gentlemen, welcome to the ball tonight. My thanks to the Duke and Duchess of Kirkburton, who have kindly allowed me to lead you in thanks." He toasted. Everyone drank.

Downholland stayed on his feet. "If I may tax your patience a moment longer, I have a small announcement to make. This ball tonight is partly to introduce my goddaughter to the ton and so it seems appropriate. My lady and I have recently made some adjustments to our will." Dankworth smiled indulgently at his fiancée reaching out to touch her hand. He had done that frequently throughout the meal, his touches almost amounting to pawing.

Lord Downholland glanced at him and continued. "Our goddaughter and niece Constance Rattigan has been like a true daughter to us, especially since the sad demise of her father some years ago. We have always welcomed her whenever she chose to visit us. We have been considering how to show Constance how much we care for her and her happiness." Jasper's smile froze and he shot a sharp glare at Connie. Downholland gave Connie a fond smile, which she returned. "Consequently, we have decided that she should receive the bulk of our estate on my death, apart from a few personal bequests."

Dankworth's jaw dropped. Apart from that, he sat completely still.

"We will, of course, offer Mrs. Rattigan a home with us if she should wish it and a commensurate amount on her marriage, should she wish to enter that estate for a second time." Lord Dankworth glanced around, and sat.

Silence fell then Lady Stobart laughed, a little too shrilly.

Alex groused to himself. What Lord Downholland had said was, "Here's my goddaughter. She's rich, she's single, so have at her, lads." Undoubtedly what would happen once they entered the ballroom. Word would flow from here to there seamlessly.

The attention of the dinner guests went from Lord Downholland to his nephew, to a softly blushing Connie and back to his lordship.

The complete omission of his name had struck Dankworth dumb.

The Duke and Duchess appeared unsurprised but he'd expect that anyway. The old buzzard—her, not him—never showed a scintilla of emotion. Alex doubted she had any, other than the passionate desire to control everything and everyone who came her way. He met his father's gaze and the old main raised a brow. Alex nodded. He hadn't told his father the news, he had no right to but now surely his old man wouldn't object to his courting Connie.

Julius raised his glass and smiled at Connie. "Congratulations, my dear. I can't imagine it happening to a better person. I'm sure you'll take care of your inheritance." He drank and that broke the spell.

The other people did the same, inured by years of good manners and childhood training.

The duchess regarded Connie with fresh appreciation, visibly assessing as a future asset for her family, as did many others here tonight.

Alex was part of her family, her sister's son and the duchess was nothing if not dynastically minded. He could use this and he had every intention of doing so. Her approval would go a long way towards furthering his case and Connie's acceptance in society. Especially since Julius wouldn't enter the lists against him and Julius's brother was currently away from home, visiting a friend in Rome.

Lines of fury delineated Dankworth's face. He set his jaw and lifted his glass with everyone else, and after a few minutes, actually found something to say. "Congratulations, dear Connie. I'm deeply jealous but maybe you need the estate more than I do."

Because if he married his seventeen-year-old heiress, he could bring his estate right up to scratch.

After a couple more toasts, the ladies left the room. Alex watched Connie go, her shapely body beautifully on show tonight, if not as beautifully as he could remember that time at Mother Dawkins's. His groin ached from need of her.

The gentlemen lingered long enough to discuss the Parliamentary war in more detail and hash out where each of them stood on the recent turmoil. Allies must be made and in the next few weeks, the coffeehouses, dining rooms and clubs would be abuzz.

Alex had already decided to support the irascible Pitt as the best of the worst but he had also made up his mind not to tell anyone yet. Besides, he had no seat in the Commons or the Lords, so his support was merely influence. He prided himself that he had some of that. For all his self-imposed indolence, when he spoke, people listened.

Except for one exasperating woman who thought she could tame him. And the worst of it was that she was right. If she crooked her finger, he'd arrive at her side like a panting dog, eager for the smallest titbit.

After an hour, they joined the ladies in the drawing room. On the surface, the scene appeared perfectly civilized, with a young woman playing the harpsichord and pretty groupings sitting in the arrangement of sofas and chairs, chatting in low voices. Nobody shouted, nobody showed any obvious passion, and the harpsichord player had another young woman standing just behind her, to turn the pages of the music. Zoffany would have made a charming conversation piece from the scene. He'd have begged to do it, because this room contained some of the wealthiest and most influential people in the country.

Only nothing was ever that simple. The groupings told some of the story, with the mothers only concerned with matching their daughters sitting together, no doubt discussing the latest prospects, which would include him, others discussing the political situation, some just gossiping. And a group that fell silent for a second or two when he entered, then hastily talked about something else.

They had a couple of hours before the first guests would arrive for the ball. Alex accepted tea, not his beverage of choice for the evening. He wanted to space out his drinks tonight. He'd need all his wits about him for what lay ahead.

The news was probably winging its way around London even now, transported by the servants who were standing silently in the dining room but they had ears. It would bring the fortune hunters slavering at Connie's heels.

He crossed the room to stand behind her chair. Since she was sitting next to Helena, Julius joined him, leaning his hand down to press his sister's shoulder gently. Alex had no right to touch Connie in that way. Not yet. And at the moment she'd flinch away from him.

He would just have to gaze his fill on her pearly skin and the brooch he'd sent her glittering from under its veil of lace. At least he had that and her tolerance of him standing just behind her, watching her. He enjoyed the artistry that had led her to mask the brightness of the cut with lace. He'd give her more diamonds. He'd promised and she would have them.

Helena lifted her hand and covered her brother's, so briefly it was hardly a gesture at all and anyone not watching them would have missed it. "So are you for Pitt?" Julius asked.

Alex grinned. "What do you think?"

"I think he lives on Brook Street and his house has been very busy of late. And yes, I'm for Pitt but I'm also for Newcastle. He's a steadying influence and we need that now."

"And the Jacobites?"

"Where there's a Jacobite, there's a scheme," he said promptly. They had every reason to know that. "Not the spent force some people believe them to be. There's still a lot of support in the country."

"The Tories are moving away from them," Julius remarked. He was gathering opinion, offering leading questions to assess the views of people around him.

"I love this."

Connie had spoken quietly but Alex remained attuned to her every word. He wasn't even sure she'd meant to speak aloud. "What do you love?"

"The discussions and knowing the people you're talking to have a real influence on how the world works. It's exciting." She flicked open her fan and employed it vigorously. "I should claim that I'm bored, shouldn't I?"

She turned her head and glanced up at Julius, carefully avoiding looking into Alex's eyes. Good, that was good. He still affected her, she still cared enough not to meet his eyes coldly. "Enjoying the view, Lord Ripley?"

"Immensely." Why should he hide it?

"What do we do now? About—the announcement?"

Alex spoke calmly. "You'll stand with Lord and Lady Downholland when they greet people. Then you let me lead you out for the first dance."

"That would be too particular, my lord. Besides, his grace has already asked me to dance with him." She fanned. He'd made her blush after all. Ah well, a man could try.

Later, when they moved to the extremely large salon set out for tonight as a ballroom, Julius escorted her and didn't leave her until she was standing by her aunt's side. Alex ostensibly chatted to several people but took a position where he could keep her in his sights. If that bastard Dankworth addressed one foul word to her, he'd beat him senseless.

Dankworth must have known, because when he did exchange a few words with her, Connie was poised and gracious.

Alex was proud of her.

They only stayed until the small orchestra engaged for the occasion began to play. Then Lord and Lady Downholland, Dankworth and Louisa and the Duke of Kirkburton and Connie led out the dancing.

Connie danced adequately. She didn't have the sweet elegance and delicacy that other dancers had and Alex could swear she was minding her steps under her breath. Her mouth moved once or twice.

The ball led out with two minuets. Connie danced them both but with different partners. Alex bided his time. He'd been close to her, smelled her sweetness, heard her voice and that had to be enough for now. Unless Dankworth touched her, of course.

Her partner led her towards her godparents but Dankworth intercepted them. Alex moved fast, and murmured a hasty excuse to the people he was standing with. He scooted across the side of the ballroom in her directions. Interested murmurs followed and he heard a few snatches of conversation. "Ballroom steeplechase," was the gist of them.

He wasn't doing that nonsense tonight. Probably never again, as it happened, because others had taken up the sport and they were growing a trifle tedious. Besides, he wouldn't do that to Connie. This was her night.

But he was too late.

Dankworth had already led Connie on to the floor. They went through the careful, elegant steps of the bourré, making the required pattern while people murmured in their wake.

"Heir,"

"Marriage,"

"Possible match."

Alex wanted to stamp his foot and scream like a small child. Or hit someone hard like a bad-tempered adult.

Neither would help, but at least he'd have the sting of pain to distract him from his heartache as Jasper Dankworth guided Connie around the floor and people speculated about a future match between them. After all, it would be a practical move and perhaps the Downhollands meant for it to happen and were just providing Connie with a suitable portion to bring to her marriage. So they said.

Much they knew.

The dance had an elaborate pattern, which the dancers must execute. Alex had already worked out where they would end up and he was careful to station himself there.

Dankworth bowed to her, murmuring.

Connie glanced at Alex, then back at Jasper, so it wasn't difficult to guess what he'd asked her.

Miss Stobart in a fetching pink gown stood before him. "Why, Lord Ripley, how pleasant to see you again."

He couldn't ignore her. He bowed over her hand and reconciled himself to half an hour of tedium. He felt compelled to lead her on to the floor for the next dance, another bourré. Not to do so would have given her a snub and much though he wished she'd find someone else to chase, he wouldn't wish her to be known as one of the women Alex Ripley had snubbed. Not that he'd snubbed that many. He'd left that to Julius.

Miss Stobart kept glancing in Alex's direction but she danced as well as any society lady and unfortunately, she didn't have to mind her steps, so she had no distraction to stop her flirting and sending him seductive smiles and glances. She'd been performing the formal courtly dances since she was a small child, so she did it as well as she could flirt. Better.

Her skirt swayed enticingly and when the dance called for it, she curtseyed with grace. She'd make some man a perfectly adequate wife. Just not him. She tried all the weapons in her armory. She'd already tugged down her bodice to allow him to see more than her cleavage and now she glanced up at him, gave him a small, secretive smile and let her hand linger in his a tiny bit too long.

After the dance, when he would have bowed to her, she placed her hand on his arm and leaned forward, as if sharing a confidence. "Would you escort me to my mother?" She looked around. "I don't see her here but she might be sitting in the far corner. Would you mind, sir?"

Frantically Alex looked around for someone else to perform the task. He couldn't bear this. If he didn't speak to Connie soon, he'd explode. He imagined pieces of green velvet and human flesh scattered around the ballroom for people to exclaim over. But he dismissed the vision and concentrated on his task. The sooner he could do as she asked, the sooner he could go in search of Connie.

Miss Stobart led him around the ballroom and they had traversed three sides of it before they discovered her mother, talking to her friends in a corner of the ballroom. He had to conclude that his erstwhile dance partner had known where to find her mother and deliberately led him the wrong way. She'd chattered and flirted the whole time, until his head rang with words but he had no idea what she'd said. She'd tapped his arm with her fan, flicked it open as if sharing secrets from behind it and generally made play, so it appeared they were intimate, friendly to the point of being closer.

Damn it.

When he'd extricated himself from the Stobarts' clutches, he headed off at a pace to find Connie. And nearly bumped into her. She was standing to one side of the room, chatting to a lady he vaguely recognized. When he reached her side, he remembered where he'd seen the lady before, and who she was. He swept into a deep bow. "Your highness, how good to see you here."

Princess Amelia graciously inclined her head. "I find I enjoy the company of Mrs. Rattigan. She is a lady of great good sense." From the princess, that was great praise. She rarely gave compliments. "You must visit us in Ealing, Lord Ripley. We have always found you most amusing."

He could hardly excuse himself from her presence. Royal protocol demanded that he remained until she dismissed him or moved on but at least Connie was stuck, too. The band struck up for a country-dance, a lively tune and Alex tapped a foot to the rhythm.

Princess Amelia continued to discuss the weather and then the rights of the common man to go where he would, despite damaging valuable property. After her attempt to restrict access to Windsor Great Park a few years ago, she'd taken the cause for her own. As arrogant as most of the royal family but with a kindness some of them lacked, Alex found her tolerable. Eventually she got the gentle hint.

"You should dance," she said as the country-dance came to a close. "Here is your partner, my lord."

"A royal decree, my dear." With another bow, he turned to Connie and offered her the support of his arm. He led her on to the floor.

With the ball well under way, people were moving around more freely. "I had no idea who she was," Connie confessed. "I nearly made the most dreadful faux-pas." Then she glared at him. "I still haven't forgiven you."

"I would appreciate a few words in private," he said.

She pokered up. "I hardly think that would be a good idea."

"Please?"

"No."

So much for begging. He tried another tack. "If you do not, I'll say what I have to in the middle of the dance floor. I'll sweep you off your feet and propose extravagantly. See if that won't start a rash of men proposing to you. You're an heiress now, Connie and the hounds are off the leash."

She choked but she had no time to reply, for the dance was starting and when they executed the first steps, she fell to glaring at him again.

The good thing about a country-dance was that couples could leave the floor part way through and not interfere with the more boisterous romping. The bad part was that a couple wouldn't spend the whole of a dance together. This was one of those dances, when they changed partners and eventually met up with each other again right at the end. Alex kept his attention firmly fixed on her. When he could do it without his manners falling short, he caught her gaze and it was as if that instant of perfect shock happened again, just like the first time they met, as intense as ever. Surely, she couldn't ignore that pull between them.

But she could. At the end of the dance, she was forced to hold his hands while they danced down the floor together, with the others forming an arch then formed their place in the arch, fingers linked. When it was done, he didn't release her so she could applaud, but dragged her closer and laid her hand firmly on his arm.

The call came from the end of the room. "My lords and ladies, supper is served."

"Are you hungry?" he murmured to her.

She had to lean closer to hear him, which had been his objective in not speaking up. "No."

"Then come." He tried to lead her in the opposite direction to the supper room. "Or should I make good on my promise?"

"You wouldn't."

"Try me."

She sighed and gave in, letting him take her out of the room.

Chapter 19

Alex knew Kirkburton House well and without hesitation, he led her to a small salon on the same floor as the one where the ball was taking place but not opened for tonight's festivities. He had the key, purloined from one of the footmen in return for a hefty vail. The bribe had also paid for several lit candles, set in candelabra placed on the furniture around the room.

The room was formally arranged, the effect gloomy, with heavy, William Kent furniture, the upholstery and drapery dark green, relieved only a little by mustard.

Not the best surroundings but he didn't care. They were on their own for the first time that evening and the relief overwhelmed him, rushing in on him like the unstoppable tide. He clenched his fists, hiding them behind him. She turned with a smile, one he wanted to kiss off her face. "They'll miss us if we take too long."

"I waited. They've been dancing and drinking, they've spread all over the public rooms. They'll all think you're in another room. The shock of the announcement has worn off a little and they're talking about it."

Her smile turned wry. "I should have known you'd have considered all that."

He opened his hands, and spread them before him. "That's what I am." It was important she understood that, considering what he was about to say. "But sometimes I do go too far. As I did with you. I'm sorry, Connie, more than I can say."

She folded her arms. "What are you sorry for?"

He might have known she'd want him to talk it out with her. Any other woman would have counted the apology as done but she wanted to pin him down. She wanted him on his knees? Then he'd do it. Whatever she wanted.

"I'm sorry I didn't consult you before I confronted Dankworth. But I'm not sorry I confronted him. You couldn't have helped, Connie. I did it playing piquet with him, a two-player game and in any case, I did it at Mother Dawkins's. He needed bringing down. He was upsetting a lot of people, not just you and me. Considering I never intended to force him to make good on his debts, he got off lightly, better than if some others had got hold of him. Connie, will you accept my apology? I'll do whatever you want."

A smile curled her lips and relief swept through him. "Anything?"

"Anything," he said firmly. "I know you asked me and I promised. I should have visited you and discussed it first. But the opportunity arose and I did it." He paused and yes, he had to tell her anything. "You no doubt heard that Julius and I were attacked in the street by footpads."

"Yes I did." He hoped it was anxiety for him that shaded her gaze now.

"It wasn't footpads, it was paid ruffians. Dankworth had paid them to do it. Oh, they mentioned a shady overlord but I believe that was an attempt to set us off the trail. If he'd take that risk, he must be getting desperate, I thought. I wanted to speed matters up. Get him gone. That's why I didn't have time to tell you about my plan to take him."

"You should have told me." She frowned, seemed to recall it would crease her face powder. "I was worried about you."

She glanced away, bit her bottom lip and released the plump morsel pinker than before. He wanted to soothe it, then arouse it, coax it to open for him. Yes, anything. He'd say anything if she'd come closer, if she'd let him kiss her.

"I've never wanted to protect someone so much before. And I know it's irrational sometimes and I know it's wrong because I promised you but it's done now and I want your forgiveness."

Was that a smile that flickered across her face so briefly? "There is a way you can earn forgiveness."

"What? Tell me." He dared to reach forward and grasp her hands. She let her fingers lay in his palms and he loosely closed his fingers over them, covering her but she could pull away any time she wanted to. She chose not to.

"Promise to remember that I prefer to make decisions for myself. Never do it again."

He tugged and she took a step closer, so that the front of her gown brushed the fall of his breeches. His cock came to instant attention. "I promise. But you have to be there to ensure I never do it again, don't you?"

"Ah." She hadn't thought of that. Doubt clouded the guileless blue of her eyes.

Softly, he drew her closer, heard the *shush* of her gown as her skirts compressed against him. "You'll have to stay with me, just to be sure I'm not doing something to protect you. Hiding the truth."

As her mouth opened to reply, he stopped it with his lips.

After one languorous kiss, he drew away, opened his eyes and gazed down at her face. He never wanted to see anyone like this again, except her. Her eyes glowed, her skin begged for his touch, his kiss. He could do nothing but oblige. Her mouth opened as he touched her lips, inviting him inside. There was no way on earth he could resist her now. He was lost and he rejoiced in the fact. Hunger for her rose and overwhelmed him, destroying sense and gentility.

* * * *

Connie couldn't refuse him. It was some kind of spell, the result of his years of seducing women, of learning their ways. But this was special, it belonged to them alone. She'd let herself believe it. He'd said all the right things, except for the last, which her mind tussled with while her body slid into unimaginable delight. He slid his hands around her waist, urged her to step back but he came with her, his aroused body pressing against her, revealing in explicit detail what he felt for her right this minute.

Between her thighs, her body melted for him. Her breath came sharper and she exhaled down her nose as he kissed her, longing for his touch, everywhere.

When the sharp realization came to her, she'd gone too far to care. She felt him so well because he'd lifted her skirts and only a few layers remained between them and nakedness.

They couldn't do this now. She jerked away, staring up at him in shock.

He trailed his fingers down her cheek. "Hush, sweetheart. I'm going mad for you here. You've bewitched me completely. Let me have a taste, a small flavor of paradise." His low growl vibrated against her neck when he kissed it, tongued the pulse at the base, which was throbbing so hard she could hardly breathe.

He pushed the lace aside and kissed the upper slopes of her bosom, long and lavishly. Her nipples hardened into sensitivity and the soft silk of her stays felt like sand when she moved restlessly. He groaned and lifted a breast free, drawing her nipple into his mouth with a hunger only rivalled by hers. She wanted him to touch her more than she wanted her next breath.

Tingles spread through her, increasing in intensity, so she reached out and gripped. Her hands met velvet and the buckram shaping his coat scrunched under her fingers.

"Hold on to me," he murmured, his breath hot against her skin.

With a movement she hadn't expected and couldn't have stopped if she had, he went down on to one knee and kissed her thigh, high up, close to where she wanted him. Sensation shivered through her body, rendering her helpless.

He held her legs, pushed her against the wall behind them and then reached for something and dragged it across the polished floorboards. "Lift up, precious."

He grasped her ankle, lifted it and put it down on what felt like a small footstool. That meant her legs were open to him and he could see everything, do what he wanted. Oh, that made her melt. Already the tops of her thighs were wet with her arousal. He could do anything to her, no matter how undignified she looked. She even helped him by scooping up handfuls of her skirts and holding them out of the way. She'd missed him, missed this, and if he stopped now she'd kill him.

He kissed her, his tongue flickering against her as he tasted her most intimate juices, sliding along the crease at the heart of her body.

Thrills spread up her spine, and she clenched and unclenched her hands. He licked, and she pressed closer. "More," she said, her voice breathless.

He obliged.

She cried out and lifted a fist to push it into her mouth, afraid someone might hear, heedless that the movement lifted her skirts even further, exposing more of her body to him. He could have it all, if he carried on doing this marvelous thing she had no name for, if he never, ever, stopped drinking from her and teasing her with the tip of his tongue.

Then he took that knot he'd told her was her clitoris into his mouth. She sobbed as shards of agony shot through her. Agonizing pleasure, such that she writhed against him, trying to get away then pushed closer.

The pleasure coalesced, became an impetus she couldn't deny. He continued his wonderful torture, holding her steady but driving her into such bliss that she leaned back, her head thudding against the paneled wall behind her head.

Mercilessly he worked her, heightening the sensations until she thought she couldn't bear any more then she *knew* she couldn't bear any more and then she hung, pausing for one fraught, unbelievable moment before she fell.

Plunged into the abyss, landed on a hard surface, bounced. She opened her hands, reached, clutched, found something soft, something she pushed aside and vaguely registered a *thump* before she found purchase in the short strands of his midnight hair.

He pushed fingers into her, how many she couldn't tell and she clenched viciously against them, cried his name and let him take her wherever he wanted.

She couldn't fight it anymore. She was his.

A sharp sound rent the air when he pulled away, cursed softly when she took a few strands of his hair, too sluggish to release him in time and then stood to catch her as she almost fell into his arms, helpless in her excess of passion.

He half carried, half dragged her to the nearest sofa and leaned her against the rigid back, while he put her and himself to rights. She watched him in a dream as her throbbing body returned to normal. Let him care for her.

He tucked her breast back into her bodice, lingering to deliver one last kiss to the upper curve, then fluffed her skirts before smoothing them back into place over her elegant side-hoops one by one, ensuring they were all straight. It was more than she could do. He'd make a good lady's maid.

"How did you learn to do that?"

His eyes widened and he stared at her. "That's new to you?"

She shook her head in disbelief. She hadn't imagined it possible. "Nobody—that is, John, my husb—"

He put one hand over her lips. "Connie, no. Don't call him that."

"But that's what he was."

"Was, sweetness, was." He glanced down and frowned. "Damn, I thought I heard a rip. I've torn the lower flounce of your petticoat. Do you have pins?"

"Of course." She reached into her pocket and found the small packet that most women had about them for just such an emergency. He took it with a smile. "Now what did you do with my wig?" He looked around. "Ah yes." He picked it up and paused before a large pier-glass ensuring it was properly in place. It took him but a second or two, then he was back with her, kneeling at her feet and lifting her petticoat but not for the same reason he had done earlier.

The door opened.

Connie, lost in a dream, started in alarm. He stared up at her, a warning in his dark eyes. She had to trust him now, because that was what he was asking her. To trust him.

Expressions of shock marked the various people crowding around the doorway. Some smiled. They were crowding in to view her downfall. At their head stood Miss Stobart, triumph on her face. "I knew they'd come in here." she said shrilly. "I saw them. He makes a habit of luring females into empty rooms at balls. Or maybe *she* lured *him*, don't you think, sir?"

She'd brought Lord Downholland with her. Her last attempt to regain the inheritance for her betrothed. Lord Downholland merely stared at them.

What astonished Connie was the sight of Alex swiftly closing his hand over the packet of pins. They were his excuse. He only had to say he was helping her mend her skirt and he was free to leave, unhindered.

He stayed where he was, kneeling before her.

Heat flooded through her when she realized what the people staring at them would think. By not insisting they lock the door, she'd taken the decision away from him, just as he had her, even though she hadn't meant to do it. He didn't look as unhappy as she imagined he would.

"I hadn't planned to perform this before an audience."

Amusement lacing his low tones, he turned back to her. He took one of her hands and placed a kiss on the back of it, then retained it, pressing it warmly between his own. "Mrs. Rattigan, would you do me the honor of becoming my wife?"

She gaped then remembered to close her mouth. It took her a moment to find her voice. "You can't mean that." Not in public, where her rejection could mean his public ridicule.

"Never more serious. You have stolen my heart and my senses. I want nothing more in this world. Please say yes."

His gentle urging melted her but it was the expression in his eyes that convinced her. He meant it. This wasn't for sport, wasn't to avenge himself against Miss Stobart, wasn't because he'd been forced into this situation in any way. He meant every word.

And because she wanted this more than anything else in her life, she said, "Yes. Yes please. Oh, Alex!"

He got to his feet, clasping her hands.

She wanted more, to celebrate the moment with a full embrace. She laughed shakily. "I should have said, 'Lord Ripley, you honor me with your proposal. I can do nothing but accept your most flattering offer.'"

She tore her gaze away from his, to her godfather. "Will you say I said that the first time, if you please?"

Miss Stobart colored an interesting shade of plum and she'd forgotten to school her expression. She scowled, revealing her age, appearing as nothing more than a child in her mother's clothes.

Connie almost felt sorry for her, but Louisa's act of spite negated that. "Well what did you expect?" she snapped. "For his lordship to get to his feet and walk away? Do you really know him so little?"

Stobart really was a stupid woman. Or wilfully blind, which amounted to the same thing.

Alex wouldn't have left her. She'd seen his sincerity. He would have asked her, had perhaps been planning to all along. If she'd seen any doubt in his face, any at all, she'd have refused him. That would have been acceptable, except they'd been alone but she was a widow, not an innocent miss and a little latitude could be allowed before she would have compromised herself.

They could have pulled it off. Nobody would have known what had transpired here tonight. But he'd wanted to and the thought warmed her from the inside out.

"Do you wish us to announce the happy event tonight?" asked Lord Winterton.

She hadn't noticed him coming in. Strange how a man dressed so flamboyantly could move so discreetly when he wanted to.

"If you wish it. I think it might be best, because I have plans for our marriage sooner rather than later." Alex glanced at her, smiling fondly. "Now I have her, I'm not letting her go."

She saw an intent in his gaze she wasn't at all sure about but the dark, glowing promise heated her desires.

Julius took her free hand and bowed over it formally. "May I be the first to offer my heartiest congratulations?" He turned. "Perhaps we could leave the happy couple with Lord Downholland to hammer out the details." He walked towards the door and then turned back at the last moment, as the spectators had reluctantly filed out. "I haven't congratulated my best friend and one of my dearest new friends." He offered his hand and wrung Alex's comprehensively when he gave him it. "You won't regret it." He released Alex and leaned in to kiss her cheek. "Welcome to the family, Connie. Such as it is."

She noticed the subtle but delicious scent of citrus and musk. On the whole, she preferred Alex's scent. Alex smelled of male arousal and sandalwood. It aroused her just thinking of it.

Julius turned and left.

Alex gazed down at her, smiling. "I want the wedding as soon as possible. Do you have anything planned for tomorrow?"

She gaped at him for a bare moment.

Her godfather took that moment to speak. "It might have escaped your notice but tomorrow is Sunday, so you can't marry then. But you can sign the contract on Monday, if I call on my man of business. I had one drawn up for Connie's marriage to—" He cleared his throat. "It was a fair and reasonable contract and we may, if you like, use it as the basis for the new one."

Alex gave a nod. "Then that's what we do." He spared Lord Downholland a glance. "Without that morality clause. I want Connie cared for and sure she's going into the marriage with all her rights protected. We'll marry on Tuesday."

"Sir, the banns!" Lord Downholland protested.

"I have a special license. I obtained it when I arrived in London from the visit to your house. It has Connie's name on it. My other task for tomorrow is to arrange for the ceremony."

"Alex, are you…" Connie tried, overwhelmed by the speed of events and her own emotions.

"Perfectly." He raised her hand and kissed it. "I should also inform my father. I told him of my intention to court you, so this won't come as a surprise to him."

"He's on his way," said Lady Downholland as she entered the room. "Word is already spreading but I sent a messenger to the house he is visiting tonight." She swept forward and enclosed an overwhelmed Connie into her soft, scented embrace.

Connie didn't think she could take much more. Her head spun with recent developments. She'd reconciled herself to going home to Cumbria, managing without Jasper and most of all without Alex. Now she doubted she'd see her house in some time, or, from the way Alex was looking at her, anywhere but the inside of a bedchamber. She didn't feel sorry about that part at all.

"We should steel ourselves for the congratulations of our friends and acquaintances." Alex lifted his arm, an invitation for her to rest the tips of her fingers on his forearm. Instead, she put her palm over it and squeezed a little. She needed proper support and she needed to know that he was under all that magnificence. Some connection with reality. "Shall we face the terrifying marauding hordes?"

The thought of comparing polite society to ancient warrior tribes made her smile and she was still smiling when he took her back into the main room. Although they were not so vulgar as to give them a round of applause, Connie felt the approbation of several people, mostly the ones without eligible females in their immediate family. Several congratulated them as they moved through the crowd, Connie inching a little closer to Alex as they passed through to the supper room and Alex found cool glasses of wine for them both. In that short journey, Connie began to grow aware of what it would be like to not only be the wife of Alex as Lady Ripley but in time, the Countess of Leverton. She didn't know how she felt about any of it but decided to give herself time, not to accept it all so quickly.

Except that on Tuesday, dreams would become reality.

Julius appeared, a plateful of delicacies in his hand. "I ordered this made up for you."

Immediately Alex led her to a table and made her sit. "I should have thought of that."

Julius grinned. "I think I know why you didn't." He reached out and when Alex held out his hand, Julius dropped a key into it. "I don't use it much these days. It's yours, if you wish. Although I know you don't care about discretion, I think Connie might."

"Thank you, Julius."

"We'll expect you when we see you, Connie." He bent and brushed his lips over her hand. "Welcome to our distinctly odd and reprehensible family."

"Thank you."

Alex glanced at her and leaned closer to speak to her alone. "Would you stay with me tonight?" Considering the measure of interest shown in them by the other people in the room he took a considerable risk even saying that much.

Her mind went back to those blissful hours in the small room in the house in Covent Garden. She could be true to her upbringing or true to her heart. "Yes."

"Then we leave soon."

"Yes." She wanted to bury her face in the welcome darkness of his coat, forget everything else except him.

She applied herself to the food Julius had thoughtfully acquired for her and she was just finishing the last tiny pastry when Alex, who had been conversing quietly with Julius said, "Ah, father."

She found a napkin and touched it to her mouth before glancing up. She'd never thought of Lord Leverton as formidable before, but she did now.

Clad in the society wear of elaborate, flared coat, embroidered waistcoat, breeches and clocked stockings, Lord Leverton looked like what he was, an aristocrat, born of aristocrats, sure of his place in the world.

All things that Connie was not. She stumbled when she got to her feet and Alex was quick to cup her elbow and steady her.

"Tomorrow, Ripley, I want to speak to you."

"Yes, sir. Mrs. Rattigan is staying here tonight as the guest of the duke and duchess. She is tired by the day's events and she needs to rest."

Leverton nodded. "I see. Very well."

"You might want to attend the Downhollands' house at noon on Monday, sir. We're signing the contract. We've agreed to marry on Tuesday."

Chapter 20

It appeared someone had apprised the Duchess of Kirkburton of Connie's presence in her house that night. She also knew about Alex. The subtle way the lady glanced at him after she said she was delighted to offer the shelter of her humble house to a weary guest—all said in the iciest tones—told her that. A maid took her to the room and she wasn't entirely surprised to find Saxton there.

She'd brought Connie's nightclothes, her dressing case and a change of clothes for the morning. "They said to bring them here, ma'am. I'm to sleep upstairs." She usually slept in a room close to Connie's but this wasn't an ordinary London town house. This was more like a grand country house somehow transposed to the city. A very grand house.

On her journey here from the main state rooms Connie had glimpsed the gleam of gold in rooms quiet and unoccupied and the glitter of crystal. This room was just as grand, dominated by a huge four-poster, made of old wood heavily carved and gilded. The rest of the furniture was to match, with heavy red velvet drapery. Worse, it was all spotless, even under the bed. That meant the duchess was a hard mistress, something Connie had suspected once she'd met the diminutive virago.

Saxton divested Connie of her evening clothes, helped her into her night-rail and a loose robe and washed the powder out of her hair and the cosmetics from her face.

Feeling better, more like herself, Connie leaned back in the chair before the dressing table, with its formidable array of crystal bottles and silver brushes and pots and closed her eyes to allow Saxton to brush her hair and braid it ready for the night. She still wondered what she was doing here and if he would come but at least she had some respite to try to make sense of her life. "You're a good lady's maid, Saxton."

"Thank you," said a warm male voice she knew well.

She jerked forward, yanking the brush from her hair. "Where's my maid?"

"If you want her back, I'll call her for you." His eyes gleamed.

"She won't gossip."

"I know that but it went against the grain for me to creep in once she'd gone and you were in bed. You're mine, Connie. After Tuesday I'll have the right to say so publicly."

A thrill passed right through her but she suppressed it and tried to think of the practical. "You meant it? Tuesday?"

"Assuredly. I'd do it on Monday if I could but I want to ensure it's all done as it should be. But tonight, sweetheart, belongs to us."

"What would her grace say if she caught us?" Despite her determination to face this business like the lady she would shortly become, Connie quailed at the thought of it.

"That's the beauty of this room," Alex said. "When Julius lived here, he chose this room for a reason. Most of the rooms in this house communicate in a way that the maids can go from room to room in the morning and clean more efficiently. But this room is at the corner of the house and it only has three doors. The jib door, which I'll lock, the outer door, which I'll also lock and the powder room door, which is a dead end. No way in except through this room. Nobody comes in here, except the people I say and you'll be perfectly safe. With me."

He leaned forward and put the brush down on the table, the click sounding unnaturally loud in the quiet room. He swept her hair aside and touched his lips to her neck. "Or you can sleep alone and I won't come near you again until Tuesday night. If that's what you want." He straightened. "You see? I'm doing my best to give you the choices you ask for."

That surprised a laugh out of her. "You'll kill yourself if you keep on doing it." She got to her feet and turned to face him, one hand on the back of the chair. "Alex, be yourself. It's you I want. We might argue and I'm sure we will but I don't want you to be—careful—around me."

He stiffened, gazed at her. Anyone seeing him now wouldn't recognize him as the indolent aristocrat. Every line of his body was taut and tense, his eyes wild with need, the same need she was experiencing. "Beware of what you ask for. I have never felt so powerfully for any woman before in my life."

"I am. I want you. All of you."

He remained very, very still, so much that she knew he was fighting not to reach out for her, because when he did, there wouldn't be any more talking for a long time. "You'll get it, Connie my love."

Something took hold of her heart and her breath stuttered. This wasn't a figure of speech or a casual endearment. "Wh-what did you say?"

"You heard but just in case, I'll make it clear." He gazed into her eyes, sincerity patently obvious. "I love you, Connie. I started to fall in love with you the moment I saw you. Every day since has only confirmed it." He grinned, his body more relaxed now. "You have to forgive me, sweetheart but I doubted what my heart was telling me. I didn't believe that it could be possible. But it is and now I don't want to wait to marry you a moment longer than I have to." He reached out and caught her hand, twining his fingers between hers. "You don't have to say anything in return. I want the truth, Connie, no more. No lies, ever, between us."

"Not even a tiny lie about a gown costing half what it actually did?" She knew her mother had done that to her father a time or two. He'd recounted it to her fondly, trying to remind her that her late mother wasn't a saint but a human being.

He grinned, gave her the bright, devil-may-care smile that lit up a room for her. "I might allow that. Neither of us are saints. But the truth, the honesty of our feelings. That I want clear."

"So if I confess I love you, will you believe me?"

"I'll believe you and be glad to."

She gathered all her courage together, feeling the tension tighten. She'd told one other man that and been proved wrong. This time she was certain. "I love you, Alex. Though perhaps not as long as you've loved me. It was our first kiss that made me realize what life without you would mean."

He tugged her hand, urging her closer. "What would it mean?"

"Boredom. Toleration, or so I thought at the time. When Jasper asked to visit my room but went to London instead, all I felt was relief. That was when I knew I didn't want to marry him, but I had committed myself by then so I could say nothing."

Alex's dark eyes gleamed with incipient ire but he cupped her cheek gently. "I wouldn't have allowed it. I felt jealous when I had no right to be. When I heard he'd become engaged to Miss Stobart, I was glad and angry. It meant she wasn't pursuing me anymore, but I couldn't wish the fate of Jasper Dankworth on anyone. My father isn't exactly pleased I'm marrying you but he can do nothing about it and I want you, Connie. For my own, to have the right to care for and love."

He lowered his head and kissed her. Gently at first, testing her lips, his tongue touching her, exploring. She opened her mouth and he slipped in. Not passionately, so much as lovingly. Appropriate for their first kiss after confessing their love.

She knew what he meant. There was no doubt possible between them. She could ask herself why, try to reason but it wouldn't work because it just was. It existed.

He finished the kiss and gazed at her, his eyes adoring now. "So what do you want for tonight, my love? Would you prefer to spend three nights on your own, waiting for our wedding night?"

She shook her head. "How foolish that would be, when I have you now. Will we have separate rooms after we're married? Will you behave like a polite husband and ask permission to visit my chamber?"

"No." He grinned. "If you're expecting that, you're in for a disappointment, my lady. Separate rooms, yes, because you will have a mountain of gowns and jewelry to store and care for. You'll have levées, when the petitioners and dressmakers will visit you in your chamber." He touched his lips to hers and smiled tenderly. "It's not compulsory. At least, the levée part isn't. The gowns and the jewels I'm afraid you'll have to put up with. But there's no reason we can't spend every night in each other's arms."

He put her away a little and touched the brooch, which she'd pinned to her robe after Saxton had helped her to undress. "This gave me hope that you'd forgiven me. But we can dispose of it for the time being, can't we?"

Careful not to let the pin prick her, he unfastened the brooch and laid it on the dressing table behind them. Her robe was easily dispensed with, as it fastened only with a couple of toggled frogs at her neck and a sash at her waist. That left her in her virginal white night-rail.

He undid the buttons at her neck and cuffs and pulled it over her head. She only moved to lift her arms. Her hair, still unbound, fell in a cascade around her shoulders and halfway down her back.

"You know you're beautiful." He watched her, his cheekbones tinged with pink, his eyes gleaming with desire.

She shook her head. "Not to everyone. But that I am to you is more than enough."

"I'll have the world declare you a beauty. They'll all see what I do." He paused, touched the tip of her nipple, which beaded at his command. "Not quite all. This sight is mine and mine alone." His expression turned fierce. She loved that about him that he didn't hide what he was feeling in front of her, as he did to the rest of the world.

She was naked. He was not. She didn't understand why that made her feel powerful, except, perhaps, that he was letting her know how much her nudity affected him. Always a modest woman, wonder filled her when she realized she wanted to show him her body, to give him the pleasure he so obviously took from her.

He took her hand once more and led her to the high bed. "Get in, sweetheart. I'll join you in a moment."

A small set of steps stood by the side of the old-fashioned bed and she climbed in, pushing down the elaborate coverlet, the blankets and the top sheet. They might need them later but not now. She lay on her side, her cheek propped on her hand, and watched him undress.

He pulled off his dress wig and dropped it on the post of the chair in front of the dressing table. Then he stripped off his neckcloth, winding it around his hands and pulling it taut before smiling at her. "Maybe one day—" he broke off. "What is it?" He tossed the neckcloth to the floor and would have crossed the room to her but she shook her head.

"It doesn't matter. It reminded me of something long ago. Don't ask me now, Alex, please. I'll tell you but not now."

He stared at her, then gave an abrupt nod. "We will speak of it. But, as you say, not now. Because now I want to show you how much I love you. Forget everything else but me, everyone else but me. Because in a way we are starting afresh, are we not? I've never asked anyone to marry me before and—I've never loved anyone like this before."

As he spoke, he removed his heavy evening coat and then his waistcoat, before dragging his shirt over his head and attending to the diamond buckles at his knees, stockings and shoes. His underwear came off with his breeches and then he was as naked as she, his erection rising eagerly to meet her. It bobbed as he approached the bed, climbed the steps and joined her.

His warmth and strength overwhelmed her. If she wanted to, she could melt against him and let him take control but she wanted to show him her love, as he said he wanted to show her.

He rolled her on to her back and she opened her legs to let him kneel between them. He gazed down at her. "If this is the only sight I'm granted for the rest of my life, I'll die happy."

Threading his fingers through her hair, he tugged it gently so it lay across the pillow. "Like a skein of gold. I love that you wear it unpowdered but you look marvelous with it powdered, too. I never expected that. Very dignified, my lady." He paused. "My lady. The more I say it, the more I like the sound of it."

"I am." She reached up and he turned his head, pressed a kiss into the palm. "As you're my lord. My love."

A rush of heat enveloped her as she said it and he bent his head and kissed her. This kiss had less to do with emotion, more of passion. He tasted her, then pushed into her mouth, tasting and exploring, as if he'd never done it before.

She'd fallen in love with him after he'd kissed her for the first time. She'd fall a little bit deeper every time his lips touched hers. Which meant she was already deep and the end of the journey was fathomless, because she intended to keep kissing him for the rest of her life.

He drew away after a long time and gazed at her, his eyes glazed with desire. Lifting her hand, she threaded her fingers through the short strands of his hair. "I love you like this, knowing that I see you at your most intimate."

He chuckled. "It doesn't get much more intimate, my sweet. But I hope I've shown you that I'm never safe." At his reminder of what had happened downstairs, Connie heated and made a small sound at the back of her throat.

His expression softened and he bent, kissed her ear, the hollow below it and down her neck to the spot at the base where she was particularly sensitive. By now, she wanted him, badly. Her body yearned to feel him again, to have him close and then deep inside her body.

Alex wasn't done with caressing her yet. He swept his hand from just under her arm to her hip, stroking her skin into high awareness then returned to her breast, where the movements of his hand were soon joined by his mouth, as he touched tiny kisses to the soft skin there. "So pretty," he murmured. "So tasty." Without warning, he took her nipple deep into her mouth, sucked hard then released it again so cool air washed over the wet tip.

Connie couldn't have repressed her moans if she tried to but now she had the opportunity to make all the noise she wanted to.

"That's it, sweetheart, moan for me. Show me how much you want me."

She cried out when he fingered her other breast, pinched it and then stroked it, so it peaked for him, the tip going tight and hard. When he touched it, his caress was almost unbearable and she wanted him to press harder, stroke her everywhere. Opening her legs wider, modesty abandoned, she pressed her back against the bed and pushed her pelvis up, urging him to take her.

He kissed as far as her navel, licked it and kissed her stomach, before returning to her. His cock stood close to the plush hair between her legs and when she arched, she grazed the damp tip. Now he moaned and kissed her, as she felt his shaft come into contact with her clitoris.

Already those names seemed almost natural to her, the way he'd taught them to her by showing her, exploring her body with the delight she felt when he did it. He lifted her head and watched her. "I live to serve you, my lady." He slid further down, then drew away to do it again. "Do you like that?"

"Oh yes, Alex, yes I do." The movement stimulated the pearl of flesh, made it swell against him, as it had earlier against his tongue.

"One day I might find something you don't like. Until then, we can carry on, trying out positions and going on sensual journeys together. But tonight we're going to make love. Pure and simple."

She curled one arm around his neck, gazed up into his eyes and knew there was nothing simple about Alex Ripley. "I want to feel what it's like to hold you inside me, everything you are."

He slid down once more but this time he slipped inside her. He forged his own way and didn't stop until he had sunk his shaft deep into her body and his balls touched the base of her buttocks. "Everything I am," he murmured. He filled her totally and he watched her as he withdrew and plunged inside, making her his.

Everything outside this room fell away. She'd do anything for him, now and forever and although she knew how dangerous it was to think like that, she still gave herself to him.

His smile told her he knew. "I will serve nobody but you and I will spend the rest of my life showing you how much you mean to me."

He drove inside her. When she responding with a moan, pushing her body up to his, he lifted up to rest on his elbows and changed his position slightly.

That made him graze her sweet spot with every stroke. She cried out, then she arched up. More, she wanted more. Like a helpless addict, she'd take it all and still hunger for more. He gave it to her and took for himself.

"You know how good this feels?" he murmured. "No, how could you? Better than anything else I can remember. My love, oh, my love," which wasn't a very extraordinary thing to say but it pleased her more than she could articulate.

So she showed him. She cupped her breasts, offered them to him, then dragged him close so he could feel her hardened nipples against his chest, rubbed them to increase the sensation, until he groaned and lifted again.

Lynne Connolly

This time he balanced easily on one hand and used the other to touch her clitoris. Shards of heightened awareness radiated through her, and her breath shortened to desperate gasps.

"Ah!" Her cry was sharp and hard, her arousal rocketing into a higher level, something she hadn't thought possible. But he worked her, moved his finger against her clitoris while he thrust in and out in a rhythm she couldn't resist, didn't want to. And all the time she watched him, stared up into those dark, searching eyes, let him see everything he was doing to her. And in return, he opened himself to her. It humbled her, excited her and drove her to the precipice.

He removed his hand and rested his body on his hands, lifting his upper body off hers to drive hard. He watched her breasts as they responded to his drives and she loved the way his gaze heated. Then she forgot everything as her body became his, as she fell into clear space, empty of everything but him and her. She cried his name, screamed, as her body convulsed around him, milked him, the hot spasms of his essence jetted into the depths of her.

He slumped over her and she welcomed his weight but in a moment he rolled away but slung his arm around her waist and took her with him. She snuggled close, lifted one leg to place over his and he kissed her once more. "A busy day," he murmured, "And it's late. Sleep now, darling."

She didn't need any more urging than that. Held safe against his strong body, she slid into the most blissful slumber she could remember.

* * * *

Connie wasn't sure what woke her. She lay in the gloom, not even a fire to light her vision, just the faint outlines of the great bed and the heavy furniture. She blinked and spread her arm to feel the empty space next to her. But it was warm. He hadn't been gone long.

The sound of a door opening startled her and she sat upright, drawing the sheet up around her. But Alex, stark naked and smiling came through the small door he'd told her led to the powder room. "Miss me?"

"I must have because I woke up."

He crossed to a table that held some decanters. "Are you thirsty?"

"Water, something like that?"

He glanced at her and smiled. "No wine to toast our agreement?"

"Not wine."

He laughed softly and poured a glass of rich red wine and another of a pale liquid she only recognized when he gave it to her and she sniffed before drinking. A cordial, like the one her grandmother used to make. The scent of elderflowers took her back to simpler times, when she'd laughed and played in her father's garden, before any cloud had crossed her horizon.

He touched his glass to hers. "To our long and prosperous union. May we give my father a nursery full of children."

Tears filled her eyes and she stared at him as her world tumbled around her. He gently took her glass and put it with his on the table by the bed. Cursing, he climbed off the bed and pulled aside the curtains, which opened on to the back of the house. The pink light of dawn filtered into the room and he would see her tears when he returned to bed.

He took her in his arms. "Now what on earth have I said to upset you, dear heart?"

Before now, she'd thought herself perfectly reconciled to her fate but his reminder brought her sharply down to the earth she should never have left. If this night was all they ever had, it was beautiful. She had never told him, assuming they'd never come to this point but they had.

He stroked her but he paused when he touched the ridge just below her hips, that line above her bottom. It hardly showed any more and the ridge wasn't very pronounced but a smooth stroke would make it apparent. He just hadn't touched her that way before. He paused then traced the line with his fingers, to where it stopped just above one buttock. "Who did that?"

Not, "How did that happen?" or "How did you get that?"

She wouldn't hide anything from him. She'd promised and it was probably better now, while he could still change his mind. She'd have to jilt him of course, but since she had no intention of marrying anyone else, that didn't matter very much to her social standing.

She lifted her head and he crooned something soothing, before picking up his handkerchief, which was lying on the nightstand with the two glasses. He gently wiped her tears away and kissed the corners of her eyes. "Now tell me. Is the mark anything to do with those tears?"

She swallowed. "In a way. Let me tell you about my marriage to John. It's time you knew everything about me." His arm stiffened around her but he jerked a nod. He had braced himself to listen.

"John was the son of the local squire, Stephen Rattigan. He went away on the Grand Tour. Not quite as grand as the one you aristocrats go on but it kept him away from home for a year. Before, I'd taken him for granted but when he returned, I saw him with new eyes. I followed him around like a puppy after its master. In retrospect, I must have seemed gentle and biddable, the perfect answer for his dilemma. So he wooed me and married me. He was gentle and kind and handsome and I thought I loved him."

She kept Alex's gaze. "I discovered I was wrong. He encouraged my feelings, believing an acceptable match would work for him, no consideration for anyone else. He'd fallen in love with the daughter of the local innkeeper before he went abroad. It wasn't an entirely respectable inn." Her mouth tightened when she remembered. "They harbored the ne'er-do-wells, the thieves and cutpurses but Eliza wasn't like that. She was sweet and kind and not very bright. And John loved her. That was the real reason his father had sent him away, the real reason he married me."

She lifted her hand, flattened the palm against Alex's strong, hair-roughened chest. "At first it was fine, because I didn't realize John had taken up with Eliza again. He really loved her, you see. If he'd been stronger, he could have defied his father, maybe they could have run away but they didn't. And I became pregnant. John didn't do any of the things with me that you and I—" she broke off in confusion, still too shy to articulate what they'd done.

Alex kissed her forehead. "I know. You think I didn't realize how innocent you are?"

"I carried the baby for five months then I lost it as I entered the sixth." She could hardly bear to think about the details of that terrible, painful time but she had to. He needed to know.

She drew a shaky breath. "I lost the baby because Eliza came to see me and begged me to let him go. She wanted him all to herself. I hadn't realized John was seeing her. The shock made me stumble and I fell. A bad fall."

He murmured something and cupped the back of her head, stroking her hair.

She leaned her head on his shoulder. "They were all very kind but I didn't want John near me. They thought it was shock and when they finally left me alone to recover, John came to me and we had the first honest talk of our lives. It made me very sorry for him but worse for myself. He should have stood up to his father then I'd have married someone else and had a simple, tranquil life."

"Then I wouldn't have met you. Go on. I didn't intend to stop you."

"Well that's about it. Except that my doctor told me the miscarriage might affect my ability to have children. It was a blow but John swore to give Eliza up. Of course, he didn't and he never came back to my bed, coming up with excuse after excuse. When I saw her, pregnant, walking across the village green on Mayday, I knew John had fathered her baby. I confronted him that night, said he hadn't fulfilled his side of the bargain, and if he didn't put his heart into it, there was no point going on. He yelled at me as if it was my fault. He took his crop to me." She swallowed and ignored Alex's low curse. "It wasn't the first time. He started after I lost the baby, told me everything was my fault. He said he should have married Eliza and she was fertile, more than I was. And he rode off to join her."

She paused, remembering the night in vivid detail and set her jaw firmly. "That night one of those summer storms whipped up out of nowhere. I had the windows and doors locked and barred and although we lost a chimney to the wind, came out of it more or less intact. Not so John. They found him in the morning. He'd been riding to her when a branch had fallen from a tree and struck him. He fell off his horse, landed on a rock and he died. Either the rock or the branch killed him."

She took a breath and spared a thought for her unhappy husband. Too weak to fight for the woman he wanted, he'd taken her without telling her first. If he had, she'd have refused, but at least he'd have given her the choice. "When John's father died a few months later, broken hearted, I discovered he'd left the estate to me, in recompense, he said, for what John did to me. I sold some of it and gave the money to Eliza. It was only fair. She'd suffered as much as I and the child she carried should have been John's heir, if he'd had the courage to follow through his desires, instead of doing what society and his family wished."

"My poor love." Alex's gentleness brought her to tears again. But he held her and stroked her and afterwards went and found a damp cloth in the powder room, which he used to clean her face.

He wouldn't let her speak but when she tried to push him away, he brought her closer, nestling her against him. "Now it's my turn. First of all, I am not John. When I made love to you for the very first time, it was with the full knowledge that we'd reach this point. That we'd marry. I wouldn't have taken the risk without making that decision. The only thing that would have stopped me was you, if you took a dislike to me or if you wanted to go elsewhere."

"No, Alex, no—"

"Be quiet," he said fondly. "I said it was my turn to speak." He tapped a finger against her lips and she kissed it, unable to stop herself. "That's better," he murmured. "When I heard Dankworth was courting Miss Stobart I felt sorry for her but overwhelmingly glad you were free. I warned my father that I had every intention of visiting you when you came to town with the Downhollands and trying to discover a way to break the engagement if you wished it. He grumbled but he knew he couldn't do anything. I'd made my mind up. Then you disappeared and I went frantic. After I found you, when you were staying at Brook Street, I got to woo you in the full light of Society's amused gaze. And in case you didn't recognize it, that was what I did. Miss Stobart only sped things up a little by interrupting us tonight."

He gave a short laugh. "She had meant it to happen as it had happened with her, that I'd back off and make you seem foolish, or worse. But it didn't and if she'd stopped for one moment and given the matter some thought, she'd have realized it for herself."

His hold on her tightened, his muscles enclosing her. She felt so safe she wanted to stay there forever. Dangerous to think that way. "Connie, I love you. Don't you understand that by now? You are the only woman I will marry and I made that clear to my father. If you wish it, we'll try to get you pregnant but if you don't, there are ways of preventing it. I don't believe you are barren. One miscarriage and the say-so of one country doctor, who only said 'may' and not 'will' is no proof. If that doesn't happen, I will still love you and want to stay with you. You complete me, darling."

"But—"

"I have two brothers," Alex continued relentlessly. "If we don't produce offspring, then they probably will. It doesn't matter. I won't say I don't care. I do, because it obviously hurts you to think of it. I would love a child with you, sweetheart but our happiness isn't dependent on it."

"I'll be thirty soon."

"And I'll be thirty-six." He kissed her. "My father was right that I left it rather long to marry but I'd never met anyone I wanted to stand by my side, anyone I'd give up the rest of my active social life for. When I look at you, I can't imagine ever wanting anyone else. Why drink milk when you can have cream? You, my love, are the cream."

His warmth and reassurance suffused her, driving out her anxiety and her tears. He kissed her and made everything better. "So let's prove it, sweetheart. Let's make love."

"Yes." She wanted that closeness again. She'd never stop wanting it.

He lifted her and turned her, so she sat astride him. His cock had grown erect again, ready for her. Connie studied it, fascinated. The smooth head gleamed from a drop of pure essence that seeped from the tiny opening at the top.

John had always conducted his hasty couplings with her in the dark, when they were both wearing their nightclothes. Like a guilty secret, one with no joy.

She'd seen Alex naked more times than she'd ever seen her husband. Her *last* husband, her *late* husband, her *first* husband. She tried the words out in her mind, decided on one and then put John away. First was probably the most tactful.

Hesitantly, she opened her hand and spread it over Alex's chest, feeling the powerful muscles tense when she did so. He watched her with a slow smile curling his lips. "I love it when you touch me. Will you do this often? Will you enjoy it?"

"Of course I'll enjoy it. How could I not?" She moved her hand and he moaned his encouragement.

"Touch me, sweetheart. All of me."

Although she still felt some hesitation, she knew it stemmed from her lack of experience, not from her desire.

Alex leaned against the stacked pillows, blatantly gazing at her body. Under his scrutiny her nipples beaded and hardened, their sensitivity increasing all the time. Her eyelids flicked shut, then opened. She watched him, while she explored.

No more hasty lovemaking. They could take all night, as long as they wished. "We'll go into the country after the wedding," Alex said hoarsely. "I have a hunting box in Leicestershire that should be suitably lonely at this time of the year."

"I heard you had a house in Hampstead."

He laughed. "Ah, that. A remnant of my wicked past. It's gone, my sweet. I gave it to someone who could make better use of it."

"Your last mistress?"

He laughed again, fuller and longer and covered her hand with his. "My very last. You are not, nor will you ever fill that position. You're my lover and soon to be my wife. Nobody else will ever be in my bed. And I can't wait until I have the right to share your bed every night."

Lifting his hand, he stroked her breast, just one gentle caress, before he moved it to her waist and shaped the curve. "So learn me. Find out what I like, what I don't like, although it's hard to imagine anything you do wouldn't please me." He traced a line from her navel to where her curls half covered her most intimate secrets. He watched her reaction as he slipped his finger deeper, into the wet heat of her crease. He tweaked the pearl of flesh at the front. "What's this called?"

"My clitoris."

"And this?" He tweaked one of the folds of flesh on one side.

"I don't know."

"Labia. Lips, protecting that delicate skin. And this?" Gently, he touched her opening, slipped inside just a tiny bit.

Connie caught her lower lip between her teeth and sucked in a breath.

"It has many names, some coldly clinical, some so euphemistic you can't tell what is meant. Some frankly crude. And they can all be exciting, in the right situation. When we join our bodies, what would you call that?"

"Making love." She didn't need to think to tell him that.

"And fucking, too. Straight, ordinary, honest fucking."

She thrilled to the forbidden words. Of course, she'd heard that word, on the streets, or when people thought she wasn't by. Now he was talking to her, looking at her as he said it and she smiled at him.

"I hope we'll do both," he said. "We'll take each other for the sheer pleasure, just to stimulate and enjoy each other's bodies. But we'll also do it because we want to get closer to each other, to share the ultimate intimacy. We have a long journey ahead of us, my dearest dear, owner of my heart and we should explore everything. I will take you again at a ball, in a side room, I can promise you that, because that time excited me beyond measure and I want to do it again. I know you enjoyed it, too. But then we'll go to our bedroom and we'll undress each other slowly and enjoy each other to the full."

"And everything in between." She slid her hand down his chest and, smiling, he moved his hand away from her. She was sorry he'd done that.

He had remarkable skills with his fingers.

She touch his cock, circled it with her fingers and squeeze.

He gasped, as he'd made her do a moment earlier. "It's a talented woman, I'm marrying."

Taken by a sudden urge, remembering what he'd done to her in that room downstairs, she bent her head and licked the head of his cock, that shiny, damp cap that fascinated her so much. Sliding smoothly against the buds of her tongue, it tasted salty, good.

Alex seemed to like it, too. He cried out then threaded his fingers through her tousled hair, cupped the back of her head and urged her down. Eagerly, she accepted his unspoken invitation and lowered her head more, opened her mouth, let her tongue rub against the ridge at the base of the cap, then further, the looser skin lower down. She closed her lips around him and he groaned. "Sweetheart, oh, dear God, Connie."

Loving his almost inarticulate murmurs, she sucked and then lifted one hand, rested it on his thigh and cradled the part under his cock in her hand.

They felt like balls, loose in a small, hairy bag. She explored and he let out a long, sighing, "Ah!"

His cock heated and hardened, she sucked and released and gasped air when he lifted her off him, only to bring her back down and impale her, his cock in her—he still hadn't given her the names for that part.

Her inner walls embraced him, welcoming him back as if he'd been away for weeks and she knew they would never let it go that long if it were humanly possible.

Alex grasped her waist and lifted his legs, urging her to lean back against them. His mouth half open, he panted as he worked her, then he tweaked her clitoris and it was her turn to cry out.

Shots of pure sensation shot from where they joined through her whole body in staccato bursts. She failed to find her balance and found purchase on the mattress below. If she pushed, she could respond to his deep thrusts, push down so he went deeper with every stroke.

Mercilessly he worked her, tweaked her and the increasingly wet sounds of their bodies coming together sounded like the sweetest music she'd ever heard and his voice, murmuring encouragement, sometimes without words, urged her internal turmoil, bringing her to the climax, along a road she was becoming used to expecting.

She gripped the sheet under them when she came, her passage clenching him in rhythmic ripples, her whole body shuddering with the impact. But she could lose control because he would keep her safe, the man she adored with everything she was.

He lifted his legs further, tilting her forwards, so she all but fell into his arms, with him still deeply embedded inside her. He kissed her, treating her gently now but when he would have lifted her off him, she protested and planted her feet firmly on either side of him, sliding them down so her knees touched the bed. She could find control now and she wanted to bring this to him, to make him come as he'd done for her.

"You, my love, will kill me," he said but he lay back and watched her. "Take me, Connie. I'm all yours."

Laughing, she did as he asked and as she wanted. Letting her take control delighted her and with the remnants of her recent climax thrumming through her, she began again and lifted and lowered her body until she found a motion that pleased them both.

Alex wasn't backwards in telling her what he liked, how he liked it and he caressed her breasts, claiming he'd neglected them for long enough.

Time no longer meant anything as they worked together, enjoyed each other. Alex was a strongly built man and now he was all hers, to caress, to hold and to love.

The thought sent her over once more but this time she took him with her. Roaring her name, he came in strong, hard jets, flooding her with his essence.

He dragged her down, into his arms, so she lay on top of him, his cock still inside her. "You are a miracle, my love, my Connie."

"So are you."

Chapter 21

Alex heard a sound from the bed, a gentle sound of waking and he turned to greet her. "Good morning, love of my life."

"Mphn."

"Interesting." Waistcoat in hand, he strolled to the bed and gazed down at her.

She grabbed a handful of her hair to cover her eyes. "I must look awful."

He leaned down and pushed the hair aside. "You look wonderful. Well-loved and beautiful. I'm looking forward to seeing you like this a great deal more in the near future."

He kissed her, making it gentle and loving, when already he wanted to shove the sheets aside and climb in with her. Waking with her in his arms had been one of the best experiences of his life.

But he wouldn't relax until he had his ring on her finger and he could claim the right to take her home with him and love her until neither of them could stay awake anymore. "It's early, sweetheart. I'm going home to change, then church, then I'll see you at the Downholland's house to discuss the contract. After that, it's the offices of Makepeace, George and Simms on Monday to formalize the betrothal."

"How will I get there?"

"I'll send a carriage for you. You can spend your last two nights at the Downhollands, if you want to, or with Julius and Helena. Or you can spend them with me."

She blinked and rolled on to her back. "How?"

"Here. If you stay here, as a guest of the Kirkburtons, I can slip upstairs to you." He shrugged into his waistcoat. "One of the reasons Julius chose this room, apart from the limited access, is that it's close to a side door. The servants became quite used to seeing him going in and out."

"They'll gossip."

"We'll be married soon enough."

She swallowed and reached her hand out to him. He took it and raised it to his lips. "What about Helena? Won't her mother insist on her returning home?"

The very thing Julius and his sister dreaded.

"He's interviewing professional companions. He is thinking of employing one as a companion to Helena and a governess for his daughter."

"So they will cope?"

"Julius is determined on it." He smiled. "Think about us now. What would you like to do? No one will gossip, I swear." He paused. "Or we can be good and you can stay with the Downhollands until Tuesday. Then you're coming home with me. Of that I'm certain."

"I am, aren't I?" She frowned. "If nobody objects, I'd like to stay here. I want to get to know the duchess a little. I'll have to meet her more often and if I can win her over, it would be better for both of us, would it not?"

He frowned. "I'm not sure you can win her over but if you try, she will walk over you."

"No she will not." The duchess would not intimidate her, she decided. "She's no worse than the vicar's wife at home, all starch and superiority. I will not turn tail and run, I can promise you that."

"And no more nonsense about age or children. We love each other, we have promised ourselves to each other." He leaned in and stole another kiss.

He reached under the covers and found one of her sweet breasts, caressing it before teasing the nipple into a peak. He loved her breasts. Soft, responsive and the most delicious nipples he'd ever tasted. He was completely besotted and didn't care. "You aren't particularly interested in mornings, are you?"

"I can cope with mornings, as long as they come with tea. You think I sleep until noon in the country?"

"No more than I do." He took one more kiss. "I'll see you this evening, my love. If the duchess doesn't ask me to dinner, I'll come after. Don't be late coming to bed."

He tucked the sheets around her, picked up his coat and left the room by the jib door. He should really not feel quite so cheerful at the prospect of putting his head in the marriage noose but he felt stupidly happy as he rattled down the uncarpeted, narrow stairs, startling a maid carrying a clean chamber pot up to the bedroom floor.

But he winked at her and continued on his way.

* * * *

Three hours later Alex wasn't quite so happy. His father called around before he had the chance to pre-empt him. He'd washed, shaved and changed before attending church at St. Georges' and suffering the congratulations of society, then changed into something suitable for a visit to his father, although he was tempted to wear the red figured velvet. Julius would have, but it wasn't Alex's style. He let people think he was a harmless, easy-going man, all the while learning their secrets. People underestimated him at their peril and not a few had done just that.

Not his father. Unfortunately, Lord Leverton had his character worked out to the last degree. He offered his father some of the coffee that was almost everything he'd left of his breakfast. Lovemaking gave him an appetite. He'd had time to think and plan—and remember. Leverton took a seat at the breakfast-room table and the coffee. He filled his cup with five chunks of sugar. Alex inwardly shuddered. He wanted his father in a good mood, because he guessed what was coming so he didn't comment on his father's sweet tooth.

"Alexander, while I'm pleased by your decision to marry, I wonder at your choice."

Alex leaned back. Hell and damn. Not "Ripley" or "Alex," but his childhood name of "Alexander." "Nevertheless, sir, it's my choice."

"Why, boy? I've been making enquiries you know."

"I'd have expected nothing less."

His father took a sip of his over-sweetened brew and replaced his coffee can in the saucer with a sigh of satisfaction. He always did that with coffee. "Mrs. Rattigan was married for five years to her first husband and had only one pregnancy, which ended in miscarriage. Did you know that?"

"Yes, sir, as it happened, I did. She told me because she thought it might mar her fertility. And that she is nearly thirty. If you've come to tell me those things, you've had a wasted journey." He waited for the explosion but it didn't come. Yet. His father's greatest fault was his hasty temper and his sons had learned to disregard anything said to them in the heat of anger. He would throw them out of his house and then ask for them a day later, as if the incident had never occurred.

"You are the oldest son and it is your duty to provide heirs. That's all I ask of you, boy. Your brothers don't want to be burdened with that, when they have to make their own way in the world."

Alex turned his empty coffee can in the saucer. The fine porcelain made a scraping sound he knew his father detested. So he desisted. Perhaps later. No sense aggravating the old boy yet. "I think we have every chance of producing children." He decided to tell his father an amended version of what Connie had told him last night. "I probably dug a little deeper than you. Connie had a pregnancy and after that, her husband didn't touch her. He found a mistress instead."

Leverton grunted. "It's often the way. So you have a rival. A dead one. They're the worst, or so I've been told." He took another scalding gulp, as if gathering strength. "Why, Alex, when you could have anyone you chose?" At least they were back to Alex. "I've a good mind to forbid the match. I want you married to some pretty young thing, not a scrawny widow."

Alex held his temper by a thread. If he lost it, he'd lose the argument. People who lost their tempers always did and that had been a lesson he'd learned the hard way. "She's hardly scrawny, father. She's my choice and now the Downhollands have made her their heir, you can't complain about her portion, either." He shrugged. "I'd have taken her with nothing."

"Still, Alex, you could have done so much better for yourself."

"No I could not." He tested the coffee pot but it was nearly empty and he didn't feel like ringing for more. "She's everything I want. She's a partner, father. Remember what that's like? You told me that you wouldn't marry again because you had the children you needed and you didn't want to weaken the estate by having more. But that's not the only reason, is it?"

He hated the stricken look on his father's face but he carried on. "You didn't want to replace my mother. I'm the eldest and I remember what it was like. You adored her. I want that, father. I've always wanted that and all your talk of practicalities hasn't deterred me. That's why I waited for so long. I've met perfectly charming young women, who would have made me excellent partners but none of them moved my heart. This one does."

His father got to his feet a trifle unsteadily. "Then there's nothing left to say. I wish you well, my son."

* * * *

Early the next day, Monday, they met at the offices of their men of business. They were ushered into the largest room in the place, which wasn't as large as Alex's drawing room but was already full.

He sought out Connie first, looking perfectly lovely in a gown of apple green. Fresh and beautiful, as if they hadn't spent the night loving each other. Today she wore her hair unpowdered and it glinted in the sunlight streaming through the admittedly dusty windows.

He took her hand and bowed over it, dropping a soft kiss on the back and turned, retaining her hand to place on his arm.

Mr. Mills, who still had to get his name on the board but was the sharpest knife in the drawer in this place, had already laid out the contracts, big, crackling monstrosities of documents which Alex didn't intend reading. "Outline the agreements and we'll take it from there."

All of it was ordinary, in his world but Connie gasped quietly once or twice at the sums mentioned. He guessed she hadn't realized how much the Downhollands were investing in her, especially as they preferred to live modestly. But Downholland had a finger in many pies and most of them had proved fruitful. When children were mentioned, she blushed adorably and he lifted her hand to his lips, an acknowledgement that they'd do their best.

His father behaved, even greeted Connie with a kiss on her cheek and a gruff, "Do you have plans for the wedding?"

"That's next," Alex admitted. "We marry tomorrow. I've already sent word to the vicar."

His father didn't seem surprised but he was the only one in the room. The others exclaimed and when Connie opened her sweet mouth to protest—he saw it in her eyes—he was tempted to stop it with a kiss but instead, he said, "Tomorrow at ten. That wasn't empty rhetoric when I said it before. I won't wait any longer. I have the special license ready. If anyone else protests, I swear I'll carry her off in a closed coach to Gretna Green."

The earl raised a bushy brow. "You might have collided with Dankworth. He made a botched attempt to make off with Miss Stobart last night."

"He abducted her?" Connie said, startled. Abduction seemed to be Jasper's weapon of choice.

"I said he tried," his lordship said. "Mrs. Stobart had decided to break off the connection and she put a watch on her daughter. Dankworth had a coach further up the street but all the doors were barred and guarded."

"Who told her?" Alex said suddenly.

"Who do you think? Winterton, of course. That man knows everything and is everywhere. Or it seems so sometimes."

The earl shrugged and moved toward the huge desk on which lay the documents they had to sign. As a caveat, he added, "Dankworth must have known it was all up. He used the coach to flee to the docks, where a packet took him abroad. Winterton tells me it was headed for the continent. I don't doubt his august relative aided his escape."

He'd gone. Alex had planned to take care of the man but with less finesse than Julius had shown. He'd planned a little more brutality. But if the Duke of Northwich had become involved that demonstrated intent. It was tantamount to a declaration of war. Interesting times lay ahead.

They signed and Alex felt the weight lift off his shoulders. Another hurdle jumped. One more and she would be his, to love and to cherish for the rest of their lives. Both of which he fully intended to do but not always at the same time.

"If my future bride is in agreement, I'd like to attend Lady Franklin's ball tonight," he said.

"It's one of the biggest events of the season," his father remarked.

Alex smiled down at Connie. "I want to declare my intentions in public, sir." She would spend her time until our wedding in perfect comfort and happiness. He would ensure it. He no longer had to hide how he felt about her and so he smiled at her, his heart in his eyes.

The happy sigh came from Lady Downholland's direction.

Meet the Author

Lynne Connolly lives in England with her family and her mews, Jack the cat. She comes to the USA every year to visit her publishers and readers. She was born in Leicester, England and was brought up in a haunted house. She is part Romany, and in her spare time, she loves reading the Tarot as her grandmother taught her, and making and filling dollhouses.